Feast of Fools

The Morganville Vampires

RACHEL CAINE

Allison & Busby Limited
13 Charlotte Mews
London, W1T 4EJ
www.allisonandbusby.com

A CIP catalogue record for this book is available from
the British Library.

First published in Great Britain in 2009 (ISBN 978-0-7490-7979-6).
Reissued in 2011.

First published in the US in 2008.

10 9 8 7 6 5 4 3 2

ISBN 978-0-7490-1053-9

Typeset in 10/14 pt Century Schoolbook by
Allison & Busby

Printed and bound by
CPI Group (UK) Ltd, Croydon, CR0 4YY

RACHEL CAINE is the international bestselling author of over thirty novels, including the *New York Times* bestselling Morganville Vampires series. She was born at White Sands Missile Range, which people who know her say explains a lot. She has been an accountant, an insurance investigator and a professional musician, and has played with such musical legends as Henry Mancini, Peter Nero and John Williams. She and her husband, fantasy artist R. Cat Conrad, live in Texas with their iguana Pop-eye, a *mali uromastyx* named (appropriately) O'Malley, and a leopard tortoise named Shelley (for the poet, of course).

www.rachelcaine.com

Available from
ALLISON & BUSBY

The Morganville Vampires series

Glass Houses
The Dead Girls' Dance
Midnight Alley
Feast of Fools
Lord of Misrule
Carpe Corpus
Fade Out
Kiss of Death
Ghost Town
Bite Club

Morganville Vampires Omnibus:
Glass Houses, The Dead Girls' Dance, Midnight Alley

The Weather Warden series

Ill Wind
Heat Stroke
Chill Factor
Windfall
Firestorm
Thin Air
Gale Force
Cape Storm
Total Eclipse

To the Time Turners,
who keep me moving forward...
And to PN Elrod, who knows why.

THE STORY SO FAR

Claire Danvers was going to Caltech. Or maybe MIT. She had her pick of great schools...but her parents were a little worried about sending a wide-eyed sixteen-year-old into such a high-pressure world. So they compromised and sent her to a safe place for a year – Texas Prairie University, a small school located in Morganville, Texas, just an hour or so from their home.

One problem: Morganville isn't what it seems. It's the last safe place for *vampires*, and that makes it not very safe at all for the humans who venture in for work or school. The vampires rule the town... and everyone who lives in it.

Claire's second problem is that she's gathered enemies, major ones, human and vampire. Now she lives with housemates Michael Glass (newly made a vampire), Eve Rosser (always been Goth), and Shane Collins (whose absentee dad is a vampire killer).

Claire's the normal one...or she would be, except that she's deep into the secrets of Morganville. She's become an employee of the Founder, Amelie, and befriended one of the most dangerous, yet most vulnerable, vampires of them all – Myrnin.

And just when she thinks things can't get any worse...they have.

Amelie's vampire father has come to town, and he's not happy.

When Daddy's not happy...nobody's happy.

CHAPTER ONE

It was hard to imagine how Claire's day – even by Morganville standards – could get any worse... and then the vampires holding her hostage wanted breakfast.

'Breakfast?' Claire repeated blankly. She took a look at the living room window, just to prove to herself that, yes, it was still dark outside. Getting darker all the time.

The three vampires all looked at her. It was bad enough having that kind of attention from the two she hadn't properly met yet – man and woman, eerily pretty – but when the cold, old Mr Bishop's eyes focused her way, it made her want to curl up in a corner and hide.

She held his stare for a full five seconds, then looked down. She could almost feel him smiling.

'Breakfast,' he said softly, 'is something to be eaten in the mornings. Mornings for vampires are not controlled by sunrise. And I like eggs.'

'Scrambled or over easy?' Claire asked, trying not to sound as nervous as she felt. *Don't say* over easy. *I don't know how to make eggs over easy. I don't even know why I mentioned it. Don't say* over easy...

'Scrambled,' he said, and Claire's breath rushed out in relief. Mr Bishop was sitting in the comfortable chair in the living room that her housemate Michael normally occupied while he was playing his guitar. Unlike Michael, Mr Bishop made it look like a throne. Part of it was that everybody else stayed standing – Claire, with her boyfriend, Shane, hovering protectively by her side; Eve and Michael a little distance away, holding hands. Claire risked a glance at Michael. He looked...contained. Angry, sure, but under control, at least.

Claire was more scared about Shane. He had a pretty well-documented history of acting before thinking, at least when it came to the personal safety of those he cared about. She took his hand, and he sent her a quick, dark, unreadable glance.

No, she wasn't sure about him at all.

Mr Bishop's voice pulled her attention back to him with a cold snap. 'Have you told Amelie that I've arrived, girl?'

That had been Bishop's first command – to let his daughter know he'd come to town. *His daughter?* Amelie – the head vampire of Morganville – didn't seem human enough to have family, not even family as scary as Mr Bishop. Ice and crystal, that was Amelie.

He was waiting for an answer, and Claire hastily got one together. 'I called. I got her voice mail,' Claire said. She tried not to sound defensive. Bishop's eyebrows drew together in a scowl.

'I suppose that means you left some sort of a message.' She nodded mutely. He drummed his fingers impatiently on the arm of the chair. 'Very well. We'll eat while we wait. Eggs, scrambled, as I said. We shall also have bacon, coffee—'

'Biscuits,' drawled the woman leaning on the arm of his chair. 'I love biscuits. And honey.' The vampire had a molasses-slow accent, something that wasn't quite Southern and wasn't quite not, either. Mr Bishop gave her a tolerant look, the kind a human would give a favourite pet. She had the icy glitter in her eyes, and moved so smoothly and quietly that there was no way she was regular-flavoured human. Not hiding it, either, the way some of the vampires of Morganville tried to do.

The woman kept smiling, dark eyes fixed on Shane. Claire didn't like the way she was looking at him. It looked – greedy.

'Biscuits,' Mr Bishop agreed, with a quirk of a smile. 'And I'll indulge you further by agreeing to gravy, child.' The smile vanished when he turned back to the four standing in front of him. 'Go about your business, then. Now.'

Shane grabbed Claire's hand and practically dragged her toward the kitchen. However fast he was moving, Michael was there first, pushing Eve through the door. 'Hey!' Eve protested. 'I'm walking here!'

'And the faster, the better,' Michael said. His normally angelic face looked stark, all sharp edges, and he closed the kitchen door once they were safely inside. 'Right. We don't have a lot of choices. Let's do exactly what he says and hope Amelie can sort all this out when she gets here.'

'I thought *you* were all Big Bad Bloodsucker these days,' Shane said. 'It's your house. How come you can't just throw them out?' That was a reasonable question, and Shane managed to say it without making it seem like a challenge. Well, much of one. The kitchen felt cold, Claire noticed – as if the temperature of the whole house was steadily dropping. She shivered.

'It's complicated,' Michael said. He yanked open cabinets and began assembling the makings of fresh coffee. 'Yeah, it's our house' – emphasis, Claire noted, on the *our* – 'but if I revoke Bishop's invitation, he will still kick our asses, I guarantee you.'

Shane leant his butt against the stove and crossed his arms. 'I just thought you were supposed to be stronger than them on home ground—'

'Supposed to be. I'm not.' Michael spooned coffee into the filter. 'Don't be an asshole right now – we don't have time for it.'

'Dude, I wasn't trying to be.' And Claire could tell he actually meant it this time. Michael seemed to hear it, too, and sent Shane an apologetic glance. 'I'm trying to figure out how big a pile of crap we're in. Not blaming you, man.' He hesitated a second, then continued. 'How do you know? Whether or not you have a chance?'

'Any other vampire I meet, I know where I stand with them. Who's stronger, who's weaker, whether or not I could take them in a straight-up fight if it came to that.' Michael poured water into the machine and switched it on to brew. 'These guys, I know I haven't got a chance in hell. Not against one of them, much less all three, not even with the house itself backing me up. They're badass, man. Truly black hat. It's going to take Amelie or Oliver to handle this.'

'So,' Shane said, 'landfill-sized pile of crap. Good to know.'

Eve pushed him out of the way and began getting pots and pans out of the cabinets, clattering everything noisily. 'Since we're not fighting, we'd better get breakfast ready,' she said. 'Claire, you get the eggs, since you volunteered us for short-order cooks.'

'Better than volunteering us for breakfast,' Shane pointed out, and Eve snorted.

'You,' she said, and pressed a finger into the centre of his well-worn T-shirt. 'You, mister. You're making gravy.'

'You do want us all to die, don't you?'

'Shut up. I'll do the biscuits and bacon. Michael—' She turned, looking at him with big dark eyes, made almost anime-wide by the Goth eyeliner. 'Coffee. And I think you have to be the private eye here. Sorry.'

He nodded. 'I'll go make sure I know what they're doing when I finish here.'

Assigning Michael the barista and spy duties made sense, but it left the three of them the majority of the work, and none of them were exactly future chefs in training. Claire struggled with the scrambled eggs. Eve cursed the bacon grease in a fierce whisper, and whatever Shane was making, it didn't really look that much like gravy.

'Can I help?'

They all jumped at the voice, and Claire whirled toward the kitchen door. 'Mom!' She knew she sounded panicked. She *was* panicked. She'd forgotten all about her parents – they'd come in with Mr Bishop, and Bishop's friends had moved them into the not-much-used parlour at the front of the house. In the great scheme of scary things, Bishop had taken the forefront.

But there was her mother, standing in the kitchen doorway, smiling a fragile, confused smile and looking...vulnerable. Tired.

'Mrs Danvers!' Eve jumped in, hurried over, and guided her to the kitchen table. 'No, no, we're just – ah – making some food. You haven't eaten, right? What about Mr Danvers?'

Her mother – looking every year of the forty-two she claimed not to be – seemed tired, vague, kind of out of focus. Worried, too. There were lines around her eyes and mouth that Claire couldn't remember seeing before, and it scared her.

'He's—' Claire's mom frowned, then leant her forehead on the palm of her hand. 'Oh, my head hurts. I'm sorry. What did you say?'

'Your husband, where is he?'

'I'll find him,' Michael said quietly. He slipped out of the kitchen with the grace and quickness of a vampire – but at least he was *their* vampire. Eve settled Claire's mom at the table, exchanged a helpless look with Claire, and chattered on nervously about what a long drive it must have been to Morganville, what a nice surprise it was that they were moving to town, how much Claire was going to enjoy having them here. Etc., etc., etc.

Claire numbly continued to rake eggs back and forth in the skillet. *This can't happen. My parents can't be here.* Not now. Not with Bishop. It was a nightmare, in every way.

'I could help you cook,' Mom said, and made a feeble effort to get up. Eve glared at Claire and mouthed, *Say something!* Claire swallowed a cold bubble of panic and tried to make her voice sound at least partly under control.

'No, Mom,' Claire said. 'It's fine. We've got it covered. Look, we're making extra in case you and Dad are hungry. You just sit and relax.'

Her mom, who was usually a control freak deluxe in the kitchen, prone to take command of something as error free as boiling water, looked relieved. 'All right, honey. You let me know if I can help.'

Michael opened the kitchen door, and ushered in Claire's father. If her mom looked tired, her dad just looked...blank. Puzzled. He frowned at Michael, like he was trying to work out exactly what was happening but couldn't put his finger on it.

'What's going on around here?' he barked at Michael. 'Those people out there—'

'Relatives,' Michael said. 'From Europe. Look, I'm sorry. I know you wanted to spend some time with Claire, but maybe you should just go on home, and we'll—'

He paused, then turned, because someone was standing in the kitchen door behind him. Following him.

'Nobody's going anywhere,' said the other one of Bishop's vampire companions – the guy. He was smiling. 'One big happy family, eh, Michael? It's Michael, isn't it?'

'What, we're on a first-name basis now?' Michael got Claire's dad inside the kitchen and closed the door in the other vampire's face.

'Right. Let's get you guys out of here,' he said to Claire's parents, and opened the back door, the one that led out into the backyard. 'Where's your car? Out on the street?'

Outside the night looked black and empty, not even a moon showing. Claire's dad frowned at Michael again, then took a seat at the kitchen table with his wife.

'Close the door, son,' he said. 'We're not going anywhere.'

'Sir—'

Claire tried, too. 'Dad—'

'No, honey, there's something strange going on here, and I'm not leaving. Not until I know you're all OK.' Her father transferred the frown back to Michael again. 'Just who are these...relatives?'

'The kind nobody wants to claim,' Michael said. 'Every family's got them. But they're just here for a little while. They'll be leaving soon.'

'Then we'll stay until they do,' Dad said.

Claire tried to focus on the scrambled eggs she was making.

Her hands were shaking.

'Hey,' Shane whispered, leaning close. 'It's OK. We'll all be OK.' He was a big, solid, warm presence next to her, stirring what could not possibly *really* be gravy. She knew this mainly because Shane's sole culinary ability came in the genre of chilli. But at least he was trying, which was new and different, and probably showed just how seriously he was taking all this.

'I know,' Claire said, and swallowed. Shane's arm pressed against hers, a deliberate kind of thing, and she knew if his hands weren't full, he'd have put his arms around her. 'Michael won't let them hurt us.'

'Weren't you listening?' Eve joined them at the stove, whispering fiercely. She scowled at the frying bacon. 'He can't stop them. Best he can do is get himself really hurt in the process. So maybe you ought to call Amelie again and tell her to get her all-powerful ass over here *now*.'

'Yeah, good idea, piss off the only vampire who can help. Look, if they were going to kill us, I don't think they'd ask for eggs first,' Shane said. 'Not to mention biscuits. If you ask for biscuits, clearly, you think you're some kind of a guest.'

He had a point. It didn't really stop the trembling in Claire's hands, though.

'Claire, honey?' Her mom's voice, again. Claire jumped and nearly flipped a spatula full of eggs out onto the stove top. 'Those people. What are they really doing here?'

'Mr Bishop – he's, uh, waiting for his daughter to come pick him up.' That wasn't a lie. Not at all.

Claire's father got up from the table and went to the coffeepot, which had wheezed itself full; he poured two mugs and took them back to the table. 'Have some coffee, Kathy. You look tired,' he said, and there was a gentle note in his voice that made Claire look at him sharply. Her dad wasn't the most emotional of guys, but he looked worried now, almost as worried as Mom.

Dad drained his coffee like it was water after a hot afternoon of lawn mowing. Mom listlessly creamed and sugared, then sipped. Neither of them spoke again.

Michael slipped out the kitchen door, taking mugs of coffee out to the others. When he came back, he closed the door and leant against it for a minute. He looked bone white, strained, worse than he had in the months since he'd been transformed fully into a vampire. Claire tried to imagine what they'd said to him to make him look like that, and couldn't even begin to guess. Something bad. No, something *horrible*.

'Michael,' Eve said tensely. She nodded toward Claire's parents. 'More coffee?'

He nodded and moved away from the door to pick up the coffeepot, but he never made it to the breakfast table. The kitchen door opened again, and Mr Bishop and his entourage entered the room.

Tall and haughty as nineteenth-century royalty, the three vampires surveyed the kitchen. The other two vampires were pretty, young, and frightening, but Mr Bishop was the one in charge; there was no mistaking it. When his gaze fell on her, Claire flinched and turned back to the sizzling eggs.

The female vampire strolled over and dipped her finger in the gravy Shane was stirring, then lifted the finger slowly to her lips to suck it clean. She stared at Shane the whole time. And Shane, Claire realised with a helpless, unpleasant shock, stared right back.

'We'll sit for the meal now,' Bishop said to

Michael. 'You will have the pleasure of serving us, Michael. And if your little friends decide to try to poison me, I'll have your guts out, and believe me, a vampire can suffer a very, very long time when I want him to.'

Michael swallowed and nodded once. Claire sent an involuntary look toward her folks, who could not *possibly* have missed that.

And they hadn't. 'Excuse me?' Claire's father asked, and began to rise out of his chair. 'Are you threatening these kids?'

Bishop turned those cold eyes toward them, and Claire desperately thought about whether a hot iron skillet with a panful of frying eggs might be a useful weapon against a vampire. Her dad froze, halfway up.

She felt a wave of something go through the room, and her parents' eyes went blank and vague. Her dad sank down again heavily in his chair.

'No more questions,' Bishop said to them. 'I tire of your chatter.'

Claire felt a surge of utter black fury. She wanted to leap on that evil old man and claw his eyes out. The only thing holding her back, in those two long seconds, was the fact that if she tried, they'd all end up dead.

Even Michael.

'Coffee?' Eve broke the silence with a desperate, brittle brightness in her tone. She grabbed the coffeepot from Michael and bore down on Claire's mom and dad like the avenging dark angel of caffeine. Claire wondered what her parents made of Eve, with her rice-powder makeup and black lipstick and raccoon eyeliner, and her dyed-black hair teased into fierce spikes.

Then again, she had coffee, and she was smiling.

'Sure,' Claire's mom said, and tried a tentative smile in return. 'Thank you, dear. So – did you say that man is a relative of yours?' She cast a look toward Bishop, who was exiting the kitchen and heading for the dining table in the living area. The handsome younger male vamp caught Claire's look and winked, and she hastily focused back on Eve and her parents.

'Nope,' Eve said, with fear-fuelled cheer. 'Distant relative of Michael's. From Europe, you know. Cream?'

'Eggs are done,' Claire said, and turned down the burner. 'Eve—'

'I hope we have enough plates,' Eve interrupted, more than a little frantic. 'Jeez, I never thought I'd say this, but where's the good china? *Is* there good china?'

'Meaning plates without chips in the edges? Yeah. Over there.' Shane pointed to a cabinet about four feet higher than Eve's head. She gave him a stare. 'Don't look at me – I'm not reaching for it. Still wounded, you know.' He was. Claire had forgotten that, too, in the press of all the other stuff – he was doing better, but he'd been out of the hospital only a short while. Hardly enough time to really heal up from the stab wound that had nearly killed him.

That was another good reason not to make waves unless they absolutely had to – without Shane, their ability to fight back was seriously compromised.

Eve climbed up on the counter, found the plates, and handed them down to Claire. Once that was done, Claire took Shane's place at the stove, stirring the lumpy stuff that was supposed to be gravy. It looked like something an alien would barf.

'That girl,' Claire said to Shane.

'What girl?'

'The – you know. Out there.'

'You mean the bloodsucker? Yeah, what about her?'

'She was staring at you.'

'What can I say? Irresistible.'

'Shane, it's not funny. I just – you should be careful.'

'Always am.' Which was an absolute lie. Shane's eyes fixed on hers, and she felt a burst of heat inside that crept up to burn in her cheeks. He smiled slowly. 'Jealous?'

'Maybe.'

'No reason. I like my ladies with a pulse.' He took her hand and pressed his fingers gently against her wrist. 'Yep, you've got one. It's beating pretty fast, too.'

'I'm not kidding, Shane.'

'Neither am I.' He stepped closer, and they were barely a breath apart. 'No vamp's going to come between us. You believe me?'

She nodded wordlessly. For the life of her, she couldn't have forced out a single word just then. His eyes were dark, the colour of rich brown velvet, with a thin rim of gold. She'd looked into his eyes a lot recently, but she'd never noticed just how *beautiful* they were.

Shane stepped back as the door opened again. Michael turned first toward them, offering up a mute apology, then faced Claire's parents.

'Mr and Mrs Danvers, Mr Bishop would like for you to join him for dinner,' he said. 'But if you have to go home—'

If Michael was hoping they'd changed their minds, Claire could have told him that wasn't going to happen. As long as her dad had the idea something funny was going on, he wasn't about to do the sensible thing. Sure enough, he got to his feet, holding his coffee cup. 'I could do with some breakfast. Never tasted Claire's eggs before. Kathy? You coming?'

Clueless, Claire thought in despair, but then again, she'd been just as bad when she'd first come to Morganville. She hadn't taken the strong hints, or even the outright instructions, seriously. Maybe she'd gotten that from her parents, along with the fair skin and slightly curly hair. In their defence, though, Mr Bishop was playing with their heads.

And they were scared for *her*.

She watched as her parents followed Michael into the other room, and then helped Eve get the eggs and bacon and biscuits onto serving dishes – nice ones at that. The lumpy gravy couldn't be helped. They poured it into a gravy bowl and hoped for the best, then silently carried it out into the dining area, which was really a corner of the living room.

Claire was struck again, as she was at the oddest times, how the mood of the house could change at a moment's notice. Not just the mood of the people in it – the house itself. Right now, it felt dark, cold, foreboding. Almost hostile. And yet all that dark emotion seemed directed at the intruding vampires.

The house was worried, and on guard. The solid Victorian furniture crouched hunched and deformed, nothing warm or welcoming about it. Even the lights seemed dimmed, and Claire could feel something, almost a *presence* – the way she'd been able to sometimes sense Michael when he'd been trapped in the house as a ghost. The fine hair on her arms stood on end, and her skin pebbled into gooseflesh.

Claire set the eggs and bacon down on the wooden table and backed away. Nobody had asked her, Eve, and Shane to take seats, although there were empty places at the table; she caught Eve's eye and retreated back to the kitchen, grateful to escape. Michael stayed by the table, putting food on plates. Serving. There was a tight, pale set to his face and a cold fear in his eyes, and God, if Michael was panicking, there was definitely reason for a total freak-out.

As soon as the kitchen door closed again, Shane grabbed her and Eve and hustled them to the farthest corner of the room. 'Right,' he whispered. 'It's official – this is getting way more than creepy. Did you feel that?'

'Yeah,' Eve breathed. 'Wow. I think if the house had teeth, it'd be chomping down right now. You have to admit, that's cool.'

'Cool isn't getting us anywhere. Claire?'

'What?' She stared at him blankly for a few long seconds, then said, 'Oh. Right. Yeah. I'll call Amelie again.' She dug the cell phone out of her pocket. It was new, and came with a few important numbers preloaded on it. One of them – the first on speed dial, in fact – was a contact number for Amelie, the Founder of Morganville.

The head vampire. Claire's boss, sort of. In Morganville, the technical term was *Patron*, but Claire had known from the beginning that it was just a more polite word for *owner*.

It rang – again – to voice mail. Claire left another hurried, half-desperate message to *'come to the house, please, we need your help,'* and hung up. She looked mutely at Eve, who sighed and took the phone, then dialled another number.

'Yeah, hi,' she said when she got someone on the line. 'Let me talk to the boss.' A longish pause, and Eve looked like she was steeling herself for something really unpleasant. 'Oliver. It's Eve. Don't bother to tell me how nice it is to hear from me, because it's not, and this is business, so save the BS. Hold on.'

Eve handed over the phone to Claire. Frowning, Claire mouthed, *Are you sure?* Eve made an emphatic thumb-and-little-finger phone gesture at her ear.

Claire reluctantly took the call.

'Oliver?' she asked. On the other end of the line, she heard a low, lazy chuckle.

'Well,' he said. The owner of Common Grounds, the local coffee shop, had a warm voice – the kind that had made her think he was just an all-around nice guy when she'd first met him. 'If it isn't little Claire. Eve didn't want to hear it, but I'll tell it to you – it's nice that you turn to me in your moment of need. It is a moment of need, I assume? And not an invitation to socialise?'

'Someone's here,' she said as softly as she could. 'In the house.'

The warmth drained out of Oliver's voice, leaving a sharp annoyance. 'Then call the police if you have a prowler. I'm not your security service. It's Michael's house. Michael can—'

'Michael can't do anything about it, and I don't think we should call the cops. This man, he says his name is Mr Bishop. He wants to talk to Amelie, but I can't get her on the—'

Oliver cut her off. 'Stay away from him,' he said, and his voice had grown edges. 'Do nothing. Say *nothing*. Tell your friends the same, especially Michael, yes? This is far beyond any of you. I will find Amelie. Do as he says, *whatever* he says, until we arrive.'

And Oliver hung up on her. Claire blinked at the dead phone, shrugged, and looked at her friends. 'He says do what we're doing,' she said. 'Take orders and wait for help.'

'Fantastic advice,' Shane said. 'Remind me to stock a handy vampire-killing kit under the sink for times like these.'

'We'll be OK,' Eve said. 'Claire's got the bracelet.' She grabbed Claire's wrist and lifted it to show the delicate glitter of the ID bracelet circling it – a bracelet that had Amelie's symbol on it, instead of a name. It identified her as property, someone who'd signed over life and limb and soul to a vampire in return for certain protections and considerations. She hadn't wanted to do it, but it had seemed like the only way, at the time, to ensure the safety of her friends. Especially Shane, who was already on the bad side of the vamps.

She knew that the bracelet could bring its own brand of hazard, but at least it obligated Amelie (and maybe even Oliver) to come to her defence against other vampires.

In theory.

Claire slipped the phone into her pocket. Shane took her hands in his and rubbed lightly over her knuckles, a gentle, soothing kind of motion that made her feel at least a little safe, just for a moment.

'We'll get through this,' he said. When he tried to kiss her, though, he winced. She put a hand lightly on his stomach.

'You're hurting,' she said.

'Only when I bend over. When did you get so short, anyway?'

'Five minutes ago.' She rolled her eyes, playing along, but she was worried. According to the rules of Morganville, he was off-limits to vampires during his convalescence; the hospital bracelet still around his wrist, glowing white plastic with a big red cross on it, ensured that any passing bloodsucker would know he wasn't fair game.

If their visitors played by the rules. Which Mr Bishop might not. He wasn't a Morganville vampire. He was something else.

Something worse.

'Shane, I'm serious. How bad is it?' she asked in a low whisper, just for Shane's ears. He ruffled her short hair, then kissed it.

'I'm cool,' he said. 'Takes more than a punk with a switchblade to put a Collins down. Count on it.'

Unspoken was the fact that they were up against a hell of a lot more than that, and he knew it.

'Don't do anything dumb,' she said. 'Or I'll kill you myself.'

'Ouch, girl. Whatever happened to unconditional love around here?'

'It got tired of visiting you in the hospital.' She held his eyes for a long few seconds. 'Whatever you're thinking about doing, don't. We have to wait. We have to.'

'Yeah, all the *vampires* say so. Must be true.' She hated hearing him say the word quite that way, with so much loathing; when he said it, she always thought of Michael, of the way that he suffered when Shane's hatred boiled out. Michael hadn't *wanted* to be a vampire, and he was trying as best he could to live with it.

Shane wasn't making that any easier.

'Look.' Shane put his hands around her face and stared earnestly into her eyes. 'What if you take Eve and get out of here? They're not watching you. I'll cover for you.'

'No. I'm not leaving my parents. I'm not leaving *you.*'

And they didn't have time to talk about it, because there was a tremendous crash from the living room. The kitchen door flew open, and Michael stumbled backward through it, held by the throat by the handsome young vamp who'd come in with Bishop. He slammed Michael up against the wall. Michael was fighting, but it didn't seem to be doing him a lot of good.

The other vampire opened his mouth in a snarl, and his big, sharp vampire teeth flashed down like switchblades.

So did Michael's, and Claire involuntarily backed up against Shane.

Shane yelled, 'Hey! Let him go!'

Michael choked out, 'Don't!' but of course Shane wasn't listening, and Claire's grip on his arm wasn't going to stop him, either.

What did stop him was Eve, holding a big, nasty-looking knife. She gave Shane a wild warning look, then spun around and levelled the knife at the vampire holding Michael. 'You! *Let him go!*'

'Not until this one apologises,' the vampire said, and emphasised it by banging Michael against the wall again, hard enough that every piece of glass in the room rattled. No – it wasn't the impact; it was a low-level vibration coming from the room itself. The walls, the floor...the house. Like a warning growl.

'You'd better let him go,' Claire said. 'Can't you feel that?'

The vampire frowned at her, and his pretty green eyes narrowed even as the pupils expanded. 'What are you doing?'

'Nothing,' Eve said, and gestured with the knife. '*You're* doing it. The house doesn't like it when you play dirty with Michael. Now step away from him before something bad happens.'

He thought they were bluffing – Claire could

see it in his eyes – but he also didn't see much of a reason to push his luck. He let Michael go, his full lips curling in contempt. 'Put that away, silly girl,' he told Eve, and before any of them could even blink, he slapped it out of her hand – slapped it so hard it flew across the room and stuck in the wall. Eve grabbed her hand and cradled it close, backing away from him.

'Apologise,' he told her. 'Beg my forgiveness for threatening me.'

'Bite me!' she snapped.

The vampire's eyes flared like hot crystal, and he lunged for Eve. Michael moved faster than Claire had ever seen him, just a confusing blur, and then the stranger was hurtling into the stove. He caught himself with both hands out, and she heard the sizzle as his palms hit the burners, followed by an enraged cry of pain.

This was going to get really bad, and there was nothing, *nothing*, they could do.

Shane grabbed Eve by the shoulder, Claire by the arm, and he hustled them into the corner by the breakfast table, where they had at least partial cover. But that left Michael on his own, fighting out of his weight class against something more like a wildcat than a man.

It didn't take long, maybe a few seconds, before Michael's strength failed. The stranger threw Michael to the kitchen floor and straddled him, fangs down and gleaming. The temperature in the kitchen plummeted to icy chill, cold enough that Claire could see her own breath as she panted in fear. That low-frequency rumble began again, jittering plates and glasses and pans.

Eve screamed and fought to get free of Shane's hold, not that she could do anything, anything at all—

The back door shuddered and crashed open under a single, overpowering blow. Wood splinters flew across the room, and Claire heard the locks snap like ice breaking.

Oliver, the second-scariest vampire in town (the first, some days), stood at the back door, staring inside. He was a tall man, built like a runner, all wiry muscles and angles. Tonight, he'd dispensed with his usual nice-guy disguise; he was in black, and his hair was pulled back in a ponytail. His face looked like carved bone in the moonlight.

He slapped an open palm against the empty air of the doorway, and it smacked into a solid barrier. 'Fools!' he shouted. 'Let me in!'

The stranger laughed, and yanked Michael up to a sitting position, fangs poised just over his neck. 'Do it and I'll drain him,' he said. 'You know what that will do. He's too young.'

Claire didn't know, but she knew it couldn't be anything good. Maybe not even survivable.

'Invite me in,' Oliver repeated, in a deadly soft voice. 'Claire. Do it now.'

She opened her mouth, but she was interrupted.

'No need for that,' said a cool female voice. The cavalry had finally arrived.

Amelie moved Oliver aside and walked through the invisible barrier like it wasn't there – which, to her, it wasn't, as Amelie was technically the creator and owner of the house. She was without her usual attendants and bodyguards, but there was no mistaking that she, not Oliver, was in charge by the way she swept across the threshold.

As always, Claire thought of her as a queen. Amelie was wearing a perfectly tailored yellow silk suit, and her pale hair was piled in a glossy crown on top of her head and secured with gold and diamond pins. She wasn't especially tall, but the aura she gave off was as powerful as an unexploded bomb. Her eyes were cold and very wide, and focused completely on the intruding vampire threatening Michael.

'Leave the boy alone,' she said. Claire had never heard her use that tone, not ever, and she shuddered even though it wasn't directed toward her. 'I rarely kill our own, but if you test me, François, I'll destroy you. I only give one warning.'

The other vampire hesitated only for a second, then let go of Michael, who collapsed back full length on the floor. François rose to his feet in a single smooth, graceful motion, facing Amelie.

And then he bowed. Claire didn't have a lot of experience with seeing men bow, but she didn't think that one looked exactly respectful.

'Mistress Amelie,' he said, and the vampire teeth folded back into his mouth, discreetly hidden. 'We've been waiting for you.'

'And amusing yourself at my expense while you do,' she said. Claire didn't think she'd blinked at all. 'Come. I wish to talk with Master Bishop.'

François smirked. 'I'm sure he wishes to speak with you, as well,' he said. 'This way.'

She swept in front of him. 'I know my own home, François – I don't require a guide.' A quick glance over her shoulder, to where Oliver still stood silently at the door. 'Come inside, Oliver. I will replace the Protections against you later, on behalf of our young friends.'

He raised his eyebrows and crossed the threshold. Michael was just sitting up. Oliver extended a hand to him, but Michael didn't take it. They exchanged a look that made Claire shiver.

Oliver shrugged, stepped over him, and followed Amelie and François into the other room.

When the kitchen door swung shut, Claire let out a long, relieved breath, and heard Eve and Shane do the same. Michael rolled painfully to his feet and braced himself against the wall, shaking his head.

Shane put a hand on his shoulder. 'OK, man?' Michael gave him a thumbs-up answer, too shaken to do anything more, and Shane slapped his back and grabbed the collar of Claire's shirt as she rushed past him, heading for the door of the kitchen. 'Whoa,

whoa, Flash, where do you think you're going?'

'My parents are in there!'

'Amelie's not going to let anything happen to them,' Shane said. 'Get your breath. This isn't our fight, and you know it.'

Now *Shane* was talking sense? Wow. Was it opposite day? 'But—'

'Your parents are OK, but I don't want you rushing in. Got it?'

She nodded shakily. 'But—'

'Michael. Help me out here. Tell her.'

Michael was doing the vampire equivalent of gasping for air, but he nodded, eyes unfocused and vague. 'Yeah,' he said weakly. 'They're OK. That's why François came after me, because I got between him and your mom.'

'He went after my *mom?*' Claire flung herself toward the door of the kitchen, and this time Shane barely managed to hold on.

'Dude, that was not the kind of help I was looking for,' Shane said to Michael, and wrapped both arms around Claire to hold her in place. 'Easy. Easy, Amelie's in there, and you know she'll keep things under control—'

Claire did. After a second's thought, it made her struggle harder, because Amelie was perfectly capable of seeing Claire's parents as expendable if it served her needs. She saw *Claire* as expendable, off and on. But Shane didn't let go until she jabbed an elbow back and felt him stagger and release his grip. She didn't realise what she'd done...until she saw a thin line of red on his T-shirt, and Shane thumped himself down hard in the nearest available chair.

She'd hit him where he'd been stabbed.

'Dammit!' Eve hissed, and yanked Shane's shirt up to expose his chest and stomach – still bruised – and the white bandages, which were staining fresh with blood. Claire could even smell it...

...and as if she were in a dream, or a nightmare, she turned to look at Michael.

His eyes weren't vague and unfocused anymore. No, they were wide and intent and very, very scary. His face was still and white, and he wasn't breathing at all.

'Get the bleeding stopped,' he whispered. 'Hurry.'

Michael was right. Shane was bait in a shark tank, and Michael was one of the sharks.

Shane was staring back at him as Eve poked and probed at his bandages, making sure they were tight. 'I think it's OK, but you need to be careful,' she said. 'These bandages need to be changed. You might have popped a stitch or something.'

She put her shoulder under Shane's and helped him to his feet. Shane was still watching Michael, and Michael didn't seem to be able to physically look away from the bloody slash of bandage on Shane's stomach.

'Want some?' Shane asked. 'Come and get it,

bat boy.' He was almost as pale as Michael, and his expression was tight and furious.

Michael somehow managed to smile. 'You're not my blood type, bro.'

'Rejected again.' But some of the wildness in Shane's eyes eased. 'Sorry.'

'No problem.' Michael turned toward the closed kitchen door for a moment. 'They're talking. Look, I'm going to go in and get your parents, Claire. I want everybody together who's still—'

'Breathing?' Shane asked.

'In danger,' Michael said. 'Back in a second.' He hesitated just a breath, then added, 'See if you can fix him up while I'm gone.'

And then he was out the door, moving unnaturally fast, as if it was a relief to get away from the smell of Shane's blood. Claire swallowed and exchanged a look with Eve. Eve looked just as shaken as she felt, but she moved quickly on with priorities. 'OK. Where's the first aid kit?'

'Upstairs,' Claire said. 'In the bathroom.'

'Nope, it's down here,' Shane said. 'I moved it.'

'You did? When?'

'Couple of days ago,' he said. 'Figured it would be better where I could get to it, since I'm the one who's usually getting bandaged. Look under the sink.'

Eve did, and hauled out a big white metal box marked with a red cross. She opened it up and pulled out supplies. 'Shirt off.'

'You only love me for my abs.'

'Shut up, loser. Shirt off.'

With a glance toward Claire, Shane pulled it over his head and tossed it on the breakfast table next to him. Claire took the shirt to the sink, where she rinsed it in cold water, watching as Shane's blood tinted the water light pink. She didn't like to watch what Eve was doing; seeing the damage that Shane put himself through made her feel sick and frail, because he'd done it – as always – for other people. For her, and Eve.

'Done,' Eve pronounced a few minutes later. 'You'd *better* not bleed all over my nice clean bandages, or I'll stick a sale price on you and put you on the corner for the next neck-muncher.'

'You're such a bitch,' Shane said. 'Thanks.'

She gave him an air kiss and a wink. 'Like most girls wouldn't line up to play nurse with you. Right.'

Claire felt an unwelcome, completely surprising surge of jealousy. *Eve?* No, it was just Eve's usual teasing. Nothing else, right? She wasn't – she wouldn't. She just wouldn't.

Claire wrung out the shirt until her hands ached, then pressed it between two towels to try to get it as dry as possible. She handed it to Shane while Eve was busy putting the unused supplies back in the box, and helped him drag the damp fabric over his head and down his chest. She couldn't help but let her fingers brush down his skin, and to be honest, she didn't really try. In fact, she might have moved a little more slowly than she should have.

'Feels good,' Shane said, very quietly, in her ear. 'You OK?'

Claire nodded. He touched her lightly under the chin to lift it, and studied her face closely.

'Yeah,' he said. 'You're OK.' He brushed her lips with his and looked past her at the kitchen door as it opened.

Michael, with Claire's parents in tow. The knot in Claire's chest, the one tied tight around her heart, eased a couple of precious notches.

Her parents looked...blank. Frowning, as if they'd forgotten something important. When her mother's eyes focused on her, Claire dredged up a smile.

'Weren't we going to have dinner?' her mother asked. 'It's getting very late, isn't it? Were you going to cook, or—'

'No,' Michael said. 'We'll go out.' He grabbed his car keys from the hook next to the door. 'All of us.'

CHAPTER TWO

There weren't a lot of choices for late-night dining in Morganville for those who weren't of the fanged persuasion, but there were a few places near the campus, most notably a twenty-four-hour diner. They ended up in an uncomfortable bunch around a table, the four of them plus Claire's parents, after an even more uncomfortably close ride in Michael's big vampire-tinted car.

The hamburgers were good, but Claire couldn't concentrate on the taste. She was too busy watching the people outside the diner. Some were college students, laughing in groups in the parking lot, ignoring the occasional pale-looking strangers walking nearby. Claire was reminded of videos of lions pacing along with antelopes as they grazed, waiting for one or two to fall behind.

She wanted to warn those kids, and she couldn't. The gold bracelet on her wrist made sure of that.

Michael, predictably, had to bear the brunt of parental conversation. He was just better at it, and he had a soothing kind of presence that made everything seem...normal. Claire's parents didn't exactly remember what had happened back at the house; more of Mr Bishop's influence, Claire was sure. She hated that he'd messed with their heads, but in a way she was relieved, too. One less thing to have to worry about.

Her dad's attitude with Shane was enough.

'So,' Dad said, as he pretended to concentrate on his pot roast, 'how old are you again, son?'

'Eighteen, sir,' Shane said, in his most blandly polite voice. They'd been over this. Repeatedly.

'You know my daughter's only—'

'Almost seventeen, yes sir, I know.'

Dad frowned more deeply. '*Sixteen*, and sheltered. I don't like her living in a house with a bunch of hormone-crazy teenagers – no offence, I'm sure you mean to do right, but I was young myself once. Now that we're in town, with a place of our own, it's probably better that Claire move in with us.'

Claire had *not* been expecting that. Not at all. 'Dad! You don't trust me?'

'Honey, it's not about trusting you. It's about trusting the two adult *men* you're living with. Especially one I can see you're getting very close to, even though you know that's not very smart.'

Fury burst open inside of her, and all she could see beyond the haze of red was Shane, standing between her and Eve, defending their lives while putting his own at risk.

Shane, turning away from her time after time because he was better – better by far – than she was at self-control.

Claire sucked in a deep breath and was about to let it out in a torrent of words, at top volume, when Shane's hand came down over hers and gripped it.

'Yeah,' he said. 'You're right about that. You don't know me, and what you do know you probably don't much like. I'm not really parent friendly. Not like Michael.' Shane jerked his chin at Michael, who was trying to shake his head *no, don't do it*. 'I think maybe you're right. Maybe it would be better if Claire moved back in with you for a while. Give you a chance to get to know all of us, especially me.'

'What the hell are you doing?' Claire whispered fiercely. She didn't care that Dad could probably hear, and Michael certainly could. 'I don't want to go anywhere!'

'Claire, he's *right*. You'd be safer there. Our house isn't exactly a fortress, in case what happened today didn't sink in yet,' Shane replied. 'Hell, between strangers cruising in and out, my dad's threat to come back and finish what he started—'

Claire threw down her fork. 'Wait just a minute. You're telling me it's for my own good, is that it?'

'Yes.'

'Michael? Jump in anytime!'

Michael held up his hands in surrender. He'd

had enough, and Claire couldn't really blame him.

Eve, though, cleared her throat and waded right into the conversational swamp. 'Mr Danvers, honest, Claire's perfectly fine with us. We all look after her, and Shane's not the kind of guy who'd take advantage—'

'Wouldn't say that,' Shane said, way too mildly. 'I'm exactly that kind of guy, really.'

Eve sent him a dirty look. ' – And besides, he knows we'd both kill him if he tried. But he wouldn't do it. Claire's fine where she is. And she's happy, too.'

'Yes,' Claire agreed. 'I'm *happy*, Dad.'

Michael still hadn't spoken. He was, instead, watching Claire's father with a strange kind of intensity; at first she thought, *He's trying to put some kind of vampire whammy on him*, but then she changed her mind. It was more like Michael was honestly puzzled, and trying to figure out what to say next.

Her father hadn't heard a word that anyone had said. 'I want you to move home, Claire, and that's that. I don't want you staying in that house anymore. End of discussion.'

Her mother wasn't talking, which was unusual, too; she just stirred her coffee slowly and tried to look interested in the food on the plate in front of her.

Claire opened her mouth to shoot back a heated, not very respectful reply, but Michael shook his head and put his hand over hers. 'Don't waste your breath,' he said. 'This isn't their idea. Bishop planted the suggestion.'

'What? Why would he do that?'

'No idea. Maybe he wants us separated. Maybe he just likes messing with people. Maybe he wants to piss off Amelie. But the important thing is, I don't think you ought to let this get to you—'

'Not *get to me*? Michael, my father is saying I have to *move*!'

'You don't,' Michael said. 'Not if you don't want to.'

Claire's father, who'd been frowning, turned a dark, unhealthy colour of red in the face. 'You damn well *do*,' he snapped. 'You're my daughter, Claire, and until you turn eighteen, you'll do what I tell you. And *you*—' he levelled a finger at Michael, 'if I have to bring charges against you—'

'For what?' Michael asked mildly.

'For…look, don't think I don't know what's going on here. If I find out that my daughter's been… been…' Dad didn't seem to be able to work up the words. Michael continued to watch him steadily, with no sign of comprehension.

Claire cleared her throat.

'Dad,' she said. She felt colour blazing in her cheeks, and her voice was barely steady. 'If you're asking if I'm still a virgin, I am.'

'Claire!' Her mom's voice cracked sharply across the last of her sentence. 'That's enough.'

Total silence at the table. Not even Michael

seemed to know where to take the conversation from there. Eve looked like she was having a hard time deciding whether to laugh or wince, and finally dug into her chocolate sundae as the best possible response.

Michael's cell phone rang. He opened it, spoke softly, listened, and closed it without replying. He signalled the waitress. 'We have to go,' he said.

'Where?'

'Back to the house. Amelie wants to see us.'

'You're coming home with us,' Dad said to Claire, who shook her head. 'Don't argue with me—'

'I'm sorry, sir, but she has to come with us right now,' Michael said. 'If Amelie says it's the right thing to do, I'll bring her to your house myself. But we'll drop you off on the way, and I'll let you know as soon as possible.' It was said respectfully, but without any room for argument, and there was something about Michael in that moment that just couldn't be pushed.

Dad's face set, still red, and very hard. 'This isn't over, Michael.'

'Yes sir,' he said. 'That much I know. We haven't even started yet.'

The drive back was even more uncomfortable, and not just physically; Claire's father was livid, her mother embarrassed, and Claire herself was so mad she could barely stand to look at either of them. How *could they?* Even if Mr Bishop had done something to them, screwed with their heads, they'd bought into it completely. They'd always said they trusted her, always said that they wanted her to make her own decisions, but when it came right down to it, they wanted her to be their helpless little girl, after all.

Well, it wasn't going to happen. She'd come too far for that.

Michael pulled to a stop in front of her parents' new house – another big Gothic-style house, looking almost exactly like their own except for the landscaping out front. Her parents' Founder House had a spreading live oak tree towering over the property that rustled like dry paper in the evening breeze, and the trim was painted what looked like, in the dark, a dull black.

Claire's dad leant in to give her one last look. 'I expect to hear from you tonight,' he said. 'I expect you to tell me when you're coming home. And by home, I mean here, with us.'

She didn't answer. After extending the look for way too long, her dad shut the car door, and Michael accelerated smoothly away – not too quickly, but not slowly, either.

And they all breathed an audible sigh of relief when the house faded into the darkness behind the car. 'Wow,' Shane said. 'Dude's got a glare on him. Maybe he really does belong here in Morganville.'

'Don't say that,' Claire said. She was fighting with all kinds of emotions – anger at her parents, frustration with the situation, worry, outright fear. Her parents *didn't* belong here. They'd been just fine where they were, but Amelie had to uproot them and bring them here. Having Claire's parents where she could control them gave her more leverage.

And now it gave Mr Bishop leverage, too.

Shane took her hand. 'Easy,' he said. 'Like Michael said, you don't have to go if you don't want to go. Not that I wouldn't feel better if you were someplace a hell of a lot safer.'

'I don't think the Danvers house will be safer,' Michael said. 'They don't understand the rules, or the risks – they're too new here. I think Bishop's trying to play with Amelie's head, and whatever we think about her, he's worse. I guarantee it.'

Claire shuddered. 'Was it Amelie who called you at the restaurant?'

'No,' Michael said, and there was a grim tone in his voice. 'That was Oliver. I have to admit, I'm not feeling real good about this. Oliver's never really been on her side – maybe he's taken Bishop's. In which case we could be going home to a trap.'

'Do we have a choice?' Shane asked.

'Don't think so.'

'Then screw it. I'm getting tired.' Shane yawned. 'Let's go get eaten. At least then I can get some sleep.'

Nobody thought it was funny – least of all Shane, Claire suspected – but they didn't have any better ideas, and Michael drove home. Morganville was silent outside the dark-tinted windows; Claire could barely see dim gleams of lights, and they might have been the few and far-between street lamps, or the glow from house porch lights. It was a lot like being in a space capsule, but with better upholstery.

Michael parked and turned off the car. As Eve reached for her door handle, he said, 'Guys.' She waited. They all waited. 'I didn't exactly get any instant upgrade on knowledge when I – when I changed, but I'm damn sure of one thing. This Bishop, he's real trouble. Trouble like maybe we've never seen before. And I'm worried. So watch each other's backs. I'll try—'

He didn't seem to know how to finish that. Eve reached out to touch his face, and he turned toward her, lips parted. The look that went between them was so naked it felt wrong to see it. Shane cleared his throat.

'We're all on it, man,' he said. 'We'll be OK.'

Michael didn't answer, but then, Claire figured maybe there wasn't much to say. He got out of the car, and the others followed. The evening was getting cold, and the wind fluttered around Claire's hair and clothes, looking for skin to chill. Finding it, too. She wrapped her jacket closer and hurried after Michael toward the back door.

Inside, the kitchen was exactly as they'd left it – messy. Pots and pans still on the stove, though thankfully they'd remembered to turn off the burners before they'd left. The smell of stale bacon grease and rubbery gravy hung heavy in the air, barely cut by the aroma of old, overcooked coffee.

They didn't stop. Michael led them straight through the kitchen door, into the living room.

Bishop was gone. So were his two pretty hangers-on. It was just Amelie and Oliver, sitting alone at the large wooden table. They'd carelessly shoved aside plates and cups and glasses into a tottering pile, and between them was a chessboard. Nothing Claire recognised that belonged in the house; it looked old, and well used. Beautiful, too.

Amelie was playing white. She ignored their entry as she contemplated the chessboard. Across from her, Oliver leant back in his chair, crossed his arms, and sent the four of them an unreadable look. He seemed right at home, which made Claire fume, and she could only imagine how Michael felt about it. Oliver had killed Michael – ripped away his human existence and trapped him in a twilight state between human and vampire – right here in this house. In fact, almost on this very *spot*. It had been brutal, and murderous, and Michael had never for a second forgotten who and what Oliver was, however he appeared.

Amelie had offered Michael the chance to escape from that trap, and he'd taken it even at the cost of becoming a true vampire. So far, he didn't seem to regret it. Much.

'You're not welcome here,' Michael said to Oliver, who raised his eyebrows and smiled.

'Waiting for the house to evict me? Keep waiting,' he said. 'Amelie, you really should teach your pets manners. Next thing you know, they'll be clawing the carpet and spraying the drapes.'

She didn't look up. 'Do try to be civil,' she replied. 'You're a guest in their house. *My* house.' She moved a piece on the chessboard. 'Be seated, all of you. I dislike having people stand.'

It had the force of royal command, and before she could think about it, Claire was sliding into one of the dining-table chairs, and Shane was settling in next to her. Eve hesitated, then took a chair as far away from Oliver as possible.

That left one empty chair, and it was next to Oliver. Michael shook his head, crossed his arms over his chest, and leant against the wall.

Amelie gave him a glance, but didn't force the issue. 'So you have met Mr Bishop,' she said. 'And he has most assuredly met you. I wish this had not happened, but since it has, we must find ways to guard you against him and his associates.' Oliver took one of her bishops and set it aside. She had no visible reaction. 'Otherwise, I fear this house will be in the market for new tenants soon.'

Oliver laughed. He stopped laughing when Amelie made her next move, and concentrated on the chessboard with a fierce, blank expression.

'Who is Bishop?' Michael asked.

'Exactly who he says he is. He has no reason to lie.'

'So he's your father?' Claire asked. There was a long silence, one not even Oliver broke; Amelie raised her cool grey eyes and focused on Claire's face until Claire felt the urge, not just to look away, but to *run*.

Amelie finally said, 'In a sense, at least, as you might understand such things. Both my human and immortal bloodlines flow through him. Oliver, do hurry. I feel the need to go home before the sun rises.'

The sun wasn't anywhere close to rising, which must have been Amelie's bone-dry idea of a joke. Oliver moved a pawn. Amelie took it effortlessly.

Michael chimed in. 'Maybe the better question is, *where* is Mr Bishop?'

'Gone,' Oliver said. 'I packed him off in a nice limousine with a driver. He'll be staying at one of the Founder Houses.'

'Which one?' Claire felt a sudden surge of illness, one that got worse as neither of the vampires answered. 'It isn't my parents' house, right? Right?'

'I'd rather you not be aware of his exact location,' Amelie said, which wasn't an answer, certainly not the right answer. She moved her white queen in a long, deliberate scrape down the chessboard. 'Checkmate.'

Oliver studied the board, then studied her with equal annoyance as he tipped over his doomed black king. 'We need to discuss this,' he said. 'Obviously.'

'Your tragic lack of strategic skills?' Amelie's frost-coloured brows slowly rose. 'I am deliberating what to do about our guests. For now, go home, Oliver. And thank you for coming.'

She said it without a trace of irony – she could dismiss him like a servant, but at least she thanked him. Oliver's eyes went even darker, but he got up without comment and walked out into the kitchen. Claire heard the door slam behind him.

Amelie took in a deliberate breath, then let it out. She rose to her feet and nodded to Michael. 'I think you'll be safe enough here tonight,' she said. 'Let no one enter, not for any reason.' A quick, almost invisible flicker of a smile. 'Except for me, of course. Me, you cannot stop.'

'What about Oliver?' Shane asked.

'His invitation to enter has been revoked. He won't be able to bother you unless you do something foolish.' Which, from the look Amelie gave him, she considered hardly unlikely. 'Bishop is my affair, not yours. Go about your business, and stay out of this. All of you.'

'Wait, my parents—'

Amelie didn't wait. With silent grace, she left the table and walked up the stairs, and as her luminous pale figure disappeared at the top, Shane said, 'Where the hell is she going? There's no door up there.'

Claire knew. She knew all too well. 'However she does it, she's gone.' They all looked at her, even

Michael. 'There must be some way out. What's she going to do, bring her pyjamas and crash on the couch?'

'Do you think she has any?' Eve asked. 'Because I'm betting she sleeps in the nude.'

'*Eve!*'

'What? Come on. Can you really see her in flannel footies? Bunny slippers?'

Michael sank into the chair Amelie had vacated, and stared at the chessboard. He slowly reset it, but Claire could tell he wasn't really thinking about the game. 'Shane,' he said. 'Go make sure we're locked up, would you?'

Shane nodded and left, heading straight for the kitchen first. Claire sat across from Michael, in the chair Oliver had occupied. 'You're worried,' she said.

'No,' Michael said, and picked up the white knight, to turn it over and over in his pale fingers. 'I'm scared. If this guy's got Amelie and Oliver nervous, we're way out of our league. *Morganville* is way out of its league.'

He looked up at Eve, who didn't respond except to press her lips tighter together. Claire heard Shane's footsteps as he went toward the front door, checked the lock and dead bolt, and then went on to test the windows.

'We should get some rest,' Michael said. 'Could be a long day tomorrow.'

As he got up, Eve's hand grazed his, just a very

light caress, and the two of them locked stares for about a half second.

'Yeah,' Eve agreed. 'I should rest, too.'

Claire threw a stray magazine at her. 'Get a room.'

'Paying for one already,' Eve shot back. 'And I'm going to get my money's worth, too.'

She jogged up the stairs, pausing near the top to throw a glance back down toward Michael, who had the most luminous smile on his face. He shook his head, like he couldn't believe what was going through his mind, and cleared his throat when he saw Claire watching him.

'Discreet,' Claire said. 'You guys ought to hang a towel on the doorknob or something.'

'Quiet.' But Michael was smiling, and when he smiled, her heart just soared. She loved seeing him happy. He was usually so...focused. 'If you need anything, you know where to find me.'

'Yeah, you think?'

He waved and followed Eve upstairs.

Shane came back from checking all the ground-floor entry points, and dropped into the chair Michael had vacated. 'Where'd they go?'

She pointed straight up.

'Oh.' He knew, all too well. 'So. Want to play a game?'

'I want to call my parents,' Claire said. 'Do you seriously think Amelie let Mr Bishop stay in their house?'

'I don't know,' he said. 'Call if you think it'll help.'

She pulled her phone out of her pocket and dialled information; her parents had a new listing, since they'd just arrived in Morganville. While she waited for an answer, Shane reached across the table and took her free hand in his, and the warm touch of his skin made her feel a little less nervous.

Until her mom answered the phone, at least. 'Claire! I didn't expect you to call so soon. Are you ready to come home?'

She froze for a second, then said, as calmly as possible, 'No, Mom. I just wanted to make sure you were OK. Everything all right?'

'Of course everything's all right. Why wouldn't it be?'

Claire squeezed her eyes shut. 'No reason,' she said. 'I just wanted to check in and see how you were settling in. How's the house?'

'Well, it's a fixer-upper, you know. Needs some wiring, and an absolute mountain of decorating, but I'm looking forward to that.'

'That's great. And – so, you don't have any guests or anything?'

'Guests?' Her mother laughed. 'Claire, honey, we barely have sheets on our mattress right now. I'm not ready for guests!'

That, at least, was a relief. 'Great. Well – Mom, I have to go. Good night.'

'Good night, sweetheart. I'm looking forward to having you home.'

Claire hung up, and Shane slipped an arm around her waist. 'Hey,' he said. 'They're OK?'

'For now. But he could get to them, right? Anytime he wants.'

'Maybe. But he could get to us just as easily. Look, you can't help them right now, but he's got no good reason to hurt them. It'll be OK.'

Shane was the optimist. That was how you knew things were really bad…Claire forced a smile, opened her eyes, and tried to be a brave little toaster. 'Yeah,' she said. 'Yeah, it'll be fine. No problem.'

His dark eyes searched hers, and she knew that he could see she was lying. But he didn't call her on it, probably all too familiar with the concept of denial. 'So,' he said. 'Care for a nice, civilised game of chess?'

A thump, and the unmistakable sound of a muffled giggle, drifted through the ceiling from the second floor. Approximately where Eve's room would be.

'Hey!' Shane yelled up. 'Turn down the porn soundtrack! Trying to concentrate here!'

More laughter, quickly stifled. Shane focused back on Claire, and Claire felt her lips curling into a more genuine kind of smile.

'Chess,' she said. 'Your move, tough guy.'

Another thump from upstairs. Shane shook his head and tipped over his king. 'What the hell. I surrender. Let's hook up a video game and kill some zombies.'

CHAPTER THREE

In the morning, it was...the morning. For a precious few seconds when Claire woke up, nothing was wrong, nothing at all. Her body hummed with energy, and the birds were singing outside, and the sun burnt in warm stripes across her bed.

She squinted at the alarm clock. Seven thirty. Time to get up if she intended to make it to her first class and still have any margin for coffee.

It wasn't until she was in the shower, and the hot water was pounding sense back into her head, that she realised that all was not well. Her parents were in town. Her parents were on the radar screen of the monsters.

And her parents wanted her to move back in with them.

That put an end to her good mood, and by the time she padded down the steps, dragging her textbook-loaded backpack and carrying her shoes, she was frowning. The house was a mess. Nobody had done the chores, including her. The kitchen was still a wreck, with breakfast congealing in the pans. She muttered to herself as the coffee brewed, dumped filthy dishes and pans in the sink to soak in hot water, and left a snarky note for her housemates. Especially Shane, who'd slacked even more than was normal.

Then she put on her shoes and walked to school.

Morganville looked just like any other dusty, sleepy town in the daylight: people out driving to work, jogging, pushing strollers, walking dogs. College students with backpacks as she got closer to the campus. The casual visitor never knew, at least during the daytime, that this place was so vastly screwed up.

Claire supposed that was the point.

She spotted some trucks delivering to local businesses; did those drivers know? Did they just come and go without incident? Was there some off-limits rule for the vamps about whom they could hunt and whom they couldn't? There would have to be. Having the state police descend on Morganville wouldn't be helpful for the vamps...

'Hey.'

Claire blinked. A car was idling next to her, barely keeping pace as she walked. A red convertible, harsh and shiny as fresh blood in the sun. In it, three girls with identically false smiles.

The driver was Monica Morrell, the daughter of

the town's mayor. Claire's worst human enemy from day one of her tenure in Morganville. Monica had mostly recovered from her recent brush with death by drugs, or at least she looked that way – glossy as the car, and just as hard. Her blond hair was shiny and casually styled, her makeup perfect, and if she looked just a shade more pale than usual, it was hard to tell.

'Hey,' Claire said, and made sure to drift farther over on the sidewalk, out of easy grabbing range. 'How are you feeling, Monica?'

'Me? Great. Couldn't be better,' Monica said brightly. There was something way darker in her eyes than in her tone. 'You tried to kill me, freak.'

Claire stopped dead in her tracks. 'No,' she said. 'I didn't do that.'

'You gave me that drug. It almost killed me.'

'You *took it* from me!' The red crystals, the ones that she'd stolen from Myrnin. The ones that, however briefly, had seemed like a good idea. Not so much once she'd seen their effect on Monica, and her own face in the mirror after taking them. They hadn't hurt her, but their effect on Monica had been shocking.

'Don't give me that. You nearly killed me,' Monica said. 'I'd file charges, but with you being the Founder's pet and all, that won't do any good. So we'll just have to find some other way to make sure you pay. Just wanted to give you a heads-up, bitch – this isn't done. It isn't even started. It is *on*.'

She gave Claire a cold, hard smile, and accelerated away with a screech of rubber on pavement.

Claire shifted her backpack nervously and looked around. Nobody had paid attention, of course. It didn't pay, in Morganville, to get into anybody else's business.

She was on her own out here. Eve worked on campus, but Claire didn't want to drag her friends into this. They had enough problems already, and Monica was all her own.

Like it or not.

But as she passed the recessed doorway of a boarded-up shop, she sensed someone watching her.

She tried to dismiss it as imagination, but there really *was* someone watching her. She couldn't make him out for a few seconds, and then she did, with another unpleasant shock. Heroin-addict-skinny, pale, stringy hair. Wearing black. Eve's brother.

'Jason,' she said, and involuntarily looked around for help. Nobody there, nobody she could turn to. Not even a passing police car – and the police definitely wanted to talk to Jason, after his run-in with Shane.

It hit her again: *He'd stabbed her boyfriend.* Tried to kill him. The cops said it was self-defence, but she knew better.

Jason took his hands out of his coat pockets and held them up. 'Don't scream,' he said. 'Unless you really feel like it. I'm not going to hurt you.

Not in broad daylight on a busy street, anyway.'

He sounded...different. Odder than usual, and that was a pretty high standard of odd.

'What do you want?' She clutched the strap of her backpack in a white-knuckled fist. In an emergency, it would make a respectable blunt object. She might knock him down with it, or at least trip him. It was only about a block to Common Grounds – Oliver owed her protection once she was inside the building, even from human enemies.

'Stop freaking, genius. I'm not here to hurt you.' He put his hands back in his jacket pockets. 'How's Shane?'

'Why do you care?'

'Because—' He frowned and shrugged. 'Look, that was self-defence, OK?'

'You baited him. You threatened me and Eve. You *wanted* him to come after you.'

'Yeah, well, granted, I was tweaking, but the guy took a home-run swing at my head, in case you missed it.'

Uncomfortably, that was true. 'What about the other people you've killed? Were those all self-defence, too?'

'Who says I've killed people?'

'You did. Remember? You left a dead girl in our basement for Shane to find. You tried to put him in prison.'

Jason didn't say a word to that. He just stared at her, and in the shadows his dark eyes were like holes in his still, pale face. He looked…dead. Deader than most vampires.

'I need to talk to my sister,' he said.

'Eve doesn't want to talk to you, you psycho. Leave us alone!'

'It's about our dad,' he said, and even though Claire was walking away, leaving him and all his psycho problems behind, she slowed to look back. 'I need to talk to Eve. Tell her I'll call. Tell her not to hang up.'

Claire nodded, once. She didn't hate him any less, but there was something different about him right now – something that asked for a truce, but didn't get down on its knees and beg for it, either. 'No promises,' she said.

Jason nodded back. 'Didn't expect any.'

He didn't say thanks. She kept walking.

When she looked back, the doorway was empty. She caught a glimpse of a black jacket turning the corner at the end of the block. *Damn, he moves fast,* she thought, and that gave her another kind of chill. What if Jason had gotten his wish? What if someone had made him a full-fledged vampire, as hard as that seemed?

She decided she'd ask Amelie, first chance she got.

The morning classes came and went. It wasn't like any of them were especially difficult, even the high-level physics courses she'd tested herself into. She'd traded out some of her lame core classes for a mythology course, or rather Amelie had insisted on it – that was a fairly cool thing, and she found herself looking forward to it. No discussions of vampires just now, unfortunately. It was all about zombies, voodoo, and popular media on the subject. They were going to watch *Night of the Living Dead* next week. Claire didn't know nearly as much about zombies as most of the other students; except for the first-person-shooter game that Shane liked to play, she couldn't remember ever really paying attention to the idea.

Of course, since moving to Morganville, she wasn't ruling anything out as unlikely.

After mythology, which turned out to be a wealth of information about voodoo, if she ever needed that, Claire had a break before lab sessions began. She took herself off to the University Centre. It was a sprawling building, home to a large study area with long tables and groupings of chairs, and it featured a bookstore, a cafeteria that served fantastic grilled cheese sandwiches and salads, and a pretty decent coffee bar.

There wasn't a line today. Claire paid for her mocha and moved around to the barista side, where Eve was working. Eve looked great today, and not just because of the care she'd taken with her outfit and makeup; she kind of radiated satisfaction.

Oh. *Right*.

Eve gave her an absolutely stunning smile and handed over her drink. 'Hey, bookworm. Doing OK?'

'Sure. You?'

'Not bad. It's even been kind of slow and steady today, after the morning rush.' That smile had a secret.

'So? How was your night?' Claire prodded. The secret wanted to be shared, and besides, she was kind of...curious.

'Fantastic,' Eve sighed. 'I just – yeah. Since I was fourteen, I've had a crush on that boy, you know? And he never knew I existed. I went to every one of his concerts, from the time he first started playing, up to the last time he headlined at Common Grounds. I never thought – I just never thought it'd work out.'

'And how was...?' Claire raised her eyebrows and left the question open to anything Eve wanted to make it mean.

Eve's smile got wicked. *'Fantastic.'*

They shared muffled squeals. Eve did a little happy-dance behind the counter, dumped shots in a drink, and twirled. Claire had never seen her look so full-stop happy.

Reality came back, and she remembered why she'd come in the first place. She had the strong suspicion she was about to blow all that happiness sky-high.

Eve's smile was fading, like someone had turned down her dimmer switch. 'Claire, you're wearing the worried face. What's wrong?'

'I...' Claire hesitated, then plunged in. 'I saw Jason. This morning.'

Eve's dark eyes widened, but she didn't say anything. She waited.

'He wanted me to tell you that he's going to call. It's something about your dad, he says. He says not to hang up.'

'My dad,' Eve repeated. 'You're sure.'

'That's what he said. I told him, no promises.' Claire sipped her mocha, which was perfect, and watched Eve's expression. Not too easy to read, right now. 'He didn't try to hurt me.'

'Broad daylight, on a main street? Yeah, well, he's bug-out crazy, but he's not stupid.' Eve seemed very far away, suddenly. And all her happy glow was gone. 'I haven't talked to either one of my parents since my eighteenth birthday.'

'Why not?'

'They tried to sell me to Brandon,' she said flatly. 'Like a piece of meat on the hoof. I don't know why Jason's suddenly all nostalgic about the fam; it's not like there were good times to remember.'

'But they're still your parents.'

'Yeah, unfortunately. Look, here's the story of the Rosser clan: we're the original nuclear family. As in, nuclear bomb. Toxic even when it doesn't explode.' Eve shook her head. 'Whatever Dad's damage is, I don't care. And I don't know why Jason would, either.'

Another student had paid for coffee, and Eve cast him an absent, empty smile and started pulling espresso shots with mechanical precision.

'It's nothing,' she said. 'And I'm hanging up on him when he calls. If he calls. And even if it's something, I don't give a damn anyway.'

Claire just nodded. She had no idea what to say. Eve was clearly upset, a lot more upset than she'd expected her to be. She waved good-bye and took herself off to a nearby study table, and began ploughing through a book she'd borrowed from the library. Somebody's PhD paper, which read like the guy had never bothered to attend a single English Composition class.

Good equations, though. She was heavily involved in them when her cell phone rang.

'Hello?' She didn't recognise the number, but it was local, and not her parents.

'Claire Danvers?'

'Yes, who's this?'

'My name's Dr Robert Mills. I'm the one who treated your friend Shane in the hospital.'

She felt a piercing sensation of alarm. 'Nothing's wrong with—'

'No, nothing like that,' he broke in hastily. 'Look, you were the one who had the red crystals, right? The ones that nearly killed the mayor's daughter?'

Claire's momentary relief burnt away like flash paper. 'I guess,' she said. 'I gave them to the doctor.'

'Well, here's the thing: I've been looking at those crystals. Where'd you get them?'

'I – found them.' Technically true.

'Where?'

'In a lab.'

'I need you to show me this lab, Claire.'

'I don't think I can do that, I'm sorry.'

'Look, I understand that you're probably protecting someone – someone important. But if it helps, I already have approval from the Council to work on these crystals, and I really need more information about them – who developed them, how, the ingredients. I think I can help.'

Amelie was on the Elders' Council. But she hadn't said anything about working with the doctor. 'Let me find out what I can tell you,' Claire said. 'I'm sorry. I'll call you back.'

'Soon,' he said. 'I've been told the goal is to increase the effectiveness of the drug by at least fifty percent within the next couple of months.'

Claire blinked, surprised. 'Do you know what it does?'

Dr Mills – who sounded pleasant and normal – laughed. 'Do I *really* know? Probably not. This is Morganville – we invented the concept of the secret around here. But I have a pretty decent idea that whatever it is, it's not designed for human consumption.'

That was as much as Claire wanted to talk about on the phone, no matter how friendly he seemed. After a quick excuse, she hung up and called Amelie. She intended to leave a message, and that, she thought, would probably be the end of it.

Amelie picked up the call. Claire stammered, took a deep breath, and told her about Dr Mills and his request.

'I should have told you last evening. I have decided to concede to your request to have additional resources on this project,' Amelie said. 'Dr Mills is a trusted expert, a longtime resident of the town, and he won't make the kind of value judgments others might. He's also capable of keeping our secrets, and that is imperative. You understand why.'

Claire did, all too well. The crystals were a drug that helped vampires ward off the effects of a degenerative disease – a disease they all had, one that was robbing them of their ability to reproduce. Amelie was the strongest, but she was sick, too, and the worst cases were insane and locked away in cells beneath Morganville.

And so far, few of the vampires knew about the illness. Once they did, there might be nothing to stop them from lashing out, blaming others. Innocent humans, probably.

Just as bad would be the effect on the human population. Once they knew the vampires weren't invincible, how many of them would really cooperate? Amelie had long ago figured that this could destroy Morganville, and Claire was pretty sure she was right.

'But – he wants to see Myrnin's lab,' Claire said. Myrnin, her mentor and sometimes even her friend, had slipped off the edge of sanity, and he was in

one of the cells. Lucid sometimes, and other times...
dangerously not. 'Should I take him there?'

'No. Tell him that you'll bring what he needs to
the hospital. I don't want any human other than
yourself in that lab, Claire. There are secrets that
must be kept, and I rely on you to see to it. Restrict
his research only to refining and enhancing the
formula you've already created.' What Amelie
meant, in that queen-cool way, was that if Claire
spilt the beans, she'd end up dead. Or worse.

'Yes,' Claire said faintly. 'I understand. About
my parents—'

'They are safe enough,' Amelie said. That wasn't
the same thing as saying they were safe. 'You will
not see Mr Bishop for the time being. If you happen
to see his two associates, be polite, but don't fear;
they are well in hand.'

Maybe by Amelie's standards. Claire was a
little bit more worried. 'OK,' she said doubtfully. 'If
anything happens—'

'Discuss it with Oliver,' Amelie said. 'Curiously, I
find the differences between us lessened dramatically
once my sire paid a visit. Nothing like a common
enemy to unite squabbling neighbours.' She paused
for a moment, and then said, almost awkwardly,
'You and your friends? You are well?'

We're doing small talk now? Claire shivered.
'Yeah, we're fine. Thank you.'

'Good.' Amelie hung up. Claire mouthed a silent
Oooo-kay, and pocketed the phone.

As she was leaving, she saw Eve at the barista station, staring blankly at the levers as she worked. The happy glow hadn't returned. In fact, she looked grim. And scared.

Dammit. Why did I ruin her day like that? I should have just blown him off, the little psycho.

Claire checked her watch, snagged her backpack, and jogged off to her lab class.

When she met Dr Mills later that afternoon, she did it at the hospital, in his office. He was a medium sort of guy – medium tall, medium age, medium colouring. He had a nice smile, which seemed to promise that everything would be OK, and despite the fact that Claire knew it was total fiction, she smiled back.

'Have a seat, Claire,' he said, and indicated one of the blue club chairs in front of his desk. Behind him were floor-to-ceiling bookshelves – medical references in matching bindings, with some newer off-brand volumes thrown in for variety. Dr Mills had stacks of magazines and photocopied articles on one corner of the desk, and a teetering set of patient files on the other. A framed photo faced away from Claire, so she couldn't see if he had a family. He had a wedding ring, though.

Dr Mills didn't speak immediately; he leant back in his leather chair, steepled his fingers, and looked at her for a while. She fought against the urge to squirm, but couldn't keep her fingers from restlessly picking at the fabric of her jeans.

'I knew you were young,' he said finally, 'but I admit, I'm even more surprised now. You're sixteen?'

'Seventeen in a few weeks,' Claire said. She was getting resigned to having this conversation with every single adult in Morganville. She ought to just record it and play it back every time she met somebody new.

'Well, from the notes that Amelie has provided to me, you have a very solid grasp of what you're doing. I don't think I'll be so much directing your research as helping you execute your experiments. Where I see opportunities to add some value, I will. Obviously, the labs here at the hospital have much more sophisticated equipment than I imagine you have – wherever you developed your initial crystals.' He flipped through the large folder open in the centre of his desk, and Claire saw photocopies of her own neat handwriting. Her notes, which she'd provided to Amelie. 'I took the liberty of making up a set of crystals based on your formula, using the facilities in our labs. I found that if you accelerate the drying process with heat, you can increase the strength of the dosage by about twenty percent. And I also created a stronger liquid version that can be delivered directly into the body by injection.'

She blinked. 'Injection.' She tried to imagine getting close enough to Myrnin to stick a needle in his arm, especially when he was in one of his bad swings.

'It can be delivered through a dart,' he said. 'Like an animal tranquiliser, although I wouldn't use that analogy to anyone else. Wouldn't be respectful.'

She managed a smile. 'That'd be – very helpful. I didn't try the heating process for drying the crystals. That's interesting.'

'No reason you should have. I tried it because I didn't have an unlimited time to dry them – our lab's busy, and I didn't want anyone questioning what I was doing. I've asked Amelie to provide us with some secured laboratory space at the university. More convenient for you, and safer for me. I can have equipment moved there as we need it, or requisition it through the Council.' Dr Mills cocked his head and looked at her again, brown eyes bright and challenging. Like Myrnin's, only not half as crazy. 'About my request to tour the lab where you made the crystals...'

'Sorry, I can't.'

'Perhaps if you checked with Amelie—'

'I did.'

He sighed. 'Then when can I examine our patient?'

'You don't.'

'Claire, this will not work if I can't take baseline readings on the patient and determine what the measurable improvements are as we change the formula!'

She did see that, actually, but the thought of putting nice Dr Mills in grabbing distance of Myrnin made her shiver. 'I'll check,' she promised, and got to her feet. 'I'm sorry, it's getting late. I need to—'

Dr Mills glanced at his office window. Outside the blinds, the sky was darkening from faded denim to indigo. 'Of course. I understand. Here's a sample of the new batch of crystals. But before you give it to him, see if you can get baseline information – most importantly, a blood sample.'

'A blood sample,' she repeated. He opened a drawer and handed her a small, sealed kit. It had a syringe, gauze pads, alcohol wipes, and a couple of vacuum tubes. 'You're not serious.'

'I'm not saying it might not be difficult, but if you won't let me go with you to do it...'

She could do a lot of things, but she was pretty sure she couldn't hold Myrnin down and stick a needle in his vein. Not while he was...altered.

She took the kit and put it in her backpack. 'Anything else?'

Dr Mills passed her a gun – a dart gun. He opened the back to show her the fluffy end of the tube. 'It's preloaded with one dose,' he said. 'I only made up a few – it takes some time to distil. Here are two extra, if you need them.' As she stowed the gun in her backpack, he said, 'It's untested. So be careful. I *think* it will be stronger and longer lasting, but I'm not sure about the side effects.'

'And the crystals?'

He passed them over, too. They looked a little finer than the ones she'd developed – more like raw sugar. Those went into the backpack, as well.

'Claire,' he said, as she hoisted the burden, 'have you heard any rumours about a new vampire in town?'

She froze. Her gold bracelet, the one with Amelie's symbol etched on it, caught the light and glittered – not that she needed the reminder.

'Just Michael,' she said. 'But that's not news.'

'I heard there were strangers.'

Claire shrugged. 'Guess you heard wrong.'

She left before she had to lie any more. She couldn't stop herself from glancing back at him. He nodded and smiled a good-bye.

She felt bad, but there was only so much truth she was prepared to give, even to somebody who came recommended by Amelie.

'Did you bring the hamburger?'

Claire didn't even have time to drop her backpack on the hallway floor at home before Eve had buzzed in on her like a dark, caffeine-fuelled Tinkerbell, brandishing a wooden spoon.

'Uh – what?'

'Hamburger. I sent you a text.'

Oops. Claire dug her phone out and saw that, sure enough, there was a flashing message icon. 'I didn't get it. Sorry.'

'Crap.' Eve turned away and marched back down the hall, Doc Martens boots clomping with fine disregard for the safety of the wood floor.

'Michael! Guess what? You're running errands!'

Michael was playing guitar – something fast and complicated. He stopped periodically, which was unusual for him, and he ignored Eve, which wasn't normal, either. As Claire rounded the corner, she saw him standing up at the dinner table, leaning over to jot down music on a lined page.

Turned out that he wasn't ignoring Eve so much as not obeying. 'I'm busy,' he said, frowned at the paper, and played the same phrase again, then again. Shook his head in frustration and erased notes on the paper. 'You and Shane go.'

'I'm cooking!' Eve rolled her eyes. 'Creative people. They think the world stops when they think.'

'I'll go,' Claire said. The chance to be alone with Shane, even on something as boring as a trip to the all-night grocery, was too good to miss. 'Better if I do, anyway. I've got the free pass.' She held up the bracelet.

Michael pulled himself away from the music in his head long enough to give her a look. He tapped his pencil in a fast, complicated rhythm on the table. 'Thirty minutes,' he said. 'There and back. No excuses. If you guys are late, I'm coming after you, and I'm going to be pissed off.'

'Thanks, *Dad*.' She wished she hadn't said it – not so much because of the grimace on Michael's face, but because it made her think of her actual dad. And that the clock was running on how long he'd allow her to continue her current living arrangements.

Shane came out of the kitchen sucking on his fingertip. 'What's going on?'

'You have *not* been sticking your dirty fingers in my sauce,' Eve said, and pointed her wooden spoon at him.

He quickly took the finger out of his mouth. 'First off, they're not dirty. I licked them first. And second – did I hear something about the store? Claire?'

'Yeah, I'm ready.'

He grabbed Eve's keys from the hall table. 'Then let's roll.'

Shane was a good driver, and he knew Morganville like the back of his hand – of course, Morganville was just about that big, too, and there was only one all-night grocery store, the Food King, locally owned and operated. The parking lot was lit up like a football stadium. There were fifteen or so cars already there, evenly split between human vehicles and vamp-mobiles. Shane parked directly, under a blazing set of lights and turned off the car.

'Wait,' he said as Claire reached for the door handle. 'It takes us about five minutes to get here, five minutes to get the stuff, five minutes back home. That gives us fifteen whole extra minutes.'

She felt her heart stammer, and race a little faster. Shane was looking at her with fierce intensity.

'So what do you want to do?' she asked, trying to sound casual about it.

'I want to talk,' he said, which was not what she

expected. Not at all. 'I can't talk about this back at the house. I never know who could be listening.'

'Meaning Michael?'

Shane shrugged. 'It's just never exactly private.'

He wasn't wrong, but she still felt horribly disappointed. 'Sure,' she said, and knew she sounded stiff and wounded. 'Go ahead. Talk.'

His eyes widened. 'You thought—'

'Just talk, Shane.'

He cleared his throat. 'I've been doing some research on Bishop.'

The idea of *Shane* and *research* didn't seem to want to fall into the same sentence. 'Where?'

'The town library,' he shrugged. 'Special collections. I know Janice, the librarian – she was a friend of my mom's. She let me into the back to take a look at some of the older stuff, the things they don't put out for public reading.'

'The vampire collection.'

He nodded. 'Anyway, the only thing I could find out was a reference to a Bishop – maybe not the same one – who killed a whole lot of people about five hundred years ago.'

'Doesn't sound too unusual...'

'Except that he wasn't killing humans,' Shane said. 'From the way the thing was written, Bishop was killing off his enemies in the vampire community. Making himself the ruler of the world. And then something happened, and he dropped out of sight.'

'Wow. No wonder Amelie and Oliver were freaked.'

'If he's been underground all this time, and has a rep for taking out anyone who stands in his way, human or vampire – yeah. I'd be freaked, too. Anyway, I thought you should know. It could be important.'

'Thanks.'

He nodded, gaze fixed on hers.

'Anything else?' she prompted.

'Yeah.'

He leant forward and kissed her. His weight settled toward her, leaning her back against the door, and she felt all the strength and breath go out of her body, replaced with a quivering, golden vibration. *Oh*. Shane's lips were warm and damp, soft but demanding, and she heard herself make a sound like a whimper in response. His hands knew just where to hold her – one at the back of her head, one at the small of her back, pulling her closer. Fitting their bodies together.

It felt so good, it was like swimming in sunlight. Her fingers tangled in his soft, shaggy hair and traced down his back, and for a wild second she imagined what it would be like, right here, right now, in Eve's big car. It seemed to go on forever, a dreamy eternity of heat…

His hands slipped down her shoulders, traced her collarbone, then moved lower. She heard herself make a sound that was more a whine than anything else, a naked plea, as the heat of his touch reached the top edge of her bra, slid past the edge and down...

Shane broke the kiss with a gasp, leaning his cheek against hers. The sound of his breath in her ear made her shiver again. *So close. God, we're so close...*

'We'd – better go inside,' he said. It sounded like he was fighting hard to sound normal, but he was missing by a mile, and when he sat back, all she could see was the hot focus in his eyes, and his damp, reddened, totally kissable lips. She wondered what he was seeing in her, and realised with a shock that it was probably the same thing.

Shared hunger.

'Yeah,' she said. She didn't sound normal, either. She wasn't sure she could walk, in fact; her whole body felt like it had melted, especially around the knees. She took in a couple of deep breaths, then stopped when Shane's eyes focused on the rise and fall of her chest. 'We should – go shop.'

Shane checked his watch. 'No, we should get the hamburger, throw money at the cashier, and break every speed limit back to the house if we don't want Michael calling out the SWAT team.'

That sobered them up, enough to get them out of the car and into the store, but they held hands the whole way.

Inside, the place looked too bright, and yet somehow too cold. Aisles of colourful packages.

There were a few shoppers pushing carts, and some of them, Claire knew, had to be vampires, but she couldn't necessarily tell which ones, at a glance. Many of them had perfected their human disguises. Was it the twenty-something girl with the red hair and the long shopping list? Or the elderly lady with her little fluffy dog riding in the child seat of the cart? Not the dad with the two small children and the harassed look – she was sure of that one.

Claire didn't really have time to gawk. Shane let go of her hand and pointed off down one aisle; she split off toward the meat section. Choosing hamburger was mainly a decision about poundage, and Eve hadn't said how much to get. Claire settled for two packages, and headed for the aisle where Shane had disappeared. The snack aisle, what a shock.

The song on the store's speakers changed to an annoying and slightly creepy song from the 1970s, something about seasons in the sun, and she was thinking about how ironic that was when she rounded the endcap display and found Shane backed up against the shelves, with a woman pressed right up against him.

It was the female vamp Bishop had brought to town. She was wearing a tight-fitting pair of blue jeans, a formfitting maroon knit shirt, and a black leather jacket. Black ankle boots, with buckles. Feminine, but dangerous. Her dark hair flowed over her shoulders in luxurious, glossy waves, and her skin was the colour of fine porcelain, just a tiny hit of blush in her cheeks.

Her eyes were fixed on Shane's. He was crushing a bag of chips in one hand, but he'd clearly forgotten all about it.

The vampire leant forward and took in a deep breath from around Shane's neck. Shane closed his eyes and didn't move.

'Mmmmm,' she said in that slow, sweet voice. 'You smell like desire. I can feel it curling off your skin. Poor little thing, all frustrated and wanting. I could help you with that.'

Shane didn't open his eyes. 'Get away from me.'

The vampire's hand shot out to slam hard against the shelves next to Shane's head. The entire structure rocked unsteadily, but didn't quite go over. 'Don't be rude, Shane Collins. Yes, I know who you are. You've been looking us up, so I did a little reading all on my own. You've got daddy problems, don't you? I understand. I have those, too. I could tell you all about it, if you come with me. It'd be nice to have a strong man to tell my troubles to.'

As quickly as it had come, her anger was gone, and she was back to the vampire sex kitten she'd been back at the Glass House, running her pale fingers down Shane's collarbone, over his chest...

'I said go away,' Shane said, and opened his eyes to stare at her face. 'Not interested, leech.'

'My name's Ysandre, honey. Not leech, bitch, or bloodsucker. And if you want to survive my visit to this cesspool of a town, you'll learn to call me by my name, Shane.' Her pale lips curled into a smile. 'Or if you want *other people* to survive it. Now, let's be friends.'

She leant forward and brushed her lips lightly against Shane's, and Claire saw him shudder and go completely still. Ysandre laughed, reached past him, and plucked a bag of baked chips from the rack.

'Mmmm,' she said. 'Salty. Tell your girlfriend I like the taste of her lip gloss.'

She walked away. Shane and Claire stayed frozen where they were until she was out of sight, and then Claire rushed to him. When she put her hand on him, he flinched, just a little.

'Don't touch me,' he said. His voice was hoarse, and the vein in his throat was beating very, very fast. 'I don't want—'

'Shane – it's me, it's Claire—'

He reached out for her then, like a drowning man clutching a life raft, and his strength shocked her as he pulled her in. His head bent, and she felt the weight of it resting on her shoulder. The feverish, damp heat of his forehead against her neck.

She felt the shudder go through him, just one, just enough to tell her how horribly *wrong* he felt.

'God,' she whispered, and gently stroked his hair. It was wet underneath, matted with sweat. 'What did she do to you?'

He shook his head without raising it from her shoulder. He couldn't, or wouldn't, say it. His chest rose and fell, taking in breaths that felt like gasps but were too deep for that, and after what seemed like a full minute, Shane's body began to relax, uncoiling from that awful tension.

When he pulled back, she expected to get a look at his expression, but he turned away so fast it was just a blur – wounded dark eyes in a stark, pale mask. He looked down at the chips he was holding, and dropped them on the floor as he walked away.

Claire quickly put them back on the shelf and followed. He kept going, right past the registers. She shelled out cash to the impatient cashier for the hamburger, grabbed the plastic bag, and hurried out into the lamplit darkness after her boyfriend.

He was already unlocking the car and getting in. She was still at least a dozen feet away when he started the car with a roar, and she saw the flare of brake lights as he shifted into gear.

For a heart-stopping second Claire thought he was going to peel out and drive away, leaving her there in the dark, but he waited. She opened the passenger door and got in. Shane didn't move.

'Are you OK?' she asked.

He didn't so much as *look* at her.

He put the car in gear and burnt rubber on the way out of the lot.

CHAPTER FOUR

Shane went straight to his room, and didn't come down again for the dinner that Eve made – spaghetti with meat sauce, light on the garlic for the sake of the vampire at the table. It was probably delicious, but Claire couldn't taste a thing. She couldn't keep her mind off the white, rigid set of Shane's face, and the panic and loathing in his eyes. She didn't understand what had happened, and she knew he didn't want to be asked. Not now.

'Well?' Eve twirled spaghetti around her fork as she stared at Claire. 'How is it?'

'Oh – fantastic,' Claire said, with so much enthusiasm she knew nobody was fooled. She sighed. 'I'm sorry. It's just—'

Eve pointed above their heads. 'The dean of the drama department?'

Michael looked up at her, and for a second Claire

saw the blue of his eyes flicker. 'He's got his reasons,' he said. 'Let it go, Eve.'

'Pardon me, but that boy can make a paper cut seem like a mortal wound...'

'I said let it go.' Michael snapped it this time, and there was unmistakable command in his voice. Eve stopped twirling spaghetti. Stopped doing everything except watching him with narrowed, kohl-rimmed eyes.

'Let's review,' she said, and put the fork carefully down on a napkin. '*You* got all diva and decided you were too busy to go to the store. Next, Shane threw a tantrum and stomped up to his room to put on a one-man pity party. And now you're ordering me around like you own me. Are we under a testosterone storm warning?'

'Eve.'

'I'm not finished. You may think that growing a pair of fangs makes you the boss around here, but you'd better check your playlist. You're on the seriously wrong track.'

'*Eve.*' Michael leant forward, and Claire caught her breath. His eyes were all wrong, his movements too fast, and she caught a flash of teeth that were too white, too sharp.

Eve pushed her chair back from the table, picked up her bowl, and walked into the kitchen without a backward glance.

Michael put his head in his hands. 'Christ, what just happened?'

Claire swallowed. She tasted nothing but metal, as if she'd tried to chew the fork instead of the food. Her whole body felt cold, aching with the need to do...something.

She took Michael's bowl, stacking it with her own. 'I'll clean up,' she said.

Michael's hand closed around her wrist. She didn't dare look up at him. At close range, she didn't want to see the changes in his eyes, the ones Eve had seen so clearly.

'I wouldn't hurt any of you. You believe me, right?'

She heard the sudden doubt in his voice.

'Sure,' she said. 'It's just – Michael, I don't think you really know what you are yet. What's changing inside you. Eve thinks that showing you our weakness is a bad idea. I don't think she's wrong about that.'

Michael was watching her as if he'd never actually seen her before. As if she'd changed right before his eyes, from a child to an equal.

She swallowed hard. That was a powerful look, and it wasn't the vampire part of him – it was the Michael part. The part she admired, and loved.

'No,' he said softly. 'I don't think she's wrong, either.' He touched Claire's cheek gently. 'What happened to Shane?'

'You don't think it was just another pity party, like Eve?'

Michael had never looked so serious, she thought.

'No,' he said. 'And I think he may need help. But I don't think he'd take it from me right now.'

'I'm not sure he'll take it from me, either,' Claire said.

Michael took the plates from her. 'Don't underestimate yourself.'

Shane's room was dark, except for the dim glow that came in from the distant streetlights. Claire eased the door open and, in the stripe of warm hallway light, saw his foot and part of his leg. He was lying on the bed. She shut the door, took a slow, calm breath, and walked to sit down next to him.

He didn't move. As her eyes adjusted, she saw that his eyes were open. He was staring at the ceiling.

'You want to talk about it?' she asked. No answer. He blinked; that was all. 'She got to you, didn't she? Somehow, she got to you.'

For a long few seconds, she thought he was just going to lie there and ignore her, but then he said, 'They get inside your head, the really strong ones. They can make you – feel things. Want things you don't really want. Do things you'd never do. Most of them don't bother, but the ones that do – they're the worst.'

Claire reached out in the darkness, and his hand met hers midway – cool at first, then growing warm where their skin touched.

'I don't want her, Claire,' he said. 'But she made me want her. You understand?'

'It doesn't matter.'

'It does. Because now that she's done it once, it's going to be easy for her to do it again.' His fingers tightened on hers, hard enough to make her wince. 'Don't try to stop her. Or me, if it comes to that. I have to handle this myself.'

'Handle it how?'

'Any way I can,' Shane said. He shifted over on the bed. 'You're shivering.'

Was she? She honestly hadn't realised, but the room felt cold, cold and full of despair. Shane was the only bright thing in it.

She stretched out facing him. Too close, she thought, for her dad's comfort, if he'd seen them, even though they were only holding hands.

Shane reached down on the other side of the bed, found a blanket, and threw it over both of them. It smelt like – well, like Shane, like his skin and hair, and Claire felt a rush of warmth go through her as she breathed it in. She moved closer to him under the covers, partly to get warm, and partly – partly because she needed to touch him.

He met her halfway, and their bodies pressed together with every curve and hollow. Their intertwined fingers curled in on one another. Even though they were close enough to kiss, they didn't – it was a kind of intimacy that Claire wasn't used to, being this close and just...being. Shane freed his hand from hers and brushed stray locks of hair back from her eyes. He traced her slightly parted lips.

'You're beautiful,' he said. 'When I first saw you, I thought – I thought you were too young to be on your own here, in this town.'

'Not now?'

'You've made it through better than most of us. But if I could get you to leave this place, I would.' Shane's smile was dim and crooked and a little broken, in the shadows. 'I want you to live, Claire. I need you to live.'

Her fingers touched the warm fringe of his hair. 'I'm not worried about me,' she said.

'You never are. That's my point. *I* worry about you. Not just because of the vampires – because of Jason. He's still out there somewhere. And—' Shane paused for a second, as if he couldn't quite get the rest of it out. 'And there's me, too. Your parents might be right. I might not be the best—'

She moved her fingers to put them over his mouth, over those soft, strong lips. 'I won't ever stop trusting you, Shane. You can't make me.'

A shaky laugh out of the dark. 'My point exactly.'

'That's why I'm staying here,' Claire said. 'With you. Tonight.'

Shane took in a deep breath. 'Clothes stay on.'

'Mostly,' she agreed.

'You know, your parents really are right about me.'

Claire sighed. 'No, they're not. Nobody knows you at all, I think. Not your dad, not even Michael. You're a deep, dark mystery, Shane.'

He kissed her for the first time since she'd entered the room, a warm press of lips to her forehead. 'I'm an open book.'

She smiled. 'I like books.'

'Hey, we've got something in common.'

'I'm taking off my shoes.'

'Fine. Shoes off.'

'And my pants.'

'Don't push it, Claire.'

Claire woke up drowsy and utterly peaceful, and it took a slow second for her to realise that the heavenly warmth at her back was radiating from someone else, in the bed, with her.

From Shane.

She stopped breathing. Was he awake? No, she didn't think so; she could feel his slow, steady breaths. There was a delicious, forbidden delight to this, a moment that she knew she'd carry with her even when it was gone. Claire closed her eyes and tried to remember everything – like the way Shane's bare chest touched her back, warm and smooth where their skin connected. She'd negotiated for the removal of shirts, since she'd been wearing a sleeveless camisole underneath, and Shane had wavered enough to let it go. He'd insisted on keeping the pants, though.

She hadn't mentioned that she'd gotten rid of the bra, though she knew he'd noticed that right off.

Dangerous, some part of her said. *You're going to take this too far. You're not ready* – Why not? Why wasn't she? Because she wasn't seventeen? What was so magic about a number, anyway? Who decided when she was ready except her?

Shane made a sound in his sleep – a deep, contented sigh that vibrated through her whole body. *I'll bet if I turn around and kiss him, I could convince him...*

Shane's hand was resting on the inward curve just above her hip, a warm loose weight, and that was how she knew when he woke up – his hand. It went from utterly limp to careful, tensing and relaxing but not moving from its spot.

She could feel each individual finger on her skin.

She stayed very still, keeping her breathing slow and steady. Shane's hand slowly, gently moved up her side, barely skimming, and then he moved away from her and sat up, facing away toward the window. Claire rolled toward him, holding the blanket at neck level.

'Good morning,' she said. Her voice sounded drowsy and slow, and she saw a slice of his face as he turned slightly toward her. Sunlight glimmered warm on his bare skin, like he'd been dusted in gold.

'Good morning,' he said, and shook his head. 'Man. That was stupid.'

Not at all what *she* was thinking. Shane got up, and she gulped at the way his blue jeans rode low on his hips, the way his bones and muscles curved together and begged to be touched –

'Bathroom,' he blurted, and moved almost as fast as a vampire getting out of there. Claire sat up, waiting, but when he didn't come back, she slowly began to assemble her clothes again. Bra, clicked back into place. Camisole neat and demure, if wrinkled. She'd kept her jeans on. Her hair looked like she'd combed it with a blender – she was still messing with it when she heard Eve's trademark heavy shoes clopping down the hallway outside, passing Shane's door, going all the way to the end.

To Claire's own room.

Oh, damn.

Eve hammered on the door. 'Claire?'

Claire slipped out of Shane's room quietly, trying not to look obvious about it, and made sure she was several steps into neutral territory before she said, 'What is it?'

Eve, who'd opened up Claire's door and was looking inside, whirled so fast she almost overbalanced. She was ultra-Goth today – deep purple dress with skull patterns, black-and-white striped tights, a death's-head choker. Her hair was up in one scary-looking spiked ponytail, and her makeup was the usual rice paper and dead black, with the addition of dark cherry lipstick.

'Where'd you come from?' she asked. Claire

gestured vaguely toward the staircase. 'I just came from there.'

'Bathroom,' Claire said. And got a frown, but Eve let it go.

'It's Michael,' she said. 'He's gone.'

'Gone to work?'

'No, *gone*. As in, he took off in the middle of the night and didn't tell me where he was going, and he hasn't come back. I checked – he's not at the music store. I'm worried, especially—' Eve's train of thought switched tracks, and her eyes widened. 'Oh my *God*, are you wearing the same thing you had on yesterday? You're not doing the walk of shame, are you? Because I totally cannot face your parents if you are.'

'No, no, it's not like that—' Claire felt a hot blush work its way up from her neck to vividly light up her face. 'I just – we were talking, and we fell asleep. I swear, we didn't, um—'

'Yeah, you'd better not have *ummed*, because if you did, that would be—' Eve struggled not to smile. 'That would be *bad*.'

'I know, I know. But we didn't. And we aren't going to until—' *Until I can convince him it's OK.* 'Whatever. About Michael – what do you want to do?'

'Go ask some questions. Common Grounds is a place to start, much as I hate it; Sam's probably there, or we can leave a message for him. I heard he's back out in public again.' Sam was Michael's grandfather – and a vampire. He'd nearly been staked dead, and it had taken Amelie's help to save him. But he'd been left weak. Claire was glad to hear that he was better – Sam was, she felt, one of the best of the vampires. One she could trust. 'Well? Are we going or what?'

Shane still hadn't come out of the bathroom. 'Five minutes,' Claire said, resigned. No chance of a hot shower, or even clean clothes – the best she had available were cleanish, and not slept in. She might be able to find that last-picked pair of underwear hiding in a drawer...

There was a knock downstairs at the front door. An authoritative, urgent sort of knock. It was still early, and the number of drop-in visitors in Morganville was generally pretty small anyway; Claire dragged the least wrinkled of the two T-shirts over her head, pulled on the fresh underwear and old jeans, and hurried out into the hall still zipping up. Eve was ahead of her, already going down the stairs, and as Claire passed the bathroom, Shane opened the door and stuck his wet head out. 'What's going on?'

'Don't know!' she shot back, and hurried after Eve.

What was going on was the delivery of an envelope, which Eve had to sign for. As she turned it over, Claire made out the name, neatly written in an antiquely beautiful hand: *Mr Shane Collins*. There was even a decorative little flourish underneath his name. The envelope was heavy cream-colored paper. On the back flap there was a gold seal with some kind of shield on it.

Eve lifted it to her nose, sniffed, and raised her eyebrows. 'Wow,' she said. 'Expensive perfume.'

She waved it in Claire's direction, and she caught a hint of the dark, musky fragrance – full of promise and danger.

Shane padded downstairs, barefoot and wearing only his jeans except for the towel draped around his neck. He slowed as they both turned toward him. 'What?'

Eve held up the envelope. 'Mr Shane Collins.'

He took it from her fingers, frowned at it, and then ripped open the back flap. Inside was a folded card of the same expensive cream paper, with raised black printing. Shane looked at it for a long second, then put it back in the envelope and handed it back to Eve. 'Burn it,' he said.

And then he went upstairs.

Eve lost no time digging the card out, and since she did, Claire didn't feel too guilty about reading over her shoulder.

You have been summoned to attend a masked ball and feast to celebrate the arrival of Elder Bishop, on Saturday the twentieth of October, at the Elders' Council Hall at the hour of midnight.

You will attend at the invitation of the lady Ysandre, and are required to accompany her at her pleasure.

'Who's Ysandre?' Eve asked.

Claire was too busy worrying about the phrase *at her pleasure.*

They located Sam Glass at Common Grounds, sitting and talking with two others Claire didn't recognise, but Eve clearly did, from the nods they exchanged. Humans, because they were wearing bracelets. They said their good-byes and cleared the chairs for Eve and Claire.

Sam looked a lot like Michael – a little older, maybe, with a slightly wider chin. He had red hair to Michael's bright gold, but a similar build and height.

That had nearly gotten him killed, not so long ago, when he'd taken a stake meant for Michael. He still looked drawn, Claire thought – tired, too. But his smile was genuine as he nodded his greeting. 'Ladies,' he said. 'It's good to see you. Eve, I didn't think you'd ever come in here again, not voluntarily.'

'Believe me, if it wasn't for you, I wouldn't,' she said, and tapped dark purple fingernails on the scarred table in agitation. 'Do you know where Michael is?'

Sam's ginger eyebrows rose. 'He's not at work?'

'He left last night, didn't say where he was going. We haven't seen him, and he's not at work. So? Ideas?'

'Nothing good,' Sam said, and sat back in his chair. 'Does he have his car?'

'Yeah, as far as I know. Why?'

'GPS. All of our cars are trackable.'

'Wow, good to know in case I ever go into the grand-theft-auto business around here,' Eve said. 'Who's got the supersecret-spy tracking gear, and how do I get my hands on it?'

'You don't,' Sam said. 'I'll take care of it.'

'Soon?'

'As soon as I can.'

'But I need to find him! What if he's—' Eve leant even closer, dropping her voice to a whisper. 'What if someone has him?'

'Who?'

'*Bishop!*'

Sam's eyes widened, and all over the coffee shop, other heads snapped up. Mostly vampires, Claire thought, who knew the name, or at least knew *of* it. And who could hear a whisper across a crowded room.

'Quiet,' Sam said. 'Eve, stay out of it. It's nothing for any of you to get involved in. It's our business.'

'It's our business, too. The guy was in our *house*. He threatened us, all of us,' Eve said. 'Can't you find out right now? Because otherwise I'm going to call up Homeland Security and tell them that we've got a whole bunch of terrorists skulking around in the dark.'

'You wouldn't.'

'Oh, I so would. With glee. And I'd tell them to bring tanning beds and conduct interviews at noon out in the parking lot.'

Sam shook his head. 'Eve—'

Eve slammed her hand down on the table. It sounded like a gunshot, and every head turned in their direction. 'I'm not kidding, Sam!'

'Yes, you are,' he said, deliberately quiet. 'Because if you were serious, you would be making a threat against people who control the destiny of your next heartbeat, and that would be very, very stupid. Now, say you'll let me handle this.'

Eve's dark eyes didn't blink. 'Is this about Bishop? Why is he here? What's he doing? Why are you so scared of him?'

Sam stood up, and there was something remote and cold about him just then. Something that reminded Claire, very strongly, that he was a vampire first.

'Go home,' he said. 'I'll find Michael. I doubt he's in any trouble, and I doubt it has anything to do with Bishop.'

Eve stood up, too, and for the first time, Claire saw her as an adult – a woman, facing him on equal terms.

'You'd better be right,' she said softly. 'Because if anything happens to Michael, that won't be the end of it. I swear to that.'

Sam watched them all the way out of the coffee shop. So did everyone else. Some of them looked worried; some looked gleeful. Some looked angry.

But nobody ignored the two of them as they left. Nobody. And that was…unsettling.

They got in the car, and Eve started it up without

a word. Claire finally ventured a question. 'Where are we going?'

'Home,' Eve said. 'I'm giving Sam a chance to keep his word.'

That, Claire thought, was going to involve Eve chewing the corners off the walls and pacing holes in the floor. And Claire had absolutely no idea what to do to help her.

But that was basically what friends were for...to be there to keep you from doing the crazy.

They'd been home for exactly one hour when the phone rang. Shane was sitting next to the phone – he'd appropriated the place, because he was worried Eve would keep picking up the receiver to check the line – and answered on the first chime. 'Glass House,' he said, and listened. Claire watched every muscle in his body go tense and still. 'Go screw yourself.'

And he hung up.

Claire and Eve both gaped at him. 'What the hell—?' Eve blurted, and lunged for the phone. She flicked the contact switch.

'Star sixty-nine,' Claire suggested. 'Shane – who was it?'

He didn't answer. He crossed his arms over his chest. Eve frantically punched in the code. 'It's ringing,' she said – and then, like Shane, she went still.

She sank down in a chair.

'Should've left it alone,' Shane said.

Eve closed her eyes, and her shoulders slumped. 'Yeah, I'm here,' she said tightly. 'What is it, Jason?'

Claire caught Shane's look, and she must have seemed suspiciously in the know, because he frowned at her. 'Have you seen him?' Shane asked.

Truth, or lie? 'Yes,' Claire said, even though that definitely wasn't the path of least resistance. 'I saw him yesterday morning on the way to school. He said he wanted to talk to Eve.'

Oh, that look. It could have melted steel. 'And you forgot about chatting with the local serial killer? Sweet, Claire. Very smart.'

'I didn't forget. I – never mind.' There was no explaining the vibe she had gotten from Jason, not to Shane, whose most vivid memories of the little creep had to do with Jason sinking a knife into his guts. 'I'm sorry. I should have told you.'

Eve made a shushing motion at them and hunched over the phone, listening hard. 'He said *what*? You're not serious. You can't be serious.'

Apparently, he was. Eve listened another few seconds, and then said, 'OK, then. No, I don't know. Maybe. Bye.'

She put the phone back in the cradle and stared at it. Her face looked frozen.

'Eve?' Claire asked. 'What is it?'

'My dad,' Eve said. 'He's – he's sick. He's in the hospital. They don't think – they don't think he's going to make it. It's his liver.'

'Oh,' Claire whispered, and leant across the

table to take Eve's right hand. 'I'm sorry.'

Eve's fingers were cool and limp. 'Yeah, well – he asked for it, you know? My dad was an ugly drunk, and he – me and Jason didn't exactly have the greatest childhood.' She locked gazes with Shane. 'You know.'

He nodded. He took her left hand and stared at the table. 'Our dads were drinking buddies sometimes,' he said. 'But Eve's was worse. Lots worse.'

Claire, having met Shane's dad, couldn't really imagine that. 'How long—?'

'Jason said a couple of days, maybe. Not long.' Eve's eyes filled with tears that didn't fall. 'Son of a bitch. What does he expect from me, anyway? To come running and sit there and watch him die?'

Shane didn't answer. He didn't lift his head. He just…sat. Claire had no idea what to do, how to act, so she followed his example. Eve's hands suddenly closed on theirs, hard.

'He threw me out,' she said. 'He told me that if I didn't let Brandon fang me, I couldn't be his daughter. Well, so he's dying, boohoo. I don't care.'

Yes, you do, Claire wanted to say, but she couldn't. Eve was trying to convince herself, that was all, and in about thirty seconds she shook her head, and the tears broke free to run in dirty streaks down her pale face.

'I'll take you,' Shane said quietly. 'That way, you don't have to stay unless you want to.'

Eve nodded. She couldn't seem to get her breath. 'I wish – Michael—'

Claire remembered, with a shock, that they were still waiting for Sam's call. 'I'll stay,' she said. 'I'll call you when I hear from Sam. I'll get Michael to come there, OK?'

'OK,' Eve said weakly. 'I – need my purse, I guess.'

She swiped at her eyes and walked into the other room. Shane looked at Claire, and she wondered what all this was bringing up for him – memories of his father, of his dead mother and sister, of a family he didn't really even have anymore.

You're a deep, dark mystery, she'd said to him, and now, more than ever, that was true.

'Take care of her,' Claire said. 'Call me if you need anything.'

He kissed her on the lips, and in a few minutes she heard the front door bang shut. Locks clicked. Claire sat by the phone and waited.

She'd rarely felt so alone.

The phone rang after ten minutes. 'He's coming home,' Sam said, and hung up. No explanation.

Claire gritted her teeth and settled in to wait.

It took another twenty minutes for Michael's car to pull into the driveway. He crossed the short distance from garage to back door in a few fast strides, covering his head with a black umbrella he left by the steps. Even then, when he entered the kitchen, Claire smelt a faint burnt reek coming from him, and he was shivering.

His eyes looked hollow and exhausted.

'Michael? You OK?'

'Fine,' he said. 'I need to rest, that's all.'

'I – where were you? What happened?'

'I was with Amelie.' He scrubbed his hands over his face. 'Look, there's a lot going on. I should have left a note for you guys. I'm sorry. I'll try to keep you in the loop next time—'

'Eve's at the hospital,' Claire blurted. 'Her dad's dying.'

Michael slowly straightened. 'What?'

'Something about his liver, I guess because of his drinking. Anyway, they say he's dying. She and Shane went to see him.' Claire studied him for a few seconds. 'I told her I'd call when you got home. If you don't want to go—'

'No. No, I'll go. She needs—' He shrugged. 'She needs people who love her. It's going to be hard, facing her parents.'

'Yeah,' Claire agreed. 'She seemed upset.' Of course she was upset. What a stupid thing to say. 'I think she'd like it if you were there for her.'

'I will be.' Michael raised his eyebrows. 'What about you? You OK to stay here?'

Claire glanced at the clock on the wall. 'Could you drop me off somewhere?'

'Where?'

'I need to see Myrnin. Sorry, but I promised.'

Not that visiting her crazy vampire mentor was going to be any more pleasant than going to the hospital.

CHAPTER FIVE

Someone had done a makeover on Myrnin's cell, and it wasn't Claire; she'd thought about it, but she hadn't been sure about what Amelie would allow him to have.

So when she stepped through the doorway from the laboratory to the cells, where the sickest and most disturbed vampires of Morganville were warehoused, she was surprised to see the glow of electric light coming from the end...from Myrnin's cell. As she got closer, she noted other things. Music. Something classical was playing softly, from a stereo set up outside the bars. There was a television, as well, currently turned off.

Myrnin's cell, which had been as bare as a monk's in the beginning, was floored with a plush, expensive-looking Turkish rug. His narrow cot had been replaced with a much more comfortable bed. There were books stacked waist-high in the corners of the cell.

Myrnin was lying on the bed, hands folded across his stomach. He looked young – as young as Michael, really – but there was something indefinably *old* about him, too. Long, curling black hair, a sense of style far out-of-date. He was dressed in a blue silk dressing gown with dragons on it – neat and clean.

Someone had been here before her to take care of him. She felt guilty.

His eyes didn't open, but he said, 'Hello, Claire.'

'Hi.' She hung back, watching him. He seemed calm enough, but Myrnin wasn't all that predictable. 'How are you?'

'Bored,' he said, and laughed. 'Bored, bored, bored. I had no idea a cell could be such a prison.'

His eyes opened, and his pupils were huge. There was a fey look in his eyes that made the skin along her backbone shiver and tighten.

'Did you bring me anything to eat?' he asked. 'Someone juicy?'

He was definitely not right. She hated it when he got this way – cruel and lazy, willing to say or do anything. It was as if the Myrnin she liked had just…disappeared, leaving behind nothing but the dark shell.

Myrnin slithered off his bed, boneless and silent as a reptile. He took hold of the bars in his white, strong fingers and fixed his black-hole eyes on her face.

'Sweet, sweet Claire,' he murmured. 'So brave,

to come here. Come on, Claire. Come closer. You'll
have to if you want to *help*.'

He smiled, and even though he wasn't showing
vampire teeth, she felt the predator's breath on the
back of her neck.

'I have some new medicine,' she said, and set her
backpack down. She unzipped it and took out the
bottle with the crystals – a plastic bottle, thankfully,
so she could throw it without fear of breakage. She
tossed it underhand through the bars of the cage. It
skidded to a stop against Myrnin's pale feet. 'I need
you to take it, Myrnin.'

He didn't even bend down for it. 'I don't think I
like your tone,' he said. 'You don't order *me*, slave. I
order *you*.'

'I'm not your slave.'

'You're *property*.'

Claire opened up her backpack, took out the dart
gun that Dr Mills had given her, and shot him.

Myrnin staggered back, staring down at his stomach,
and brushed his fingers over the yellow bristle of a
hypodermic dart. 'You little *bitch*,' he said, and sat
down heavily on the bed.

His eyes rolled back as the drug delivered itself
into his bloodstream, and he slumped back flat on
the mattress.

'I may be a bitch, but I'm not your property,'
Claire said. She didn't move from where she stood as
she loaded a second dart, just in case. She watched

his body as his muscles twitched and contracted, then relaxed. 'Myrnin?'

His eyes blinked, and she saw the pupils begin to shrink down to normal-sized black dots. 'Claire?' He reached down and pulled the dart from his stomach. 'Ouch.' He examined the dart curiously, then laid it carefully aside. 'That was interesting.'

Well, he sounded saner, anyway. 'How are you feeling?'

'Sore?' He brushed his fingers over the healing puncture wound. 'Ashamed?' His dark gaze lifted to brush across hers. 'I have the feeling I've been – unpleasant.'

'I wouldn't know,' Claire said. 'I just got here. Hey, who brought you all the stuff?'

Myrnin glanced around, frowning. 'I – to be honest, I'm not really certain. I think it might have been one of Amelie's creatures.' He didn't sound at all sure. 'I was cruel to you just now, wasn't I?'

'A little,' she agreed. 'But then again, I did shoot you.'

'Ah, yes. By the way, is there any particular reason you shot me in the stomach rather than the chest?'

'Less bone,' she said. 'And my hands were shaking. How are you now?'

He sighed and sat up. 'Better,' he said. 'Don't trust me, though. We don't know how long this will last, do we?'

'No.' Claire put the gun away, and came closer

to the bars. Not close enough to grab, though.

'That's a new formulation? In liquid?'

She nodded. 'It's stronger, but I'm not sure it will last as long. Your body may break it down faster, so we have to be careful.'

'Start the clock,' he said. He looked down at himself and laughed softly. 'My dark side dresses better than I do.' He stood up and reached for clothes folded neatly on a table to the side as he loosened the tie on his robe. He hesitated, smiled, and raised his eyebrows. 'If you don't mind, Claire...?'

'Oh. Sorry.' Claire turned her back. She didn't like turning her back on him, even with the cell door locked. He was better behaved when he knew she was watching. She focused on the faint, distorted image of his reflection on the TV screen as he shed the dressing gown and began to pull on his clothing. She couldn't see much, except that he was very pale all over. Once she was sure his pants were up, she glanced behind her. He had his back to her, and she couldn't help but compare him with the only other man she'd really studied half-naked. Shane was broad, strong, solid. Myrnin looked fragile, but his muscles moved like cables under that pale skin – far stronger than Shane's, she knew.

Myrnin turned as he buttoned his shirt. 'It's been a while since a pretty girl looked at me with such interest,' he said. She looked away, feeling the blush work its heat up through her neck and onto her cheeks. 'It's all right, Claire. I'm not offended.'

She cleared her throat. 'Any side effects from the new mixture?'

'I feel warm,' he said, and smiled. 'How pleasant.'

'Too warm?'

'I have no idea. It's been so long since I felt anything like it, I'm not sure I'd be able to tell the difference.' He looped his hands loosely around the bars. 'How long are you going to wait?'

'The first time, we wait until the effects start to fade, so we can have a good baseline and we'll know how long it'll allow you to be out. Safely.'

'And you'll keep your dart pistol ready at all times, yes?' He leant casually against the bars, elegant and relaxed. There was still a faint glow in his eyes, just a little unsettling. 'What shall we talk about, then? How are your studies, Claire?'

She shrugged. 'You know.'

'They're still too simple, I would expect.'

'See? You do know.' Claire hesitated. 'We have visitors in town.'

'Visitors?' Myrnin didn't seem overly interested. 'Is it homecoming already? Why on earth Amelie tolerates these human traditions, I'll simply never understand—'

'Vampire visitors,' she said. That got his full attention.

For a frozen second, he didn't speak, only stared, and then he said, low in his throat, 'In the name of God, who?' His fingers tightened on the bars, squeezing so tightly she was afraid his bones might snap. Or the steel. *'Who?'*

She hadn't expected that reaction. 'His name is Bishop,' she said. 'He says he's Amelie's father—'

Myrnin's face went as still and pale as a plaster mask. 'Bishop,' he repeated. 'Bishop's – here. No. It can't be.' He took in a deliberate breath – one he didn't need – and let it slowly out. His hands relaxed on the bars. 'You said visitors. Plural.'

'He brought two people with him. Ysandre and François.'

Myrnin said something soft and vicious under his breath. 'I know them both. What's happened since his arrival? What does Amelie say?'

'She said we should stay out of it. So do Sam and Oliver, for that matter.'

'Has she made any public announcements? Is she planning any public events?'

'Shane got an invitation,' she said. 'To some kind of ball. He – it says he has to go as Ysandre's escort.'

'Jesu,' Myrnin said. 'She's doing it. She's acknowledging his status with a welcome feast.'

'What does that mean?'

Myrnin suddenly rattled the bars. 'Let me out. *Now.'*

Claire swallowed. 'I – can't, I'm sorry. You know how this works. The first time we test a new formulation you have to stay—'

'Now,' he snarled, and his eyes took on that terrifying vampire sheen. 'You have no idea what's happening out there, Claire! We can't afford to be cautious.'

'Then tell me what's going on! Please! I want to help!'

Myrnin visibly controlled himself, let go of the bars, and sat down on the bed. 'All right. Sit down. I'll try to explain.'

Claire nodded. She pulled over a steel industrial chair – left over from this facility's use as a prison, she thought – and took a seat herself. 'Tell me about Bishop.'

'You've met him?' Claire nodded. 'Then you already know all you need to know. He's not like the vampires you've met here, Claire, not even the worst of us. Amelie and I are modern predators, tigers in the jungle. Bishop is from a far colder, harder time. A *Tyrannosaurus rex*, if you will.'

'But he really is Amelie's father?'

Myrnin's turn to nod. 'He was a warlord. A murderer on a scale that you would find it difficult to fathom. I – thought he was dead, many years ago. The fact that he's come here, now – it's very bad, Claire. Very bad indeed.'

'Why? I mean, if he's Amelie's father, maybe he just wants to see her—'

'He's not here for happy memories,' Myrnin said. 'In all likelihood, he's here to have his revenge.'

'On you?'

Myrnin slowly shook his head. 'I'm not the one who tried to kill him,' he said.

Claire's breath caught. 'Amelie? Not – she couldn't. Not her own father.'

'It's best you don't ask any more questions, little one. All you need to know is that he has reason to hate Amelie – reason enough to bring him here and for him to try to destroy everything she has worked for and accomplished.'

'But – she's trying to *save* vampires. To stop the sickness. He has to understand that. He wouldn't—'

'You have no idea what he wants, or what he would do.' He leant forward, elbows on his knees, the picture of earnestness. 'Bishop comes from a time before there were concepts among vampires of cooperation and self-sacrifice, and he'll have nothing but contempt for them. As you would say, he's old-school evil, and all that matters to him is his own power. He won't tolerate Amelie having her own.'

'Then what do we do?'

'First, you let me out of here,' he said. 'Amelie is going to need her friends around her.'

Claire slowly shook her head. The minutes were ticking by, and Myrnin seemed stable, but she had to abide by the rules.

'Claire.'

She looked up. Myrnin's face was still and sober, and he seemed utterly in control of himself. This was a Myrnin she rarely saw – not as charming as the manic version, not as terrifying as the angry one. A real, balanced person.

'Don't let yourself be drawn into this,' he said. 'Humans don't exist for Bishop except as pawns, or food.'

'I didn't think we did for too many of you,' she said. Myrnin's eyes widened, and he smiled.

'You do have a point. As a species, we do have an – empathy gap,' he replied. 'But at least we're trying. Bishop and his friends won't bother.'

The formula was much, much better than the last one – Myrnin's stability lasted for nearly four long hours, a score that delighted him almost as much as it did her. But once he'd tired, and begun sliding back into confusion and anger, Claire stopped the clock, made her notes, and checked the massive refrigerator in the centre of the prison. She thought it had probably been built as central storage for the kitchens – kitchens that had gotten ripped out long ago – but it had the feeling of a giant, stainless-steel morgue.

Someone had forgotten to restock the supplies of blood inside. Claire made a note as she retrieved supplies for Myrnin, and tossed the blood packs into his cell. She didn't wait to watch him rip into them.

That always made her sick.

The other vampires were mostly beyond conversation – silent, reduced to basic survival instincts. She loaded up a cart and made the rounds delivering the last of the blood. Some of them had enough control left to nod a silent thanks to her; some only stared with mad, empty eyes, seeing her as just a giant, walking version of the blood bag.

It always gave her the creeps, but she couldn't stand to see them starve. It was somebody else's responsibility to feed them and keep the cells clean – but she wasn't sure that somebody did a very good job.

By the time she was done, it was late afternoon. Claire walked to the shimmering door in the prison wall, concentrated, and formed the portal back to Myrnin's lab. It was empty. She was tired and upset about what Myrnin had said about Bishop, and considered resetting the portal to take her directly to the Glass House...but she didn't like using it; it took too much out of her. She also didn't want to explain to the others about why she was stepping out of a blank wall, either.

'Guess I'm walking,' she said to the empty lab. She climbed the stairs to the rickety, leaning shack that covered the entrance, and exited into the alley behind Grandma Day's Founder House. It was another mirror of the Glass House – slightly different trim, different curtains in the windows. Grandma Day had a front-porch swing, and she liked to sit outside with her lemonade and watch people, but she wasn't out today. The empty swing creaked in the faint, cooling wind.

The sun still felt fierce, although the temperatures were dropping steadily, day by day; Claire was sweating by the time she'd negotiated Morganville's tortuously twisted avenues and turned onto Lot Street.

The sweat turned icy as she saw the police car parked in front of the house. Claire broke into a run, slammed through the white picket fence, and pounded up the stairs. The door was shut and locked. She fumbled out her keys and let herself in, then followed the sound of voices down the hallway.

Shane was sitting on the couch, wearing what Eve liked to call his Asshole Face. He was staring at Richard Morrell, who was standing in front of him. The contrast was extreme – Shane looked like he'd forgotten he owned a hairbrush, his clothes were rumpled from sitting in a laundry basket for a week, and his whole body language screamed *SLACKER*.

A whole different person from the one who'd been so quietly concerned about Eve earlier.

Richard Morrell, on the other hand, was a Morganville success story. Neat and sharp in his dark blue police uniform, every crease perfect, every hair at regulation length. The gun on his hip looked just as well cared for.

He and Shane both transferred their stares to Claire. She felt sweaty, dishevelled, and panicked. 'What's happened?'

'Officer Dick dropped by to remind me I'd missed some appointments,' Shane said. He had a flat, dark look in his eyes, the kind he got when he was committed to a fight. 'I was just telling him I'd get around to it.'

'You're months behind in donations,' Richard said. 'You're lucky it's me standing here, not somebody a lot less sympathetic. Look, I know you don't like this, and you don't have to. What you *do* have to do is get your ass up and down to the Donation Centre.'

Shane didn't move. 'You going to make me, *Dick?*'

'I don't understand,' Claire said. 'What are you talking about?'

'Shane's not paying his taxes.'

'Taxes—' It came together suddenly. The blood she'd just tossed into the cells of ravenous, maddened vampires. *Oh.* 'Blood donations.'

Shane held up his wrist. His hospital tag, marked with a red cross, was still on. 'Nobody gets to touch me for another two weeks. Sorry.'

Richard didn't move. He didn't even blink. 'No, I'm sorry, but that doesn't hold up. Your hospital exemption protects you from attack. It doesn't excuse you from civic duty.'

'*Civic duty,*' Shane mocked. 'Right. Whatever, man. Tell you what, you delivered your message. Go bust some crime or something. Maybe arrest your sister – she probably deserves it today, if it's a day that ends in y.'

'Shane,' Claire said, with just a little pleading in her voice. 'Where's Eve?'

'At the hospital,' Shane said. 'I left her there with

Michael. It's pretty rough on her, but she's coping. I came back to make sure you were OK.'

'I am,' she said. Not that either of them was listening to her anymore. Richard and Shane had locked stares again, and it was a guy thing. A contest of wills.

'So you're refusing to accompany me to the Donation Centre,' Richard said. 'Is that right?'

''Bout the size of it, Dick.'

Richard reached behind his back, unhooked the shiny silver handcuffs from the snap on his belt, and held them at his side. Shane still didn't move.

'Up,' Richard said. 'Come on, man, you know how this is going to go. Either you end up in the jailhouse or you spend five minutes with a needle in your arm.'

'I'm not letting any vamp eat me, not even by remote control.'

'Not even Michael?' Richard asked. 'Because when supplies run low, the younger the vampire, the lower he is in the priority list. Michael's the last one in Morganville to get blood. So you're doing nothing but hurting your own, man.'

Shane's fists clenched, trembled, relaxed. He glanced at Claire, and she saw the mixture of rage and shame in his eyes. He hated this, she knew. Hated the vampires, and wanted to hate Michael but couldn't.

'Please,' she whispered. 'Shane, just do it. I'll go, too.'

'You don't have to,' Richard said. 'College students are exempt.'

'But I can volunteer, right?'

He shrugged. 'No idea.'

Claire turned to Shane. 'Then we'll both go.'

'The hell we will.' Shane folded his arms. 'Go on, handcuff me. I'll bet you're dying to use that shiny new Taser.'

Claire dropped her backpack, crossed to him, and got in his face. 'Stop,' she hissed. 'We don't have time for this, and I don't need you in jail right now, OK?'

He stared right into her eyes, for so long that she was afraid he was going to tell her to mind her own business – but then he sighed and nodded. She stepped away as he stood and held out his wrists to Richard Morrell.

'Guess you've got me, Officer,' he said. 'Be gentle.'

'Shut up, Shane. Don't make this harder than it is.'

Claire trailed along behind, uncertain what she ought to be doing; Richard didn't seem interested in her at all. He used the radio clipped to his shoulder to make some kind of police call on the way down the hall, in code. She wasn't sure she liked that. Morganville wasn't big enough to need codes, unless it was something really nasty.

As she stopped to lock the front door behind them, a big, shiny black RV rounded the corner –

so sleek it looked almost predatory. It had a red cross painted on the nose, and on the side, below its blind, dark-tinted windows, red letters spelt out MORGANVILLE BLOODMOBILE. In cursive script below that, it said, *No appointment necessary.*

Shane stopped moving. 'No,' he said. 'I'm not doing that.'

Richard used leverage to get him going again at a stumble down the steps. 'It's this or the Donation Centre. Those are your choices, you know that. I was trying to make it easier.'

Claire swallowed hard and hurried down the steps. She got in front of Shane, blocking his path, and met his eyes. He was furious, and scared, and something else, something she couldn't really understand.

'What's wrong?'

'People get in that damn thing and don't come out,' he said flatly. 'I'm not doing it. They strap you down, Claire. They strap you down and nobody can see inside.'

She felt a little ill herself at the mental image. Richard Morrell's face was carefully blank. 'Sir?'

He didn't much care for her asking him; she could tell. 'I can't give you an opinion, but one way or another, he has to do this.'

'What if you drive us both to the Donation Centre instead?'

Richard thought about it for a few seconds, then nodded. He unhooked the radio from his shoulder again, muttered some quiet words, and the engine on the Bloodmobile started up with a smooth hum.

It glided away like a shark, looking for prey. All of them watched it go.

'Crap, I hate that thing,' Shane said. His voice trembled a little.

'Me, too,' said Richard, to Claire's surprise. 'Now get in the car.'

CHAPTER SIX

The Donation Centre was still open, even though it was getting dark. As Richard pulled his police cruiser to the curb, two people Claire vaguely recognised came out, waved to each other, and set off in separate directions. 'Does everybody come here?' she asked.

'Everybody who doesn't use the Bloodmobile,' Richard answered. 'Every human who's Protected has to donate a certain number of pints per year. Donations go to their Patron first. The rest goes to whoever needs it. Vampires who don't have anyone to donate for them.'

'Like Michael,' Claire said.

'Yeah, he's our most recent charity project.' Richard got out and opened the back door for her and Shane. She slid out. Shane, after a hesitation long enough to make her worry, followed. He stuck his hands in his pockets and stared up at the glowing red cross sign above the door. The Donation Centre didn't look exactly inviting, but it was far less terrifying than the Bloodmobile. For one thing, there were bright windows that offered a clear view of a clean, big room. Framed posters on the wall – the same kind you could find in any town, Claire thought – listed the virtues of giving blood.

'Does any of it get to other humans?' she asked as Richard held the door open for Shane. He shrugged.

'Ask your boyfriend,' he said. 'They used quite a few units on him after his stabbing, as I remember. Of course it gets used for humans. It's our town, too.'

'You're dreaming if you really think that,' Shane said, and stepped inside. As Claire followed, she felt a definite change of atmosphere – not just the air, which was cool and dry, but something else. A feeling, barely contained, of desperation. It reminded her of the way hospital waiting areas felt – industrial, impersonal, soaked with large and small fears. But it was still clean, well lit, and full of comfortable chairs.

Nothing at all scary about the place. Not even the motherly-looking older lady sitting behind the wooden desk at the front, who gave them all the same bright, welcoming smile.

'Well, Officer Morrell, it's nice to see you!'

He nodded to the lady. 'Rose. Got a truant for you here.'

'So I see. Shane Collins, isn't it? Oh, dear, I'm so sorry to hear about your mother. Tragedy has come to your door too often.' She was still smiling, but it was muted. Respectful. 'Can I put you down for two pints today? To make up some of what you're behind?'

Shane nodded. His jaw was clenched, his eyes brilliant and narrowed. He was fighting for control, Claire thought. She slipped her fingers in his where they were handcuffed behind his back.

'You remember me, don't you?' Rose continued. 'I knew your mother. We used to play bridge together.'

'I remember,' Shane choked out. Nothing else. Richard raised his eyebrows, got a mirrored look from Rose, and tugged on Shane's elbow to lead him away to one of the empty chairs. They were all empty, Claire noticed. She'd seen a couple of people leaving the building, but nobody coming inside.

One thing about the Donation Centre, they were better than most medical places about keeping their magazines up-to-date. Claire found a brand-new edition of *Seventeen* and began reading. Shane sat stiffly, in silence, and watched the single wooden door at the end of the room. Richard Morrell chatted with Rose at the desk, looking relaxed and friendly. Claire wondered if he came here to donate his blood, or if he used the Bloodmobile. She supposed that whatever he chose, the vampires wouldn't be crazy enough to hurt him – son of the mayor, respected police officer. No, Richard Morrell was probably safer than just about anybody in Morganville. Protected or not.

Easy for him to be relaxed.

The door at the end of the room opened, and a nurse stepped through it. She was dressed in bright floral surgical scrubs, complete to the cap over her hair, and like Rose, she had a nice, unthreatening smile. 'Shane Collins?'

Shane took in a deep breath and struggled up out of his chair. Richard turned him around and unfastened the handcuffs. 'Good behaviour, Shane,' he said. 'Trust me, you don't want to start trouble here.'

Shane nodded stiffly. He glanced at Claire, then fixed his attention on the nurse who was waiting. He walked toward her with slow, deliberate calm.

'Can I go with him?' Claire asked, and Richard looked at her in surprise.

'Claire, they're not going to hurt him. It's just like blood donation anywhere else. They stick a needle in your arm and give you a squeezy ball. Orange juice and cookies at the end.'

'So I can donate?'

He looked to Rose for help.

'How old are you, child?'

'I'm not a child. I'm almost seventeen.'

'There's no legal requirement for anyone under the age of eighteen to donate blood,' Rose said.

'But is there a law against it?'

She blinked, started to answer, and stopped herself. She pulled open a drawer and retrieved a small book that was titled *Morganville Blood Donations: Regulations and Requirements*. After flipping a few pages, she shrugged and looked at Richard. 'I don't think there is,' she said. 'I've just never had anyone donate voluntarily at the Donation Centre. Oh, we take the Bloodmobile to the university from time to time, but—'

'Great,' Claire interrupted. 'I'd like to donate a pint, please.'

Rose immediately became all business.

'Forms,' she said, and thumped down a clipboard and pen.

To say that Shane was surprised to see her was an understatement.

To say he was pleased would have been a lie.

As she took the couch next to his, Shane hissed, 'What the hell do you think you're doing? Are you *crazy*?'

'I'm donating blood,' she said. 'I don't have to, but I don't mind.' At least, she didn't think she minded. She'd never actually done it before, and the sight of the red tube snaking out of Shane's arm and down to the collection bag was a little bit terrifying. 'It doesn't hurt, right?'

'Dude, they're sticking a big-ass needle in your vein – of course it hurts.' He looked pale, and she didn't think it was all from the fact that he was on his second pint. 'You can still say no. Just get up and tell them you changed your mind.'

The same friendly-looking nurse who'd called Shane to the back rolled up a wheeled stool and a cart. 'He's right,' she said. 'If you don't want to do this, you don't have to. I saw your paperwork. You're a little young.' The nurse's bright brown eyes focused beyond her, to Shane, and then back again. 'Doing it for moral support?'

'Kind of,' Claire admitted. Her fingers felt ice-cold, and she shivered as the nurse took her hand. 'I've never done this before.'

'You're in luck. I have. Now, I'm going to stick your finger and run a quick test, and then we'll get started. OK?'

Claire nodded. Lying on the couch seemed to have effectively sapped away her will to move. The finger stick came as a sharp, bright flash, there and gone, and Claire lifted her head from the pillow to see the nurse using a tiny glass pipette to gather blood from her fingertip. It was about five seconds, and then the stick was bandaged up. The nurse did some things with items on her cart, nodded in satisfaction, and smiled at Claire. 'O negative,' she said. 'Excellent.'

Claire gave her a weak thumbs-up. The nurse took her arm and fastened the rubber tourniquet above the elbow. 'Talk to your boyfriend,' she advised. 'Don't watch.'

Claire turned her head. Shane was staring at

her with dark, intense eyes. He smiled slightly, just enough, and she returned it.

'So,' she asked, 'come here often?'

He laughed quietly. She felt something hot slip into her arm, a jolt that faded to discomfort, and then tape being applied. A ball was pressed into her hand, and the tight pressure of the tourniquet snapped loose. 'Squeeze,' the nurse said. 'You're good to go.'

Surprised, Claire glanced down. She had a thing in her arm, and a tube, and there was red running through it...

Her head fell back against the pillow, and she couldn't hear for the dark buzzing inside her skull. She thought someone was calling her name, but for the moment that didn't seem very important. She tried to breathe, slowly and steadily, and after what seemed like hours, the buzzing faded, and the world took on edges and bright colours again. There was a poster on the ceiling overhead, one of a kitten sitting in a teacup, looking adorable. She fixed on it and tried not to think about the blood that was draining out of her. *This is what it's like,* she couldn't help but realise. *This must be what Michael felt when Oliver was draining his blood. This is what all those people feel when the vampires kill them.*

It was only a little piece of death, hardly enough to matter.

The nurse slipped a warm blanket over her, smiled down, and said, 'It's OK. You're not the first to pass out. That's why the seats recline, honey.'

Claire hadn't passed out, not really, but she wasn't feeling her best, either. The nurse rolled her cart and stool around to Shane.

'Done,' she announced, and Claire tried to turn her head that way, but she didn't want to see the needle coming out any more than she'd wanted to see it go in. Squeamish. She was squeamish about needles, and she'd never realised that before. Funny.

A warm hand covered hers, and when she opened her eyes, she saw that Shane was standing next to her, pale and hollow-eyed but upright.

'Shane,' the nurse said. 'Go get some juice.'

'When she's done,' he said.

The nurse must have realised there was no arguing about it, because she kicked her wheeled stool over to him. 'Then at least sit down. I really don't want to be picking you up off the floor.'

It probably took less time than it felt, but Claire was desperately glad when the nurse came back to remove the needle and apply bandages. She didn't look at the blood bag. The nurse said something nice, and Claire tried to respond in kind but wasn't absolutely sure what came out of her mouth. Shane led her to the next room, which was a sitting area with a plasma television tuned to a news channel, juice and sodas and water, and trays of crackers and cookies and fruit. Claire took an orange and a bottle of water. Shane went straight for the sugar shock – Coke and cookies.

Claire rubbed her fingers over the purple stretch bandage around her elbow. 'Is it always like that?'

'Like what?' Shane mumbled around a mouthful of chocolate chips. 'Scary? Guess so. They try to make it nice, but I never forget whose mouth that blood ends up in.'

She felt a surge of nausea, and stopped peeling her orange. Suddenly, the thick pulpy smell was overwhelming. She chugged some water instead, which went down cool and heavy as mercury.

'They use it for the hospitals, though,' she said. 'For accident victims and things like that.'

'Sure. Reusing the leftovers.' Shane crammed another cookie into his mouth. 'I hate this shit. I swore I'd never do it, but here I am anyway. Tell me again why I stay in this town?'

'They'll hunt you down if you leave?'

'Good reason.' He dusted crumbs from his fingers. She peeled the rest of her orange, broke loose a slice, and ate it with methodical determination – not hungry, no sir, but well aware she was still shaky. She ate three more slices, then passed Shane the rest.

'Wait,' she said. He paused in the act of biting into the orange. 'You've never done this before, have you? I mean, you left town before you were eighteen, so you didn't have to. And then you've ducked it since coming back. Right?'

'Damn straight.' He finished the orange and chugged the rest of his Coke.

'So you've never been inside the Bloodmobile.'

'I didn't say that.' Shane got that grim look again. 'I went with my mother once – didn't have to donate, but she wanted me to get used to the idea. I was fifteen. They dragged in this guy – he was crazy, out of his head. Strapped him down and started draining him. They hustled the rest of us out of there, but when we left, he was still there. I watched. They drove away with him. Nobody ever saw him again.'

Claire swallowed more water. She felt weak, but she wanted out of here. The comfortable room felt like a trap, a windowless, airless box. She tossed the rest of her water and the orange peel in the trash. Shane three-pointed his Coke can and took her hand.

'Is Eve going to stay at the hospital?' she asked.

'Not all night. It's pretty uncomfortable; her dad's sobered up, and he's doing the amends thing.' Shane's mouth twisted. He clearly didn't think much of that. 'Her mom just sits there and cries. She always was practically a bag of wet tissues.'

'You don't like them much.'

'You wouldn't, either.'

'Any sign of Jason?'

Shane shook his head. 'If he's showing up to do his family duty, he's sneaking around in the dead of night. Which, come to think of it, would probably work for him. Anyway, Michael said he'd bring Eve home. They're probably already there.'

'I hope so. Did Michael say where he was, you know, before?'

'When he was missing? Something about this damn ball,' Shane said.

I should ask him about the invitation. She almost did – she opened her mouth to do it – but then she remembered how Shane had looked last night, how deeply Ysandre had shaken him.

She didn't want to see him look like that again.

Maybe she ought to just leave it. He'd talk about it when he wanted to talk.

There were two doors – one that said exit, one that had nothing on it at all. Shane passed the unmarked door, hesitated, and backed up.

'What?' Claire asked. Shane took hold of the handle and eased the door open.

'Just a hunch,' he said. 'Shhhh.'

On the other side was another waiting area, and there were people standing in line. This part of the Donation Centre was darker, with fewer overhead lights. Three people were standing in front of a long white counter, like at a pharmacy, and behind it stood a tall woman wearing a lab coat. She didn't smile, and she was about as warm as a flask of liquid nitrogen.

'Oh crap,' Shane breathed, and about the same time Claire realised that the blond guy first in line at the counter was *Michael*. He wasn't home...He was *here*.

He finished signing something and shoved the clipboard back, and the woman handed him over a plastic bottle, about the size of the bottled water Claire had been drinking.

This one didn't hold water. *Tomato juice*, Claire told herself, but it didn't look at all like juice. Too dark, too thick. Michael tilted it one way, then another, and his face – he looked fascinated.

No, he looked *hungry*.

Claire wanted to look away, but she couldn't. Michael unscrewed the cap on the bottle as he stepped out of line, put the blood to his lips, and began to drink. No, to guzzle. Claire was distantly aware that Shane's grip on her hand was so tight it was painful, but neither of them moved. Michael's eyes were shut, and he tilted the bottle back and drank until it was empty except for a thin red film on the plastic.

He licked his lips, sighed, and opened his eyes, and looked straight at the two of them.

His eyes were a bright, brilliant, glowing red. He blinked, and it went away, replaced by an eerie shine. Another blink, and it was all gone, and he was back to being Michael again.

He looked as horrified as Claire felt. Betrayed and ashamed.

Shane shut the door and dragged Claire toward the exit. They hadn't reached it before Michael came barrelling in after them.

'Hey!' he said. His skin had taken on a flush, a faint pink tone, that Claire remembered seeing before. 'What are you doing here?'

'What do you think we're doing? They hauled me here in cuffs, man,' Shane snapped. 'You think I'd be here if I had a choice?'

Michael stopped in his tracks, and his gaze flashed down to the stretchy bandages on their arms. Recognition flashed, and then he looked... sad, somehow. 'I – I'm sorry.'

'What for? Not like we didn't already know how much you crave the stuff.' Still, Claire heard the betrayal in Shane's voice. The revulsion. 'Just didn't expect to see you chugging it down like a drunk at happy hour, that's all.'

'I didn't want you to see it,' Michael said quietly. 'I drink it here. I only keep some at home for emergencies. I never wanted you to watch—'

'Well, we did,' Shane said. 'So what? You're a bloodsucking vampire. That's not a news flash, Michael. Anyway, it's no big thing, right?'

'Yeah,' Michael agreed. 'No big thing.' He focused on Claire, and she couldn't fit the two things together – Michael with those terrifying red eyes, gulping down fresh blood, and this Michael standing in front of her, with that sad hope in his expression. 'You OK, Claire?'

She nodded. She didn't trust herself to talk, not even a word.

'I'm taking her home,' Shane said. 'Unless that was your appetiser, and now you're looking for the main course.'

Michael looked sick. 'Of course not. Shane—'

'It's all right.' The fight dropped out of Shane's voice. He sounded resigned. 'I'm OK with it.'

'And that bugs the crap out of you, doesn't it?'

Shane looked up, startled. The two of them stared it out, and then Shane tugged on Claire's arm again. 'Let's go,' he said. 'See you at home.'

Michael nodded. 'See you.'

He was still holding the empty bottle, Claire realised. There was a tiny trickle of blood left in the bottom.

As the door shut between them, she saw Michael realise what he had in his hand, and throw it violently in the trash can.

'Oh, Michael,' she whispered. 'God.' In that one gesture, she realised something huge.

He really did hate this. He really did, on some level, hate what he'd become, because of what he saw in their eyes.

How much did that suck?

The rest of the night passed quietly. The next morning, they woke up to a ringing phone.

Eve's dad was gone.

'The funeral's tomorrow,' Eve said. She wasn't crying. She didn't look much like herself this morning – no makeup, no effort at all put into what she'd thrown on. Her eyes were veined with red, and her nose almost glowed. She'd cried all night; Claire had heard her, but when she'd knocked on the door, Eve hadn't wanted company. Not even Michael's.

'Are you going?' Michael asked. Claire thought that was a funny question – who wouldn't go? But Eve just nodded.

'I need to,' she said. 'They're right about that closure thing, I guess. Will you…?'

'Of course,' he said. 'I can't do graveside, but—'

Eve shuddered. 'So not going there, anyway. The church is bad enough.'

'Church?' Claire asked, as she poured mugs of coffee for the three of them. Shane, as usual, had slept through the phone. 'Really?'

'You've never met Father Joe, have you?' Eve managed a weak smile. 'You'll like him. He's – something.'

'Eve had the hots for him when she was twelve,' Michael said, and got a dirty look. 'What? You did, and you know it.'

'It was the cassock, OK? I'm over it.'

Claire raised her eyebrows. 'Is Father Joe a…?' She did the teeth-in-neck mime. They both smiled.

'No,' Michael said. 'He's just non-judgemental.'

Eve got through the day without too much trouble; she did the normal things – helping with the laundry, taking half the cleaning jobs for the day. It was her day off from work. Claire had a few classes, but she skipped three that she knew she'd already built up enough momentum in, and attended only the one that seemed critical. Michael didn't go in to teach private guitar lessons, either.

It was nice. It was like…family.

The funeral was held at noon the next day, and Claire found herself trying to pick out what to wear. Party clothes seemed too…festive. Jeans were too informal. She borrowed a pair of Eve's black tights and wore them with an also-borrowed black skirt. Paired with a white shirt, it looked moderately respectful.

She wasn't sure how Eve planned to dress, because at eleven a.m., Eve was still sitting in front of her vanity mirror, staring at her reflection. Still in her black dressing gown.

'Hey,' Claire said. 'Can I help?'

'Sure,' Eve said. 'Should I do my hair up?'

'It'd look nice that way,' Claire said, and picked up the hairbrush. She brushed Eve's thick black hair until it shone, then twisted it into a knot and pinned it up at the back of her head. 'There.'

Eve reached for her rice-powder makeup, then stopped. She met Claire's eyes in the mirror.

'Maybe not the right time,' she said.

Claire didn't say anything at all. Eve applied some lipstick – dark, but not her usual shade – and began searching through her closet.

In the end, she went with a black high-necked dress, one long enough to hang to the tops of her shoes. And a black veil. It was subdued, for Eve.

The four of them were at the church with fifteen minutes to spare, and as Michael pulled into the parking garage, Claire saw that several vampire-tinted cars were already present. 'Is this the only funeral?' she asked.

'Yeah,' he said, and turned off the engine. 'I guess Mr Rosser had more friends than we thought.'

Not that many, as it turned out; when they entered the vestibule of the church, it was nearly empty, and there weren't many names noted in the register. Eve's mother stood by the book, waiting to pounce on anyone who came in the door.

True to Michael's earlier description, Mrs Rosser couldn't seem to stop crying; she was wearing all black, like Eve, only it was much more theatrical – dramatic sweeps of black satin, a big formal hat, gloves.

And, Claire reflected, when you were more theatrical than *Eve*, you definitely had issues.

Mrs Rosser had gone in heavy for mascara, and it was in messy streams all down her cheeks. Her hair was dyed blond, and straggling around her face. If she was going for the role of Ophelia in the town production of *Hamlet*, Claire thought she probably had it in the bag.

Eve's mother threw herself on Claire like a wet blanket, sobbing on her shoulder and smearing mascara on her white shirt. 'Thank you for coming!' she wailed, and Claire awkwardly patted her on the back. 'I wish you'd known my husband. He was such a *good* man, such a *hard* life—'

Eve stood there looking remote and a little sick. 'Mom. Get off her. She doesn't even know you.'

Mrs Rosser drew back, gulping back another sob. 'Don't be cruel, Eve, just because you didn't love your father—'

Which was just about the coldest thing Claire had ever heard. She exchanged a stricken look with Shane.

Michael got between mother and daughter, which was damn brave of him. Maybe it was the vampire gene. 'Mrs Rosser. I'm sorry about your husband.'

'*Thank you*, Michael, you've always been such a good boy. And thank you for taking care of Eve when she went out on her own.'

Mrs Rosser blew her nose, which was how she missed Eve saying caustically, 'You mean, when you threw my ass out on the street?'

'Sign us in,' Michael said to Claire, and took Eve's arm and led her into the church. Claire hastily scribbled their names in the book, nodded to Mrs Rosser – who was staring after her daughter with an expression that turned Claire's stomach – and grabbed Shane's arm to follow.

She'd been in the church before. It was nice – not overly fancy, but peaceful in its simplicity. No crosses anywhere in sight, but just now, the focus was the big, black casket at the end of the room. She was struck by the smooth curve of the wood, and how much it reminded her of the Bloodmobile.

That made Claire shiver and grip Shane's arm

even more tightly as they slid into the pew beside
Michael and Eve.

There were about fifteen people scattered
through the sanctuary, and more arrived as the
minutes ticked by. A couple of men in suits – from
the funeral home, Claire supposed – set up more
floral displays on either side of the casket.

It somehow didn't seem real. And the sounds
of Mrs Rosser's continued sobs and wails,
responding to every mourner who entered, made
it even weirder.

Eve slid out of the pew and walked up to the
coffin. She stared down into it for a few long seconds,
then bent and put something in it and came back
to take her seat. She had her veil down, but even
with the softening blur, her expression looked frozen
and hard.

'He was a son of a bitch,' she said when she saw
Claire watching her. 'But he was still my dad.'

She leant against Michael's shoulder, and he put
his arm around her.

Mrs Rosser finally entered the sanctuary and
took a seat in the front row, ahead of where the four
of them were. One of the funeral home attendants
handed her an entire box of tissues. She pulled out
a handful and continued to sob.

And a tall, good-looking man in a black cassock
and white surplice, with a purple stole around
his neck, came out from behind the floral displays
and knelt down next to her, patting her hand. The

fabled Father Joe, Claire supposed. He seemed nice – a little earnest, and younger than she'd expected. Brown hair and golden eyes that were very direct behind a pair of square gold-rimmed spectacles. He listened to Mrs Rosser's ode to her husband with a sympathetic, if distant, expression, nodding when she paused. His glance flicked away once or twice, to the clock, and he finally bent forward and whispered something to her. She nodded.

More people had come in at the last minute, enough to fill about half the church. Claire, turning, spotted familiar faces: Detectives Joe Hess and Travis Lowe, who nodded in her direction as they took their seats at the back of the room. She recognised a few more people, including a total of four vampires in dark suits and sunglasses.

One of them was Oliver, looking bored. Of course – Eve's family had been under Brandon's Protection, and when Brandon had died, they'd come under his superior's authority. Oliver's appearance here had less to do with genuine feeling than public relations.

Father Joe stepped to the pulpit and began eulogising a man Claire had never met, and one she doubted Eve recognised; except for the facts and figures of his life, his character seemed way better than anything his daughter had ever mentioned. From the way Mrs Rosser nodded and cried, she was buying into the fiction wholesale.

'What a load of crap,' Shane whispered to Claire. 'Her dad hit her, you know. Eve.'

Claire sent him a startled look.

'Just keep that in mind,' he finished. 'And don't shed any tears. Not for this.'

Shane could, Claire thought, be one of the hardest people she'd ever met. Not that he was wrong. Just – hard.

But it helped. The emotion swirling through, amped higher by Eve's mother, washed over her and away without doing more than making her eyes sting. When Father Joe finished his eulogy, the organ started, and Mrs Rosser was the first to the casket.

'Oh, God,' Eve sighed under her breath as her mother draped herself dramatically over the wood and screamed. Bloodcurdling, theatrical screams. 'I guess I'd better—'

Michael went with her, and whether it was his male presence or his angelic face or his vampire blood, he was able to pry Mrs Rosser away and lead her back to the pew, where she sat in a complete collapse, blubbering.

Eve stood there at the casket for a few seconds, back straight, head inclined, and then walked away.

Tears dripped from under her veil and pattered on her black dress, but she didn't make a sound.

Claire filed by, but gave Eve's dad only a quick glance; he looked – unnatural. Not disgusting, but clearly not alive. She shivered and took Shane's arm, and followed Eve as she passed her mother without a word and headed for the exit.

Eve almost ran into her brother.

Jason had slipped in the back. As far as Claire could tell, the kid hadn't changed his clothes at all – ever – and the unwashed smell of him was evident from three feet away.

He looked high, too. 'Nice disguise, Sis,' he smirked.

Eve stopped, staring at him, and scraped the veil back from her face. 'What are you doing here?'

'Mourning.' He laughed under his breath. 'Whatev.'

Eve deliberately looked to the side, where Detectives Hess and Lowe were sitting. 'I think you'd better go.' They hadn't noticed him yet, but they would. All it would take would be a raised voice, or Eve snapping her fingers.

'He's my dad, too.'

'Then show him some respect,' she said. 'Leave.'

She went around him. The rest of them followed, though Shane slowed down, and Claire had to tug at his arm to keep him moving.

Jason made a *bring it* motion. Shane shook his head. 'Really not worth the trouble,' he said.

And then they were out in the vestibule, away from the choking smell of flowers and the subtle smell of death, and all Claire could think was, *How is that closure?*

But Eve looked better, and that was what mattered. 'Let's go have a burger,' she said.

As ideas went, that one was popular, and Claire's spirits lifted as they walked out of the church and into the shaded parking structure, heading for Michael's car.

They were intercepted.

Michael sensed it first – he stopped dead in his tracks, turning in a circle as if trying to pinpoint a sound the rest of them couldn't hear.

A lithe shadow leapt down from the concrete rafters above, landed in a crouch, and grinned.

Ysandre. She rose with effortless grace and strolled toward the four of them.

'Get in the car,' Michael said. 'Go.'

'Not leaving you,' Shane said. He didn't take his eyes off Ysandre.

'Don't be an idiot. She's not after me.'

Shane's eyes flicked to Michael's face.

'Go.'

Claire tugged on Shane's arm. He let himself be guided to the car. Michael tossed the keys.

Ysandre flashed across the open space and plucked them out of the air. She tossed them carelessly up and down in her palm, and the cool, metallic jingle was the only sound in the garage.

'Don't get all paranoid,' she said. 'I just stopped by to say hello. It's a free country.'

'It's car theft if you keep my keys,' Michael said.

He held up his hand, and she shrugged and pitched them back. 'What do you want?'

'Just wanted to make sure Mr Shane got my invitation,' she said. 'Did you, honey?'

Shane didn't move. Didn't speak. As far as Claire could tell, he wasn't even breathing.

'From the fast little beat of that heart, I guess you did,' Ysandre said, and smiled. 'See you on Saturday, then. You-all have a good rest of the week.'

She walked away, high-heeled boots tapping on the pavement, and vanished into shadow.

Shane let out a slow breath.

None of them knew exactly what to say. Michael unlocked the car, and the quiet ruled for at least five minutes, until he stopped at Denny's.

'We still eating?' he asked.

'I guess,' Shane said. 'I'm not letting her ruin my appetite.'

There was a shade awning stretching from the covered parking to the front door, which Claire had never thought about before – apparently, the local Denny's catered to vampires as much as humans even in the daytime. There were local flyers taped to the glass front doors, and Claire glanced at them on the way inside. She stopped so suddenly Shane ran into her.

'Hey! Walking here!'

'Look.' Claire pointed at the paper.

It said *ONE NIGHT ONLY!* and there was a

black-and-white photograph of a young man with blond hair cradling a guitar.

Underneath it said *Michael Glass returns to Common Grounds,* and the date on it was... tonight.

Shane ripped it off the door, grabbed Michael's shoulder, and held it up. 'Hey,' he said. 'Ring any bells? When were you going to tell us?'

Michael looked surprised, then embarrassed. 'I – wasn't going to. Look, it's just a tryout, OK? I wanted to see if I could still – I don't want you guys to come. It's nothing.'

Eve grabbed the flyer and stared at it. 'Nothing? Michael! You're *playing*! *In public!*'

'That's new?' Claire whispered to Shane.

'He hasn't played anywhere but our living room since—' Teeth-in-neck mime. 'You know. Oliver.'

'Oh.'

Michael's face was turning pink. 'Just put it back, OK? It's not a big deal!'

Eve kissed him. 'Yes, it is,' she said. 'And I hate you for not telling me. Were you just going to sneak off or something?'

'Absolutely,' Michael sighed. 'Because if I suck, I don't want any of you hearing it firsthand.'

Claire taped the flyer carefully back to the door. 'You're not going to suck.'

'Not at the guitar, anyway,' Shane said, deadpan. Claire punched him in the arm. 'Ow.'

CHAPTER SEVEN

Michael spent two hours tuning his guitar, which was annoying, and he left early. Eve went with him, despite his protests that it really wasn't a big thing. That left Claire and Shane to decide on their own what to do.

She made chilli dogs and was putting the shredded cheese on top when Shane, fresh from video-game triumph, came into the kitchen. 'Hey,' he said. 'Nice. Thanks.' He shoved part of the chilli dog in his mouth, standing at the kitchen counter.

'You could at least sit down,' she sighed. 'We do have tables. They even have chairs.'

'You want to go?' he mumbled 'To the thing?'

Did she? Claire ate a bite of her own hot dog, hardly even aware that she was breaking her own eating-while-standing rules, and thought about it. On the one hand, it meant going out at night, and going out to Common Grounds for recreational purposes, which was sort of not done around their house these days.

But – Michael. Out in public. Playing.

'Yeah,' she said. 'I would, if you don't mind. I know you don't like the place, but—'

'I like it better than Eve does, trust me. Besides, I don't want her down there alone. She needs somebody watching her back while he's neck-deep in groupies or whatever.'

She laughed.

'Oh, you think that's funny? Should have seen him in high school. Guy could draw the hotties every time he picked up that guitar.'

'He still can, I'll bet.'

'Exactly my point. Eat up. They usually start music sets around seven.'

Claire wolfed down her meal and ran upstairs for a quick shower and change of clothes. After some debate, she went with the short skirt and tights she'd last worn to crash Monica Morrell's disastrous house party, and a plain black top tight enough to match but loose enough that she wouldn't die if her parents saw her.

Shane blinked in surprise when she came downstairs. He'd thrown on different clothes, too, but they were still slacker-casual. The only sign that he was trying to make an impression was that she suspected he might have combed his hair. A little.

'You look great,' he said, and smiled. She stopped on the last step from the bottom, which put them on about equal levels, and he kissed her. Long and slow. He tasted of toothpaste, at first, but then he just tasted like Shane, and that was so, so delicious that she found herself rising on her tiptoes to get even closer. 'Hold up, girl. I thought we were going out. Kissing like that, you're making me think about staying in.'

Claire had to admit, it made her think of it, too. Especially since the house was empty, and they were all alone.

She saw it cross Shane's mind, too, and for a second his eyes widened, and so did his pupils.

Oh, the possibilities.

'Better go if we're going,' Claire said regretfully. 'Only – how are we getting there?'

Shane offered her his arm. 'Nice night for a walk, I hear.'

'Are you sure?'

He tapped her gold bracelet, then his own white hospital-issue one. 'This may be the only night we get to do it in this town,' he said. 'Let's live dangerously.'

It was nice, strolling arm in arm with Shane and not worrying (well, not worrying too much) about which danger was about to sweep in on them from the dark.

Tonight, at least, the dangers kept their distance. It was a short walk to Common Grounds, but a lonely one; Claire felt a little unreal, moving slowly in the dark past shut houses with lit-up windows. People didn't venture out much after sunset, and if they did, they went in groups, and in cars.

Two people out in the night like this...seemed wrong, and when they were about halfway to the coffee shop, Claire saw someone pull a car into a driveway ahead of them and jump out. The look on the woman's face was starkly panicked as she looked toward them, and Claire realised that she'd thought they were –

Vampires. Which was both funny and sad.

The woman grabbed her groceries and hurried into her house, shutting the door with a bang and locking it with a harsh rasp of metal.

Claire didn't say anything to Shane, and he didn't venture a comment, but she had no doubt he felt the same unsettling guilt. But what could they have said? *It's OK, lady, we're not here to eat you?*

Claire was glad when the hot golden spill of light from Common Grounds' front window came into view. It was obviously doing good business – cars lined the streets on both sides, and more parked as she and Shane approached the entrance. 'Going to be nuts,' Shane said, but he didn't sound displeased. 'Next time I'll take you someplace nice and quiet.'

Claire searched her memory. So much had happened since she'd met Shane, but she was almost sure that this constituted their first real, actual date on their own. Which was startling, and sweet, and precious to her in ways she suspected Shane would never imagine. She savoured the warmth of his hand in hers, smiled at him, and entered

Common Grounds while he held the door for her.

The noise level was amazing. The coffee shop was normally quiet, although never boring, but as the sun went down, the excitement level rose, and tonight it was blowing through the roof. Every table was already crowded with people – humans, mostly, but toward the corners of the room Claire saw a few vampire faces she recognised, including Sam's. Michael's only family in town had come to support him. Sam sent her a smile and a wave, which Claire returned.

Michael himself was standing in the clear area behind the coffee bar, looking tense and a little bit blank. He was dressed in a plain grey T-shirt and jeans, and he had his acoustic guitar slung around his body. Claire thought the puka shell necklace he was wearing looked new – a gift from Eve? A good-luck charm?

Eve was standing next to him, and although she couldn't see clearly, Claire thought they were holding hands.

Claire and Shane pushed through the crowd to the bar. Shane nodded to Michael, who nodded back – all very manly – and then Shane went to place some drink orders, leaving Claire to fumble for words.

'You're going to do great,' she finally said. Michael's blue eyes blinked and focused in the here and now.

'Man, I don't know,' he said. 'It was supposed to be casual – I show up and play a couple of songs. Just to get used to it again. But this—'

Somebody out in the corner of the room started clapping, and suddenly everybody was doing it, a wave of rhythmic noise.

Michael couldn't possibly get any more pale, but Claire saw the outright doubt in his eyes. Eve did, too, and gave him a quick kiss.

'You can do this, Michael,' she said. 'Come on. Get out there. It's what you do.'

Claire nodded and smiled her support. Michael lifted the hinged section of the bar and stepped out, to a thunderous wave of applause. There was a small stage set up at the far end of the room, near the closed door that said OFFICE, and as Michael moved up on it, the stage lights caught and glittered in his golden hair, sparked an unearthly blue in his eyes.

Wow, Claire thought. That wasn't Michael anymore. That was…something else.

Eve ducked under the bar and came to lean next to Claire, her arms folded. She had a wistful smile on her Evil Queen-red lips. 'He's beautiful,' she said. 'Right? He is.'

Claire could only agree with that.

Michael adjusted the microphone, tested it, played a couple of fast finger exercises she knew he used to calm himself, and then smiled out at the crowd. It was a different smile than she'd ever seen from him before – *more*, somehow. More intense, more joyous, more personal. She felt a hot flutter somewhere deep inside as his gaze brushed over her, and immediately felt embarrassed about it.

But man, he was hot. She understood now what Shane was talking about, and she wasn't immune.

Shane touched her shoulder and handed her a drink just as Michael said, 'I guess you all know who I am, right?'

And about eighty percent of the room cheered like thunder. The others – college students, who'd either wandered in or come because they were bored – looked lost.

Michael gave the mike stand one last, precise adjustment. His hands were sure now, moving with confidence. 'My name is Michael Glass, and I'm from Morganville.'

More cheers. Before they died away, Michael started to play, a fast and complicated song that Claire had heard him fooling around with at the house – but this wasn't fooling around; this was serious talent. He glittered like white gold, and music flowed out of his hands like streams of light. It wrapped around Claire like a shining net, and she didn't dare breathe, didn't move, as Michael played like she'd never heard anyone play before, ever.

She managed to glance aside at Shane, whose eyes were wide and fixed on Michael, as well. She nudged him. He gave her a dumbfounded shake of his head.

Eve was smiling, as if she'd known it all along.

Michael brought the song to a liquid, blazing finish, and as the guitar strings rang in the silence, the crowd was utterly still. Michael waited, just as motionless, and then the room spontaneously erupted in applause and cheers.

Claire thought that the smile that spread across Michael's face was worth everything about Morganville, right at that moment.

His next song was slower, sweeter, and Claire realised with a shock that it was a slowed-down version of the song he'd been writing the other night, when he'd been too busy to go to the store. It had lyrics, too, and Michael's voice transformed them into sad, aching beauty.

It was a song for Eve.

Claire realised her chest was hurting, both from the pressure of unshed tears and the fact that she wasn't breathing. She'd never known music could have that much power. As she glanced around the coffee shop, she saw the same thing in the others' faces – common rapture. Even Oliver, standing behind the bar, was transfixed. And in the shadows, Claire glimpsed someone else – Amelie, nodding thoughtfully, as if she'd known all along, like Eve.

Sam's eyes were full of tears, but he was smiling.

Michael's voice drifted to a whisper, and he finished the song. This time, the applause didn't stop, and the cheers were a full-throated roar.

'Michael adjusted the mike stand again. 'Save it, guys,' he said over the noise, and smiled. 'We're just getting started.'

* * *

It was the best night Claire had ever had in Morganville. She'd never felt so much a part of something – never seen so much *unity* in a room full of people so diverse. Clueless students were backslapping Morganville natives with bracelets, vampires were smiling impartially at humans, and even Oliver seemed affected by the general euphoria.

When Michael came offstage, it was only after three encores and thunderous standing ovations. He made a beeline straight for Eve, folded her in a hug, and then kissed her so deeply Claire had to look away. When they came up for air, Michael was still grinning.

'So?' he asked. 'Didn't suck, right?'

Shane offered his hand. 'Didn't suck. Congratulations, dude.'

Michael ignored the hand and hugged him, then turned to Claire. She didn't hesitate to embrace him. He was warmer than usual, and sweaty; she hadn't known vampires could sweat. Maybe they just usually didn't exert themselves that much. 'You were amazing,' Claire whispered. 'I just – amazing. Wow. Did I say amazing?'

He gave her a kiss on the cheek, and then turned away to the press of well-wishers coming to shake his hand. There were a lot of them, and many of them were pretty girls. Claire retreated back to Shane's side.

'See what I mean?' Shane said. 'Good thing Eve's here. This can go to a guy's head.'

'Even a vampire's?'

'Heh. Especially a vampire's.'

It took about fifteen minutes for the rush of instant fans to die down, and by then the tables had cleared out, leaving just a few hard-core caffeine addicts to close out the evening. Claire and Shane grabbed chairs and fresh drinks while Eve helped Michael get his things together.

'Hey,' Claire said, and got Shane's full attention. 'Thank you.'

His eyebrows rose. 'What for?'

'For the best date I've ever had.'

'This? Nah. Just average. I can do much better.'

She cocked her head. 'Really?'

'Absolutely.'

'You willing to prove it?'

Somehow, his hand had taken hold of hers, and his warm fingers stroked shivers down her palm. 'Someday,' he said. 'Soon. Absolutely.'

She found herself doing the not-breathing thing again, caught in all the possibilities. Shane smiled, slow and wicked, and she wanted to kiss him right then, for a very long time.

'Ready?' Michael was standing at the table, gazing down at them. Some of the brilliance he'd had onstage had faded, and he was just regular Michael again – a little tired, too. Claire gulped down hot cocoa and nodded.

Even the best nights had to come to an end.

* * *

Claire was getting ready for bed when she heard Eve scream – not the shriek of *Stop tickling me, you jerk*, but a full-out cry of alarm, one that went through the house like a buzz saw. She pulled on her pyjama top, grabbed her robe, and pelted out into the hall. Shane was already there, heading downstairs, still dressed in a pair of jeans and a loose T-shirt.

When they got to the front hall, they found Michael sitting on the floor, holding a bloody girl in his arms. Eve was snapping the locks on the front door shut.

'Miranda,' Michael said, and moved the bloody hair away from her face. 'Miranda, can you hear me?'

Claire realised with a breathless shock that it was Eve's sometime friend Miranda – just a kid, really, at that gawky stage where girls both yearned to be and feared to be women. Mir had filled out a little since the last time Claire had seen her – not quite as scary thin – but she still looked like a waif.

A wounded one. There was a gash in her head, and blood dripping down her neck to patter on Michael's blue jeans and fingers.

'Ow,' Miranda whispered, and began to cry. 'Ow. I hit my head—'

'You're OK, you're safe now,' Eve said. She dropped to her knees across from Michael and held out her arms; Michael quickly transferred the girl over. His pupils had gone to pinpoints, and he seemed – different. 'Michael, maybe you'd better go – wash up.'

He nodded stiffly and pushed past Shane and Eve, heading upstairs so quickly he was just a blur.

'Ambulance?' Shane asked.

'No! No, I can't!' Miranda sounded frantic. 'Please, don't send me there. You don't know – you don't know what they'll do – the fire—'

Eve kept hold of the girl, somehow, though Miranda was flailing like mad. 'OK, chill, we won't. I promise. Relax. Shane – maybe the first aid kit? Towels and hot water?'

'I'll help,' Claire said, and she and Shane took off for the kitchen. When she glanced back, she saw that Miranda had stopped fighting and was lying exhausted in Eve's arms. 'What the hell happened to her?'

'Morganville,' Shane said, and shrugged. He stiff-armed the kitchen door and went straight for the cabinets under the sink. The first aid kit was getting a lot of play, Claire thought as she turned on the hot water and gathered up some clean kitchen towels.

Miranda's first aid session wasn't as bad as Claire had feared – the head wound was bloody but superficial, and Eve fixed it with some butterfly bandages.

The holes in Miranda's neck looked fresh, though. When Eve asked about them, Miranda looked embarrassed and pulled up the collar of her shirt. 'None of your business,' she said.

'It's Charles, right? Son of a bitch.' Eve had a problem with vampires who preyed on the underage – in fact, from what Claire had gathered, so did a lot of the other vampires. There were laws against it, after all. She wondered whether Amelie knew about Charles and Miranda. Or cared. 'You can't let him gnaw on you like this, Mir! You know that!'

'He was so hungry,' Miranda said, and hung her head. 'I know. But it didn't hurt, not really.'

That made Claire want to throw up. She exchanged a look with Shane.

'There's a guy who needs staking,' he said.

Miranda looked up sharply. 'That's not funny!'

'Do I have on my funny face? Miranda, the guy's a paedophile. The fact that he just sucks your blood instead of—' Shane paused, staring at her. 'It is instead of, right?'

It was impossible to tell if Miranda even understood what he was getting at, but Claire thought she did, and it made the girl deeply uncomfortable. Miranda tried to get out of the chair they'd put her into. 'I need to go home.'

'Whoa, whoa, you can barely stand up,' Eve said, and managed to get her settled again. 'Claire, would you check on Michael? See if he's OK?'

In other words, there were questions Shane and Eve were about to ask, personal questions. Claire nodded and went upstairs. The bathroom door was closed. She knocked softly.

'Michael?'

No answer. She tried the handle. Locked.

Claire turned at what sounded like footsteps down the hall, but she saw no one. She didn't hear the door unlock, but when she looked back, the bathroom door was open, and Michael was standing about two inches away from her.

She stumbled backward. Instead of just washing up, he'd showered; his hair was damp and curling and darker than usual, and he was wearing a towel around his waist. There was a lot more of Michael on display than she was used to, and it was... impressive.

Claire backed away, all the way to the wall.

'Sorry,' he said. Not as if he really was. He sounded annoyed, stressed, and jittery. 'She's still here.' It wasn't a question, but Claire nodded anyway. 'She can't stay. We need to get her out of here.'

'I don't think she's in any shape to go,' Claire offered. 'She seemed pretty hysterical. Shane and Eve are—'

'I can still smell her blood,' Michael interrupted her. 'I washed it off of me. I took off my clothes. I showered. None of that matters, I can still – she has to go. *Now.*'

'What's wrong with you? I thought you'd—' She hesitated, then made a drinking motion.

'I did.' Michael rubbed his face with both hands. 'Guess I burnt it off tonight at the show. I'm hungry, Claire.'

It cost him a lot to say it. Claire gulped, and nodded. 'Wait here.'

She went downstairs, past where Shane and Eve were still earnestly talking with Miranda, and into the kitchen. At the very back of the bottom shelf of the refrigerator sat some bottles that might have been full of beer, and weren't. There were three of them. She grabbed one without looking too closely at it and made sure it was concealed against her side as she passed the little downstairs group. Nobody really looked her way; they were too intent on keeping their own secrets.

Michael was still waiting, leaning against the bathroom doorframe, arms folded. He straightened when he saw what she had in her hand. She gave it to him silently. Michael never took his eyes off her as he popped the cap with his thumbnail and lifted the cold bottle to his lips. The contents moved more like syrup than blood, and Claire almost gagged.

Michael *did* gag. But he swallowed it. And kept on drinking until the bottle was empty.

His blue eyes flushed hot red, and then cleared back to their normal colour.

She saw something like horror go through him. 'I didn't just do that in front of you.'

'Uh – yeah. You did.' And there had definitely been some kind of challenge in it, too. Some kind of come-on, even. Which was beyond yuck and creepy, and yet…

And yet.

Michael wiped his lips with the back of his hand,

looked down at the faint smear, and went back to the washbasin to rinse it off.

He stared into the mirror at himself for so long, Claire thought he'd forgotten she was there, and then he said, 'Thanks.'

Claire tried to think of something not totally idiotic to say. 'Pretty disgusting, isn't it? When it's cold?' That wasn't it.

Luckily, Michael was relieved to have any kind of conversational lifeline, after that weird moment. 'Yeah,' he said. 'But it keeps the edge off. That's what's important.' He rinsed out the bottle carefully, then threw it away and took in a deep breath. 'I'll get dressed. Be there in a second.'

It was a dismissal, but a nice one, and Claire took it at face value this time, and went back to the living room.

Where Shane and Eve were standing together, heads cocked at identical angles, staring.

'What's going on?' Claire whispered.

'Shhh,' both Shane and Eve hissed, eerily in unison.

Because Miranda was talking in a strange monotone voice, and she looked...dead. Unconscious. Only talking.

'I see the feast,' she was saying. 'So much anger... so much lying. All dead, walking dead, falling down. It's spreading. It'll kill us all.'

Claire felt a hot snap of alarm. *Walking dead, falling down. It's spreading.* Miranda had psychic episodes – Claire knew that. It was part of the reason Eve let her hang around from time to time. Sometimes her visions were fake, but a lot of the time, they were as serious as a heart attack, and Claire somehow knew this one was real.

She was talking about the disease infecting the vampires, and she was talking about it spreading to humans. *No, that can't happen. Can it?* They hadn't even really been able to pinpoint what the disease was, only what it did, and what it did was erode the vampires' sanity, carving steadily until what was left was unable to function at all.

The first thing to go – for all the vampires of Morganville – had been the ability to reproduce. To create new vampires. Only Amelie still had the strength, and creating Michael had almost destroyed her.

It's spreading. Claire thought of all the humans in Morganville, all the families, all the young people who'd been in the coffee shop tonight, and felt cold and unsteady.

It couldn't be true.

'Feast,' Miranda said again. 'You're all fools, all fools – don't let him trick you. It's not just three – it's more—'

'Who?' Eve sank down next to Miranda's chair and put a hand on her shoulder. 'Mir, who are you talking about?'

'Elder,' she said, and now there were tears leaking down Miranda's pale cheeks. 'Oh no. Oh no...they're turning. They're all so hungry, can't stop them—'

Michael, who was coming down the steps, paused. He looked calm again, but worried. 'What's she talking about?'

'Shhh!' This time, all three of them shushed at the same time. Eve bent closer to Miranda. 'Honey, are you talking about the vampires? What's going to happen with the vampires?'

'Dying,' Miranda whispered. 'So many dying. We think we're safe but we're not. They won't listen – they won't see us—' She restlessly turned the silver bracelet on her wrist and twisted in her chair. 'He's doing it. He's making it happen.'

'Oliver?' Eve asked. Because Oliver was the only male vampire Elder on the town council.

But Miranda shook her head. She didn't say another word, but she cried, cried so hard she shook herself out of her trance and clung to Eve like a thin little reed in the wind.

'Bishop,' Michael said. They all looked at him. 'It's not Oliver. She's talking about Bishop. He's going to try to destroy Morganville.'

Miranda ended up sleeping on the couch, and when Claire came downstairs the next morning, she found the girl huddled in a ball under mountains of blankets, still shivering but fast asleep. She looked even more frail. Her pale skin was translucent, and there were dark, exhausted circles around her eyes.

Claire felt sorry for her, but it was a distant kind of sorry – Miranda didn't really invite a lot of devotion. She didn't have any friends to speak of, or so Eve said; people tolerated her, but they didn't exactly enjoy her company. That was hard on the kid, but Claire could understand it. Miranda was a mixture of denial and outright creepiness, and even in Morganville, she was going to have a hard time fitting in.

No wonder she defended the vampire who was feeding on her. He was probably the only one who really showed her any kind of affection.

Claire paused to tuck the blankets more firmly around the girl's trembling frame before she went into the kitchen to make coffee and toast. As breakfasts went, it was lonely and basic, but the sun was barely up and none of the others were what you might call morning people.

There were times when signing up for early classes seemed like a really bad idea.

When the phone rang, Claire nearly jumped out of her skin. She leapt for the extension hanging on the wall by the kitchen door and got it before the second ear-splitting jangle. 'Hello?'

There was a pause on the other end, and then her mother said, 'Claire?'

'Mom! Hi – what's wrong?'

'Why should anything be wrong? Why can't I

just call because I wanted to talk to my daughter?' Oh, great. Now her mother sounded agitated and defensive. 'I know it's early, but I wanted to catch up with you before you went off to class for the day.'

Claire sighed and leant against the wall, idly kicking at the linoleum floor. 'OK. How are you and Dad settling in? Getting all unpacked?'

'Just fine,' her mother said, in so false a tone that Claire went very, very still. 'It's just – an adjustment, that's all. Such a small town and all.'

'Yeah,' Claire agreed quietly. 'It's an adjustment.' She had no idea what her mother and father knew about Morganville by now, but they had to be getting some kind of – what would they call it? Orientation? Morganville was nothing if not efficient about that, she suspected. 'Have you – met some people?'

'We went to a nice getting-to-know-you party downtown,' Mom said. 'Mr Bishop and his daughter took us.'

Claire had to bite her lip to hold back a moan. Bishop? And Amelie? Oh God. 'What happened?'

'Oh, nothing, really. It was a cocktail party. Hors d'oeuvres and drinks, a little conversation. There was a presentation on the history of – of—' With shocking suddenness, Claire's mother burst into tears. 'I swear, we didn't know – we didn't know or we wouldn't have sent you to this awful place, oh, honey—'

Claire could barely swallow around the lump in her throat. 'Don't cry, Mom. It's OK. It's all going to be OK now.' She was lying, but she had to. The sound of her mother breaking apart was just too hard. 'Look, you've met Amelie, right?'

Sniffles on the other end. 'Yes, she seemed nice.'

Nice wasn't how Claire would have put it. 'Well, Amelie's the most powerful person in Morganville, and she's definitely on our side.' An exaggeration, but it was the best she could do to describe the situation in simple terms. 'So there's really nothing to be worried about, Mom. I work for Amelie. She has some responsibility for me, and for you, to make sure we're safe. OK?'

'OK.' It was wan and muffled, but at least it was agreement. 'I was just so worried about your father. He didn't look well, not well at all. I wanted him to go to the hospital, but he said he was fine—'

Claire had a cold second of flashback to Miranda saying, *Please don't send me there. You don't know what they'll do...*She'd been talking about the hospital. 'But he's OK?'

'He seems all right today.' Claire's mom blew her nose, and when she came back to the phone, she sounded clearer and stronger. 'I'm sorry to lay this on you, honey. I just had no idea – it was so strange to think that you'd been here all this time and never said a word to us about – the situation.' Meaning, the vampires.

'Well, to be honest, I didn't think you'd believe me,' Claire said. 'And out-of-town calls are monitored. They told you that, right?'

'Yes, they did. So you were protecting us.' Her mom laughed shakily. 'Parents are supposed to protect their children, Claire. We've done a bang-up job of that, haven't we? We really thought that it would be so much safer for you here than off in Massachusetts or California on your own...'

'It's OK. I'll get there someday.'

They moved the conversation to easier things – to unpacking, to the vase that had gotten broken during the move ('Honestly, I hated that thing anyway – your aunt gave it to us for Christmas that year, remember?'), to how Claire intended to spend her day. By the end of it, Mom seemed more or less stable, and Claire's coffee was hopelessly cold. So was her toast.

'Claire,' Mom said. 'About moving out of that house—'

'I'm not moving,' Claire said. 'I'm sorry, Mom. I know it's going to upset Dad, but these are my friends, and this is where I belong. I'm staying.'

There was a short silence on the other end, and then her mother said, very softly, 'I'm so proud of you.'

She hung up with a soft *click*. Claire stood for a moment, tears prickling in her eyes, and then said to the silent line, 'I love you.'

And then she picked up her stuff and went to class.

CHAPTER EIGHT

Days passed, and for a change, there were no further emergencies. Normal life – or what passed for it, anyway – set in. Claire went to class, Eve went to work, Michael taught guitar lessons – he was a lot more in demand since the concert at Common Grounds – and Shane...Shane slacked, although Claire thought he seemed preoccupied.

It finally dawned on her that he was thinking about Saturday, and the invitation. And that he didn't want to talk to her about it at all.

'So what should I do?' she asked Eve. 'I mean, can't he just call in sick for the party or something?'

'You're kidding,' Eve said. 'You think they'd buy an excuse? If you get an invitation to something like this, you go. End of story.'

'But—' Claire, who was getting glasses out of the cabinet while Eve put out plates, nearly dropped everything. 'But that means that creepy little bi—'

'Language, missy.'

'—witch is going to make him go with her!' That made her blindly furious, and not entirely because of how upset Shane had been before. It was the whole idea of Shane going along with it. Of Ysandre putting those pale, thin fingers on his chest, feeling his heartbeat.

Shane hadn't said a word to her about it. Not a single word. And she didn't know how to help.

Eve stared at her thoughtfully for a few seconds before she said, 'Well, she's not the only one who's going, of course. Shane won't be all by himself.'

'What?'

'Michael's going, too. I recognised the invitation when it came in. Didn't open it, though.'

Still, Eve had every reason to expect that Michael would at least ask her to go with him. Claire, on the other hand, was completely shut out.

Which made her irrationally angry again, and this time for herself. *You're jealous*, she realised. *Because you don't want him going anywhere without you.*

She so did not want to be that person, but there it was. And she had no idea what to do about it.

When she set Shane's glass of Coke down in front of him, she did it with probably a little too much emphasis; he glanced up at her with a question-mark expression. Eve had already settled into her chair across the table. Michael wasn't home, but Eve didn't seem bothered about it this time. Maybe he'd talked to her about where he was going.

Nice to know somebody's talking, Claire thought.

'What?' Shane asked her, and took a drink. 'Did I forget to say thanks? Because, thanks. Best Coke ever. Did you make it yourself? Special recipe?'

'Got any plans for Saturday night?' she asked. 'I was thinking maybe we could go to the movies, or—'

Too transparent. Shane knew instantly, and Eve choked on her forkful of microwave lasagne. The silence stretched. Claire poked at her own meal, just for something to do.

'I can't,' Shane finally said. 'I guess you know why.'

'You're going to that ball thing,' Claire said. 'With Bishop's – friend.'

'I don't exactly have a choice.'

'Are you sure about that?'

'Of course I'm sure – why are we talking about this exactly?'

'Because—' She stuck the fork into her lasagne so deep it scraped the plate. 'Because Michael's going. I guess Eve is, too. And what am I supposed to do, exactly?'

'You're kidding. Are you on crack? Because I thought you just implied that you wanted to go to the scary vampire thing. Which, by the way, I don't.'

Claire tried not to glare. 'I thought you hated her. Ysandre. But you're going with her.'

'I do. And I am.' Shane shovelled food into his mouth, a blatant excuse to end the conversation, or at least avoid it.

Eve cleared her throat. 'Maybe I should, I don't know, leave? Because this is starting to sound like one of those reality shows I don't want to be in. Maybe you guys want to take turns in the confessional booth.'

Shane and Claire ignored her. 'I didn't tell you because there's nothing you can do,' Shane said. 'There's nothing anyone can do.'

'Stop talking with your mouth full.'

'Dude, you asked!'

'I—' Claire felt a sudden burn of tears in her eyes. 'I just wanted you to talk to me, that's all. But I guess you can't even do that.'

She picked up her uneaten lasagne and drink and took it upstairs to her room. It was her turn to throw a fit, slam a door, and sulk, and dammit, she was going to do it well.

She burst into tears the second the door was closed, put everything down on the dresser, and collapsed into a soggy heap in the corner. She hadn't cried like this in a long time, not over something so *stupid*, but she just couldn't – didn't –

There was a knock at the door. 'Claire?'

'Go away, Shane.' Her heart wasn't in it, though, and he must have heard that. He opened the door. She kind of expected him to rush to her and sweep her up in a hug, but instead Shane just...stood there. Looking like some mixture of annoyed and confused.

'Why is this about you?' he asked her. It was a perfectly reasonable question, so absolutely logical it made her gasp and cry harder. 'I have to get dressed up in a stupid outfit. I have to pretend I don't want to shove a stake in this bitch's heart. You don't.'

'But you're going! Why are you going? You – I thought you hated her—'

'Because she said she'd kill you if I didn't show up. And because I know it's not a threat. She'd do it. Happy now?'

He closed the door quietly. Claire couldn't get her breath. The hurt in her chest seemed to be smothering her, as if every heartbeat might be her last. She heard herself make a sound, but she couldn't tell if it was tears or anger or anguish.

Eventually, the tears stopped, and Claire wiped the wet streaks from her cheeks. She felt sore, alone, and utterly to blame for everything. Her dinner held no appeal, and all she wanted to do was curl up under the blankets with the biggest, fluffiest stuffed animal she could find.

But she couldn't do that.

When she opened her door, she found Shane sitting outside, back against the wall. He looked up at her.

'You done?' he asked. His eyes were red, too. Not exactly tearful, but – something. 'Because it's not like this floor's real comfortable.'

She sank down next to him. He put his arm around her, and her head fell against his chest. There was something so soothing about the stroke of his fingers through her hair, the soft rhythm of his breathing. The reassurance of his solid warmth next to her.

'Don't let her hurt you,' she whispered. 'God, Shane—'

'No worries. Michael will be there, and I'm pretty sure he'd get into it if she tried. But I want you safe. Promise me that while we're gone, you'll go stay with your parents or something. No—' Because she was already trying to protest. 'No, promise me. I need to know you'll be OK.'

She nodded, still miserable. 'I promise,' she said, and took a deep breath to push all that away. 'So what dumbass costume are you wearing?'

'Don't ask.'

'Does it involve leather?'

'Yeah, actually, I think it might.' He sounded like he dreaded the prospect. She managed a smile, despite everything.

'I can't wait.'

Shane banged his head back against the wall. 'Chicks.'

Her next visit to Myrnin's lab brought a surprise. When she descended the steps, she saw the glow of lamps, and her first thought was, *Oh God, he's out of his cell.* Her second was that she'd better get the dart gun ready, and she was unzipping the backpack to reach for it when she saw that it wasn't Myrnin at all.

The overcrowded, dimly lit lab – which was more like a storeroom of outdated equipment, really – held a chair and reading lamp. Seated in the chair, turning pages in one of the fragile, ancient journals, was none other than Oliver.

Claire put her hand on the butt of the dart gun, just in case, although she wasn't really sure what good a dose of antidote would do in this situation.

'Oh, relax, I'm not going to attack you, Claire,' Oliver said in a bored voice. He didn't even look up. 'Besides, we're on the same side these days. Or haven't you heard?'

She came down the remaining steps slowly. 'I guess I haven't. Was there a memo?' Granted, he'd come running when Eve had called about Bishop, but that didn't necessarily put him in the category of ally in Claire's books.

'When outsiders threaten the community, the community pulls together against the outsiders. It's a rule as old as the tribal system. You and I are in the same community, and we have a common enemy.'

'Mr Bishop.'

Oliver looked up, marking the place in the journal with one finger. 'You have questions, I'd assume. I would, in your place.'

'All right. How long have you known him?'

'I don't know him. I doubt anyone does who's still alive today.'

Claire slipped into a rickety chair across from him. 'But you've met him.'

'Yes.'

'When did you meet him, then?'

Oliver tilted his head, eyes narrowed, and she remembered how she'd once thought he was nice, just a normal kind of person. Not so much now.

Not so much a person, either.

'I met him in Greece,' he said. 'Some time ago. I don't think the circumstances would be particularly enlightening to you. Or comforting, come to think of it.'

'Did you try to kill him?'

'Me?' Oliver smiled slowly. 'No.'

'Did Amelie?'

He didn't answer, but he continued to smile. The silence stretched until she wanted to scream, but she knew he wanted her to babble.

She didn't.

'Amelie's affairs are none of yours,' Oliver said. 'I assume you've been listening to Myrnin's chatter. I confess, I find it fascinating he's still with us. I thought him dead and gone, long ago.'

'Like Bishop?'

'He's quite mad, you know. Myrnin. And he has been for as long as I can recall, though it certainly got worse in more recent times.' Oliver's eyes took on a faraway look. 'He did so love the hunt, but he

was always such a pathetic weeping idiot after.
It doesn't surprise me he wants to blame his own
weakness on some – mythical disease. Some people
simply aren't cut out for this life.'

Of all the things Claire had expected, that one
caught her off guard. 'You don't believe there's a
disease?'

'I don't believe that because Myrnin and a few
others are – defective – that it means we're all
declining, no.'

'But – you can't, um—'

'Reproduce?' Oliver said it without any emotion
at all. 'Perhaps we don't wish to.'

'You tried to turn Michael.'

Oh, she shouldn't have said that, she really
shouldn't have; Oliver's face tensed, and she saw the
skull underneath that smooth, pale skin. A flicker
of red went through his eyes. 'So Michael says.'

'So Amelie says. You wanted – you wanted your
own power base here. Your own converts. But you
couldn't do it. That surprised you, didn't it? Because
all of a sudden you're – not able to.'

'Child,' Oliver said, 'you should think carefully
about the next thing you say to me. Very, very
carefully.'

He followed up with another stretch of silent
staring, and this time Claire did look away. She
picked at invisible lint on her backpack. 'I should
get to work,' she said. 'And you aren't supposed to be
in here without Amelie knowing about it.'

'How do you know she doesn't?'

'There'd be somebody else here watching you if she did,' Claire pointed out, and got a small, cold smile in response.

'Clever girl. Yes, very well. Are you going to tell me to leave?'

'I don't think I can tell you to do anything, Oliver, but if you want me to call Amelie—' She took her cell phone out, opened it, and scrolled through the address book.

Oliver thought about killing her. She saw it flash across his face, plain as sunrise, and she almost dialled the phone in sheer reflex.

Then it was gone, and he was smiling, and he stood up and gave her a nod. 'No need to bother the Founder with such nonsense,' he said. 'I'll be leaving. There's only so many ridiculous mad ravings one can read at a sitting, in any case.'

He dropped the journal onto a pile scattered near the chair and walked away, moving with effortless grace around the piles of books and barriers of mismatched furniture. He didn't seem to move quickly, but before she could blink, he was gone, a shadow on the steps.

Claire let out a shaky breath, got the dart gun from her backpack, and went to see Myrnin.

'Magnificent,' Myrnin said, staring down at his hands. He flexed them into fists, turned them over, extended his fingers. 'I haven't felt this good in –

well, years. I had numbness in my hands – did you know?'

It was a symptom Myrnin had forgotten to mention, and Claire wrote it down in her notebook. She had the countdown clock – a new addition to the lab, one she'd ordered from the Internet – up on the wall, and the red flickering numbers reminded both of them that Myrnin had a maximum of five hours of sanity from the current formulation of the treatment.

Myrnin followed her glance at the clock, and the giddy excitement in his expression faded. He still looked like a young man, except for his eyes; it was creepy to think he'd looked exactly that way for generations before she was born, and would long after she was dead and gone. *He did so love the hunt*, Oliver had said. There was really only one kind of hunt for vampires. Hunting people.

He smiled at her, and it was the smile that had won her over in the first place – sweet, gentle, inviting her to share in some delightful secret. 'Thank you for the clock, Claire. That's a great help. There's an alarm feature?'

'It starts sounding a tone fifteen minutes before the clock runs out,' she said. 'And it has tones striking every hour, too.'

'Very helpful. Well, then. Now that I have use of my fingers – what shall we do?' Myrnin wiggled his thick black eyebrows suggestively, which was actually funny, coming from him. Not that he wasn't cute – he was – but Claire couldn't really imagine finding him sexy.

She wondered if that would hurt his feelings.

'How about if we start shelving some of these books?' she said. It really was getting to be a hazard; she'd tripped over stacks more than once even when it wasn't an emergency. Myrnin, however, made a face.

'I only have a few hours in my right mind, Claire. Housekeeping seems a poor way to spend them.'

'All right, what do you want to do?'

'I think we made great progress in this last formulation,' he said. 'Why not see if we can distil the essence further? Strengthen the effects?'

'I think we'd better do some chemical analysis on what happens in your blood before we do that.'

Before she could stop him, he strode over to a table, picked up a rusty knife, and slashed open his arm. She was just opening her mouth to scream when he grabbed a clean beaker from the rack on the table and caught the drizzling blood. The wound healed before he'd lost more than a few teaspoons.

'There are – easier ways to do that,' she said weakly. Myrnin held the beaker out to her. The blood looked darker than regular human blood, and thicker, but then she supposed it would – he wasn't as warm. She tried not to think about all those people donating blood, but she couldn't help it. Was Shane's blood going to end up in Myrnin's veins? And how did that work, anyway?...Did vampires digest the blood, or just somehow pass it whole into their circulatory systems? Did blood types matter? Conflicting Rh factors? What about blood-borne diseases, like malaria and Ebola and AIDS?

There were a lot of questions to answer. She thought Dr Mills would be in heaven over the prospect.

'Pain doesn't matter much,' Myrnin said, and yanked his sleeve down over his pale, unmarked arm after wiping away the trickles of blood that were left. 'One learns to ignore it, eventually.'

Claire doubted that, but she didn't argue. 'I'm going to take part of this back to the hospital,' she said. 'Dr Mills wanted blood samples. They've got a lot of cool equipment there, he can give us detailed information we can't get here.'

Myrnin shrugged, clearly uninterested in Dr Mills or any human beyond Claire. 'Do as you like,' he said. 'What kind of equipment?'

'Oh, all kinds. Mass spectrometers, blood-chemistry analyzers – you know.'

'We should get those things.'

'Why?'

'How can we possibly operate as we should if we don't have the most current equipment?'

Claire blinked at him. 'Myrnin, you don't exactly have room down here. And I don't think your current dinky little power situation is going to let you plug in an electron microscope. That's not the way scientists work anymore, anyway. The equipment's too expensive, too delicate. The big hospitals and universities buy the equipment. We just rent time on it.'

Myrnin looked surprised, then thoughtful. 'Rent time? But how can you schedule such a thing when you don't know what you're looking for or how long it will take?'

'You have to learn to schedule your epiphanies. And be patient.'

That got a laugh out of him. 'Claire, I am a *vampire*. We aren't known for patience, you know. Your Dr Mills – maybe we should pay him a visit. I'd like to meet him.'

'He'd – probably like to meet you, too,' she said slowly. She wasn't at all sure how Amelie was going to feel about that, but she could tell that Myrnin had it in his head to do it whether she went along or not. 'Next time, OK?'

They both glanced at the countdown clock. 'Yes,' Myrnin said. 'Next time. Ah! I meant to ask you. What did you hear about Bishop and the welcome feast?'

'Not much. I think Michael and Eve are going. Shane – Shane says he has to go.'

'With Ysandre?'

Claire nodded. Myrnin turned away from her, shoved over a stack of books with restless enthusiasm, then another. He gave a raw cry of delight and scrambled over the piled volumes to retrieve one that, to Claire's eyes, looked just like any other.

He threw it to her. Claire managed to grab

it before it smacked into her chest. 'Ow!' she complained. 'Not so hard, please.'

'Sorry.' He wasn't, really. There was a subversive, dark streak in him today.

'What is this, anyway?'

Myrnin came back to her side, took the book, opened it, and flipped pages. He paused around the middle and handed it back.

'Ysandre,' he said.

The book was written in English, but it was from the eighteenth century, and not easy to make out, considering the stains on the pages.

She was of a beauty so unusual and so marvellous that her grandfather was fascinated by the dazzling sight, and mistook her for an angel that God had sent to console him on his deathbed. The pure lines of her fine profile, her great black liquid eyes, her noble brow uncovered, her hair shining like the raven's wing, her delicate mouth, the whole effect of this beautiful face on the mind of those who beheld her was that of a deep melancholy and sweetness, impressing itself once and forever. Tall and slender, but without the excessive thinness of some young girls, her movements had that careless supple grace that recalls the waving of a flower stalk in the breeze.

'Oh,' Claire said, surprised. That was Ysandre; he was right. 'She was—'

'A very famous murderess. She helped her
husband and cousins kill a king shortly after her
grandfather's death. She was hanged, in the end,
but that was after she'd been made a vampire.
Lucky timing, for her.'

The book contained a gruesome account of the
king's murder, and a whole lot of others. Claire
shivered and closed the book. 'Why did you show
me this?'

'I don't want you to do what her grandfather
did – underestimate her because she has the look
of an angel. Ysandre has destroyed more lives than
you can begin to imagine, starting with her own.'
Myrnin's eyes were dark and very, very serious. 'If
she wants Shane, let her have him. She'll be done
with him soon enough. Amelie won't allow her to
kill him.'

'I think she wants other things,' Claire said.

'Ah. Sexual, then. Or some version of it. Ysandre
has always been a bit – odd.'

'How do I stop her?'

Myrnin slowly shook his head. 'I'm sorry. I can't
help you. My only suggestion – which I'm quite
certain you won't like – is to let him deal with this
in his own way. She'll leave him alive, and largely
intact, unless he resists her.'

'You're right. I don't like it.'

'Complain to the management, my dear.' His fit
of seriousness passed off, like a cloud from the sun.
'How about a game of chess, then?'

'How about we just analyze your blood, because you've only got a few more minutes before I have to put you back in your, ah, room?'

'Cell,' he corrected. 'Perfectly all right to say so. And you work too hard for someone so young.'

She worked too hard, Claire thought in frustration, because somebody had to. Myrnin certainly didn't.

By Thursday, the upcoming masked ball was the buzz of Morganville. Claire couldn't avoid hearing about it. At the university coffee shop, that was inevitable; people said the weirdest, most private things right out in public, like there was some invisible privacy wall around them. She'd heard way too much about her fellow students' sexual adventures over the past few weeks; apparently, it was mating season, now that everybody was settling in for the semester. Girls rated guys. Guys rated girls. Both wanted what they couldn't have, or had what they didn't really want.

But as Claire sipped her coffee and wrote out her physics essay on mechanics, heat, and fields – which didn't have to do with auto shops, weather, or farming – she heard something that made her pen come to a stuttering stop on the page.

' – invitation,' someone was saying. The someone was sitting behind her. 'Can you believe it! My God, I actually got one! They say there are only three hundred invitations being sent out, you know. It's really going to be amazing. I was thinking of going as Marie Antoinette – what do you think?'

They had to be talking about the masked ball. Claire shifted in her chair. That didn't help – she still couldn't see who was speaking.

'Well, I think somebody might have actually known her, back in the day,' the other girl said. 'So you might want to go with something safe, like Catwoman. I'll bet none of them know Catwoman.'

'Catwoman's good,' the first girl agreed. 'Tight black leather is never out of style. I would look totally hot as Catwoman.'

Claire spilt her coffee, more or less deliberately, and jumped up to gather handfuls of napkins from the common dispenser at the creamer station. On the way back, she got a look at the two who were talking.

Gina and Jennifer, Monica's ever-present friends. Only, this time, no Monica to be seen. Interesting.

Jennifer glared at her. 'What are you looking at, klutz?'

'Absolutely nothing,' Claire said, deadpan. She wasn't afraid of them, not anymore. 'I wouldn't go as Catwoman. Not with those thighs.'

'Oh, mee-yow.'

She gathered up books and coffee, and retreated to a table closer to the actual coffee bar. Eve was working. She looked perky today, bright-eyed and smiling; she had on red, and it totally worked for her. Goth, but somehow cheerful. She still grieved for her dad – Claire saw it in odd moments, when she thought nobody was watching – but Eve had pulled herself together, and was holding it together despite all the odds.

She had a break in the coffee line, so she flashed her co-worker a hand signal of five – a five-minute break, Claire guessed as Eve stripped off the apron and ducked under the bar to slip into the chair opposite her.

'So,' she said, 'I heard from Billy Harrison that his dad got an invitation to this ball thing, from Tamara – the vamp who owns all those warehouses on the north side, and runs the paper? And he said that vamps all over town are going, and taking humans as their – I don't know, dates? That's weird, right? That they're all bringing humans?'

'It's never happened before?'

'Not that I know of,' Eve said. 'I asked around, but nobody's seen anything like it. It's become the hot-ticket event of the year.' Her smile dimmed slightly. 'I guess Michael forgot to send me mine. My invitation. I should remind him.'

Claire felt a tight little knot tug inside. 'He hasn't asked you?'

'He will.'

'But…it's the day after tomorrow, isn't it?'

'He *will*. Besides, it's not like I have to come up with some elaborate costume or anything. Have you seen my closet? Half of what I wear qualifies as dress-up.' Eve glanced at her, then down. 'You?'

'Nobody's asking me to go.' Yeah, the bitterness was there in her voice. Claire couldn't keep it out. 'You know who Shane's going with.'

'It's not his fault. It's hers. Ysandre.' Eve made a face. 'What kind of a name is that, anyway?'

'French. Myrnin gave me a book about her,' Claire said. 'I knew she was dangerous, but honestly, she's worse than I thought. She might have started out just trying to get by, but she was a real player, back when politics was war.'

'What about the guy? François?' Eve rolled her eyes when she said his name, doing her best foo-foo French pronunciation. 'He thinks he's hotter than the surface of the sun. Who's he taking?'

'No idea,' Claire said. 'But – it's not a date, you know. It's—' She had no real idea what it was. 'It's something else.'

'Looks like a date, dresses like a date, dates like a date,' Eve said. 'And I intend to be arm candy for Michael and protect him from all the big, bad social climbers out there looking to grab on to the newest vamp in town.'

'He's not, though,' Claire said. 'The newest. Not anymore. Bishop and his crew are newer than he is, at least in terms of novelty factor.'

Eve frowned. 'Yeah,' she said. 'I guess that's true.'

A shadow fell across their table, but before they could look up, something hit the surface between them, and both Claire and Eve involuntarily focused on it.

It was one of the cream-colored invitations.

They looked up. *Monica*. She swept her perfect blond hair back over her shoulders, raised her eyebrows, and gave Eve a slow, evil smile.

'Too bad,' she said. 'I guess your hottie boyfriend knows where his social bread is buttered, after all.'

Eve's eyes widened. She turned the invitation around to read it, but even upside down, Claire saw the incriminating evidence.

You have been summoned to attend a masked ball and feast to celebrate the arrival of Elder Bishop, on Saturday the twentieth of October, at the Elders' Council Hall at the hour of midnight.

You will attend at the invitation of Michael Glass, and are required to accompany him at his pleasure.

The name jumped out at her like a fanged surprise attack. *Michael Glass. Michael was inviting Monica.*

Eve didn't say another word. She shoved the invitation back at Monica, got up, and ducked behind the coffee bar to don her apron again. Claire stared after her, stricken. She could see the jittery anguish in her friend's movements, but not her face. Eve was keeping carefully turned away, and even when she went to the espresso machine again to pull shots, she kept staring down, hiding her pain.

Claire's shock thawed into a nice warm glow

of anger. 'You're a total bitch, you know that?' she said. Monica raised a perfectly plucked eyebrow. 'You didn't have to do that.'

'Not my fault you freaks can't hang on to your men. I heard Shane was boy-toying around with Ysandre. Too bad. I'll bet you never even got him between the sheets, did you? Or wait...maybe you did. Because I'll bet that would drive him straight into somebody else's bed.'

Claire fantasised for a few seconds about planting her physics textbook squarely in the middle of Monica's pouty, lip-glossed smile. She glared, instead, remembering how effective Oliver's periods of icy silence could be. Monica finally shrugged, picked up the invitation, and tucked it in the pocket of her leather jacket.

'I'd say 'See you,' but I probably won't,' Monica said. 'I guess you can hold your own Loser Party on Saturday, with special shots of cyanide or something. Enjoy.'

She joined up with Gina and Jennifer, and the three girls walked away, turning heads. The golden, fortunate girls, tight and toned and perfect.

Laughing.

Claire realised she was clenching her fists, forced herself to relax and breathe, and picked up her pen again. The details of the essay kept slipping away, because all she could see was Monica preening at Michael's side, rubbing Eve's face in the humiliation. And even when she looked past that, there was Ysandre, and Shane, and that hurt even more.

'Why?' she whispered. 'Michael, *why* would you do that to her?' Had they had a fight of some kind? Eve didn't seem to think so. She acted like it had come as a bolt from the blue sky.

With a feeling that she was making a terrible mistake, she dialled the first speed-dial number on her phone.

'Yes, Claire,' Amelie said.

'I need to talk to you. About this masked-ball thing. What's going on?'

For a few seconds Claire was sure Amelie would hang up on her, but then the vampire said, 'Yes, I suppose we must talk about it. I will meet you upstairs at your home. You know where.'

She meant the hidden room. 'When?'

'I am, of course, at your convenience,' Amelie said, which was winter cold and utterly untrue. 'Would an hour suffice?'

'I'll be there,' Claire said. Her hands were shaking, fine little trembles that were a sign of the inner earthquake. 'Thank you.'

'Oh, don't thank me, child,' Amelie said. 'I shouldn't imagine you'll find anything I have to say will be of the least comfort to you.'

The house was empty when Claire got there. She checked every room, including the laundry room in the basement, to be absolutely sure. Eve was still at work; Michael was at the music store. Shane – she had no idea where Shane was, except that the house was Shane free.

Claire pressed the hidden button in the hallway on the second floor, and the panelling opened on the dusty steps leading up to the hidden room. She shut the opening behind her and trudged up, feeling sicker and more isolated with every single stair.

At the top, colour spilt across the walls: Victorian lamps, all jewelled hues and pale, watery light. There were no windows, no exits here. Only a few nice pieces of dusty furniture, and Amelie.

And the bodyguards, of course. Amelie hardly ever went anywhere without at least one. There were two this time, lurking in the corners. One of them nodded to Claire. She was on nodding terms with scary bodyguard dudes. Great. She really was moving up in the social ladder of Morganville.

'Ma'am,' Claire said, and stayed standing. Amelie was seated, but she didn't look as though she was in any mood to indulge the fantasy that Claire was her equal. It was hard to determine Amelie's feelings, but Claire was pretty sure that this one qualified as impatient, with a possible upgrade to annoyed.

'I have very little time for soothing your ruffled feathers,' Amelie said. She shifted a little, which was surprising; Amelie was usually very still, very composed. That was almost fidgeting. There was something else unusual about her today – the colour of her suit. It was still classic and beautifully tailored, but it was in a dark grey, much darker than Amelie usually preferred. It turned her eyes the colour of storm clouds. 'Yet you've done more than I asked with Myrnin. I am inclined to forgive your impertinence, if you understand that it's an indulgence on my part. Not a right on yours.'

'I understand,' Claire said. 'I just – this masked ball. Myrnin called it a welcome feast. He acted like it had something important to do with Mr Bishop.'

Amelie's eyes, which had been regarding her with impersonal focus, suddenly sharpened. 'You've spoken with Myrnin regarding Bishop's arrival?'

'Well – he asked me what was happening in town, and—' Claire broke off, because Amelie was suddenly standing. And her bodyguards had moved out of the corners of the room and were very close, close enough to hurt. 'You didn't tell me not to!'

'I told you to stay out of my affairs!' Something pale and hungry flickered in those eyes, as scary in its own way as Mr Bishop. Amelie deliberately relaxed. 'Very well. The damage is done. What did Myrnin tell you?'

'He said—' Claire wet her lips and glanced at the bodyguards hovering terrifyingly close. Amelie raised an eyebrow and nodded, and Claire felt rather than saw them move away. 'He said you both thought Bishop was dead, so he was surprised to find out that he'd come to town. He said that Bishop wanted revenge. Against you.'

'What did he tell you about the feast?'

'Only that it was part of some kind of ceremony to welcome Bishop to town,' Claire said. 'And that you weren't going to fight him if you were putting on the feast.'

Amelie's smile was quick and cold. 'Myrnin knows something about the world and its politics. No, I'm not going to fight him. Not unless I must. Did he tell you anything else?'

'No.' Claire sucked up her courage. 'Ysandre's taking Shane. And Michael – I just found out he's going, and he's taking Monica. Not Eve.'

'Do you imagine I have the slightest concern for how your friends arrange their romantic affairs?'

'No, it's just – I want you to invite me. Please. All the vampires are taking humans. Why don't you take me?'

Amelie's eyes widened. Not much, but it was enough to make Claire think she'd scored a big-time surprise. 'Why would you possibly wish to attend?'

'Monica says it's the social event of the season,' Claire said. She wasn't sure a joke was the way to go; she knew Amelie had a sense of humour, but it was obscure.

Today, it was apparently nonexistent.

'All right, the truth is, I'm worried about Michael and Shane. I just want to be sure – sure they're OK.'

'And how would you go about ensuring that, if I cannot?' Amelie didn't wait for an answer, because there obviously wasn't one. 'You want to watch the boy, to be sure he doesn't fall prey to Ysandre. Is that it?'

Claire swallowed and nodded. That wasn't all, but that was a lot of it.

'It's a waste of time. No,' Amelie said. 'You will not attend, Claire. I tell you this, explicitly, so that we are understood: I cannot risk you in this. You will not be at this event. Neither you nor Myrnin. Is that clear?'

'But—'

Amelie's voice rose to a shout. 'Is that clear?' The fury cut like knives, and Claire gasped and nodded. She wanted to take a step back from the horrible glow in Amelie's eyes, but she knew that would be a very bad idea. She'd been around Myrnin enough to understand that retreat was a sign of weakness, and weakness triggered attack.

Amelie continued to stare at her, fixed and silent, and there was a wildness to her that Claire couldn't understand.

'Mistress,' said one of the bodyguards. 'We should go.' He made it sound as if they had someplace to be, but Claire had the eerie feeling that he was intervening deliberately. Providing Amelie an excuse to back off.

'Yes,' Amelie said. There was a husky tone to her voice Claire had never heard before. 'By all means, let us be done with this. You have heard my words, Claire. I warn you, don't test me on this. You're valuable to me, but you are not irreplaceable, and you have friends and family in this town who are far less useful.'

There was no mistaking that for anything but an outright threat. Claire nodded slowly.

'Say the words,' Amelie said.

'Yes. I understand.'

'Good. Now don't bother me again. You may go.'

Claire backed away toward the stairs. She even backed down two steps before turning and hurrying down the rest, and when she was halfway there, she realised that the control to open the door from inside lay at the top, in the couch where Amelie sat.

If Amelie didn't want to let her out, she wasn't going anywhere.

Claire reached the landing at the bottom. The door was still closed. She looked back up the stairs and saw shadows moving, but heard nothing.

The lights went out.

'No,' she whispered, and fear came down like a bucket of freezing water, from head to toe. Her hand reached out blindly to stroke the closed door. 'No, don't do this—'

Something had changed in Amelie. She wasn't the cool, remote queen she'd been before. She was more – animal. More angry.

And Claire finally admitted it to herself: Amelie was more hungry.

'Please,' she said to the dark. She knew there were ears listening. 'Please let me go now.'

She heard a sharp click, and the door moved under her fingertips, swinging inward. Claire grabbed the edge with both hands and pulled it open. She was suddenly in the hall, and when she looked back, the door was closing.

She collapsed against the wall, trembling.

That went well, she thought sarcastically. She wanted to scream, but she was almost sure that would be a very, very bad idea.

Downstairs, the front door opened and closed, and Claire heard the clump of heavy shoes on the wood floor.

'Eve?' she called.

'Yeah.' Eve sounded exhausted. 'Coming.'

She looked even worse than she sounded. The red outfit that had flattered her so much before seemed to scream now, overpowering her; she seemed ready to drop, and from the state of her makeup, she'd already shed a lot of tears.

'Oh,' Claire said. 'Eve…'

Eve tried for a smile, but there wasn't much left. 'Pretty stupid to be upset about Monica, right? But I think that's why it hurts so bad. It's not like he's taking somebody halfway nice or anything. He has to pick the walking social disease.' Eve wiped her eyes with the heel of her hand. Her eyeliner and mascara had made a true Gothic mess, trickling in dirty streaks down her pale cheeks. 'Don't try to tell me he was ordered to do it. I don't care if he was – he could have told me first. And why aren't you arguing with me?'

'Because you're right.'

'Damn right I'm right.' Eve kicked open the door to her room, walked in, and threw herself facedown on the black bed. Claire clicked on the lights, which mostly consisted of strings of dim white Christmas lights and one lamp with a blood-red scarf draped over the shade. Eve screamed into her pillow and punched it. Claire perched on the corner of the bed.

'I'm going to kill him,' Eve said, or at least that was what it sounded like filtered through the pillow. 'Stake him right in the heart, shove garlic up his ass, and – and—'

'And what?'

Michael was standing in the doorway. Claire jumped off the bed in alarm, and Eve sat up with her pillow clutched in both hands. 'When did you get home?' Claire demanded.

'Apparently just in time to hear my funeral plans. I especially like the garlic up the ass. It's... different.'

'Yeah, well, I'm not finished,' Eve said. She slithered off the bedspread, dropped the pillow, and faced Michael with her arms crossed. 'I'm also going to stake you outside in the sun, on top of a fire ant mound. And laugh.'

'What did I do?'

'What did you *do*?' Eve's glare was fierce enough to rip even a vampire's heart right out of his chest. 'You can't be serious.'

Michael went very still, and Claire thought the expression in his eyes was the definition of *busted*. 'Monica. She told you.'

'Duh. Why wouldn't she take the chance to rub my face in it, you loser? And speaking of that, *Monica*! Did you lose a bet or something? Because that's really the only reason I can think of for you to humiliate me like this.'

'No,' Michael said. His gaze flickered to Claire in an unmistakable plea for her to leave. She didn't. 'I can't explain, Eve. I'm sorry, I just can't. But it's not what it—'

'Don't you even say it's not what it looks like, because it's *always* what it looks like!' Eve lunged forward, shoved Michael square in the chest, and drove him a foot backward, out of her room. 'I can't talk to you right now. Get out! And stay out!'

She slammed the door and locked it. Not, Claire reflected, that a lock would do any good, considering how strong Michael was. But he probably wouldn't go around battering down doors in his own house, at least.

'Eve, you have to listen to me. Please.'

Eve threw herself back on the bed, grabbed her iPod from the drawer, and shoved headphones over her ears as she hit the play button. Claire could hear the thundering metal all the way across the room.

'Eve?'

Claire opened the door and looked at Michael. 'I don't think she's listening,' she said. 'You really screwed this up – you know that, right? At least Shane got ordered to do what he did. You chose, didn't you?'

'Yeah,' Michael agreed softly. 'I chose. But you really don't have any idea of what my choices were, do you?'

She watched him walk away, enter his room at the end of the hall, and shut the door.

Maybe he was right. Maybe it really wasn't what it looked like. Not that Eve was going to listen. Claire stood there for a while, listening to the cold and stony silence, and then shook her head and went downstairs.

Chilli dogs weren't the same eaten alone.

Shane got home after dark, and the second Claire saw him, she knew something was wrong. He looked – distracted. Different.

And he barely nodded to her on his way through the living room to the kitchen. She was curled up on the sofa highlighting text in her English book, wondering for the thousandth time why anybody thought knowing about the Bronte sisters was important and multitasking by not really watching a cooking show on cable TV.

'Hey,' she called after him. 'I left the chilli on for you!'

He didn't answer. Claire capped her marker pen and went to the kitchen door. She didn't open it, but she stood and listened. Shane wasn't making the normal dish noises of a guy desperate for dinner; in fact, he wasn't making any noise at all.

Claire was debating whether to return to studying when she heard him open the back door of the house. Voices, hushed and muffled. She eased the door open just a little, and listened harder.

'You're lucky I don't call the cops,' Shane was saying. 'Walk away, man.'

'I can't. I need to talk to her.'

'You're not coming near either one of the girls, got me?'

'I'm not going to hurt anyone!'

She knew that voice, or thought she did. But that couldn't be right, it just couldn't be.

Shane could *not* be talking to Eve's brother, Jason, especially not at the back door. She had to be imagining things. Maybe it was someone else, someone who just sounded like Jason Rosser...

Claire eased the door open enough to get a tiny slice of a view.

No, that was Jason. There was absolutely no doubt about it. He was even wearing the same skanky, stained jeans and leather jacket. His hair was lank and even greasier than the last time she'd seen him, and he looked sallow and sick.

'Come on, man,' he said. 'Just let me talk to Claire. You keep me waiting out here in the dark, I'm lunch meat.'

'Good to know.'

Jason put out a hand to stop Shane from closing the door on him. 'Please, man. I'm asking.'

Shane hesitated. Claire couldn't really imagine why. Jason had stalked Eve; he'd killed – or at least he *said* he'd killed – innocent girls out of some misguided attempt to get the vampires to sign him up for service. He'd stabbed Shane in the guts.

Shane did swing the bat at him first, Claire's prim little voice of conscience said. She told it to shut up. Jason had engineered that fight, he'd provoked Shane into it, and it was only the fact that they'd gotten an ambulance there so fast that had saved Shane's life.

Jason didn't look like a crazy killer just now. He looked like a half-starved scared junkie kid who was terrified out of his mind. And desperate.

Claire came into the kitchen. Jason's face lit up. 'Claire! Claire, tell him – tell him it's OK. I promise, I'm not going to hurt anybody. Tell him it's OK to let me in so I can talk to you.'

'It's not OK,' Claire said. 'But he already knows that.'

Shane nodded. He shoved Jason backward, off-balance, off the porch. Jason tripped over a brick and fell flat on his ass. He glared up at Shane and rolled slowly to his feet. 'Claire, I'm supposed to tell you something. From Oliver.'

'Oliver's got nothing to tell us that we want to hear, man. Especially from you.'

'You sure about that?'

Shane grinned. 'Pretty sure. Good luck with that survival thing out there in the dark.'

Shane started to shut the door. He almost made it before Jason blurted out, 'Bishop's setting a trap. We can tell you where and when.'

Claire put a hand on Shane's shoulder, and he kept the door open, just a crack. 'What are you talking about?'

'Let me in and I'll tell you.' Jason looked desperate enough to claw paint off the door. 'Please, Claire. I swear, I'm on the level here.'

'No,' she said. 'If Oliver's got something to say, I'll talk to him, not to you.'

Resentment flickered in Jason's dark eyes like oil on fire, and he got up and shoved his hands in his pockets. 'Yeah? You gonna play it like that?'

'I'm not playing at all,' Claire said.

'I think you are. So maybe we do it the hard way after all.' Jason threw himself against the door with such force that Shane was knocked backward, and Claire lost her footing and ended up flat on her back on the kitchen floor. As she twisted around to try to get up, she felt Jason's hand close on her hair, painfully tight. He yanked her up to her knees and dragged her out into the night. She yelled and fought, but he had a lot of experience with making girls do what he wanted.

And she stopped fighting when he put a gun to her head.

'Good,' he said in her ear, and even in a blind,

black rage she thought his breath was disgusting enough to peel paint. 'Calm down, I'm not going to hurt you. I was serious. You need to listen to me.'

Shane followed them outside, moving slowly but never taking his eyes off Jason. Off the gun. 'Let her go.'

Jason laughed, and dragged her backward to the driveway, where a big black car was waiting. Shane followed at a safe distance. *Don't*, Claire mouthed. She'd seen Jason nearly kill Shane before. She couldn't stand to see it happen again. *I'll be OK*.

Jason opened the driver's-side door of the car, shoved her inside, and pushed in after. She immediately lunged for the other door.

Locked.

Jason slammed the car door and turned the key to start the engine. He took a firmer grip on Claire's hair. 'Stay still!'

Something heavy fell on the roof of the car, denting it down almost to the level of their heads; Claire and Jason both ducked, and Claire yelped at the thought that panic might make him squeeze the trigger.

It didn't.

A fist punched through the metal roof of the car, grabbed the ragged edge, and peeled it back like a tin can lid. And the face that looked down was Michael's.

No – not Michael; it was *Vampire* Michael.

Fangs completely down, eyes completely crimson.

Michael was *angry*. Also, *terrifying*.

He dropped through the hole in a fall of moonlight, took hold of Jason's gun hand, and yanked him away from Claire like a toy. A breakable one. Jason screamed. The gun went off, and Claire flinched and covered her head, trying to pull into a ball in the corner. The car shook as Michael *threw* Jason out, straight up through the opening in the roof. Jason screamed the whole way up, and the whole way down. He hit the ground with a sickening thud and rolled.

Michael launched himself up out of the car, landed lightly on his feet in the wash of headlights, and walked to where Jason was crawling to get away. Jason rolled over. He still had the gun.

He shot Michael six times, point-blank. Claire flinched with every loud crack.

Michael didn't.

He reached Jason, took the gun, ripped it in half, and threw the two pieces into the trash can leaning at the side of the house. Jason looked shocked, then resigned, as Michael reached down and grabbed him by the collar of his leather jacket.

Shane reached through the ragged sunroof, opened the car door, and grabbed Claire. He pulled her out and to her feet. 'You OK?' He sounded deeply shaken, and he kept running his hands over her, looking for bullet holes, she guessed. 'Claire, say something!'

'Stop him,' she whispered, looking past him at Michael. 'Don't let him do that.'

Because Michael was going to bite Jason, and once he did, there'd be no going back. Shane sent her a look, one that probably meant he thought she was crazy, but she forced herself to stay still and calm, even if her insides were quivering in terror.

'Shane,' she said, and tried her best to channel Amelie's cool authority. 'Stop him.'

She saw the reality of what was happening dawn on Shane, and he nodded and turned toward Michael, who didn't look as if he was in any mood to be talked off the murder ledge.

But Shane didn't have to try, because Michael looked up and saw Eve standing in the doorway, hands pressed to her mouth, dark eyes wide in horror, staring at her boyfriend threatening to suck blood out of her little brother.

Michael let go. Jason collapsed back to the ground, whimpering, and tried to crawl away.

Michael put his foot on Jason's back, holding him in place. 'No,' he said. His voice sounded low and very, very dangerous. 'I don't think so. Attempted kidnapping, assault with a deadly weapon, and attempted murder of a vampire? You're done, man. It's all over but the screaming.'

'You asshole!' Jason yelled. 'I'm working for Oliver! You can't touch me!'

He skinned back the sleeve on his jacket, and there, on his wrist, was a silver bracelet.

Michael responded by pressing his foot harder into Jason's back. 'Then you and I are going to have a talk with Oliver about how he sends his little worm to my house to shoot me,' he said. 'I think you're not going to like that very much. Because I'm pretty sure that Oliver didn't ask you to do that kind of thing.'

'Michael,' Shane said. It was a warning, and as Claire turned, she saw why – another car was arriving, a police car with lights flashing. It pulled to a stop in the driveway, blocking in Jason's half-peeled car, and Richard Morrell got out of the driver's side carrying a shotgun. Detectives Joe Hess and Travis Lowe were with him, and each of them held a drawn gun.

She'd never seen the three of them looking so grim, but she was glad to see them. At least this meant somebody would be putting a stop to Jason and his craziness at last. Michael was right: it wasn't going to be a good ending for him, but –

Richard Morrell put the shotgun to his shoulder. He was aiming at Michael. The other two men took up shooting stances.

Claire gasped.

'Out of the way,' Detective Hess ordered Shane, with a jerk of his head. Shane didn't argue. He held up his hands and backed away. Michael turned and saw the cops aiming at him, and frowned.

'Let him go, Michael,' Travis Lowe said. 'Let's do this easy.'

'What's going on?'

'One thing at a time. Let the kid up.'

Michael removed his foot. Jason scrambled to a standing position and tried to run; Richard Morrell sighed, handed his shotgun to Joe Hess, and took off after him. As fast as Jason was, Richard was faster. He took him down in a flying tackle before he was halfway to the fence. He rolled Jason onto his back and handcuffed him with brutal efficiency, yanked him upright, and marched him back to where the other two policemen held Michael at gunpoint.

'What's going on?' Michael repeated. 'He tries to kidnap Claire, and you come after *me*? Why?'

'Let's just say we're saving you from yourself,' Detective Hess said. 'You OK? You calm?'

Michael nodded. Hess lowered his gun, and so did Travis Lowe. Richard Morrell put Jason in the backseat of the police car.

'We got a tip,' Hess continued, 'that you'd gone berserk and were trying to kill your friends. But since I see they're all standing here alive and well, I'm guessing little Jason is the real problem.'

Richard came back, wiping his hands on a handkerchief. Clearly, he didn't like touching Jason, either. 'Did he break in?'

'No,' Shane said. 'He pulled a gun on us and grabbed Claire at the back door. He was trying to drive away with her. Michael stopped him.'

Michael, Claire realised as her heartbeat started to slow, had also been shot six times in the chest at point-blank range. His loose white shirt had the blackened ragged holes to prove it, each one rimmed with a thin outline of red. She remembered Myrnin swiping the knife carelessly down his arm, laying open veins and arteries and muscles just to get a blood sample.

She couldn't be sure, but it didn't look like there was a mark on Michael's chest under the shirt, and he wasn't moving like a man with bullets buried inside. Not even one in shock.

Wow.

'What did he want?' Detective Hess asked. 'Did he say?'

'He said he wanted to talk to me,' Claire said. That much was true, but she didn't want to drag Oliver into this. It was enough of a mess already. 'I think he really did want to. He just knew he wouldn't be able, to do it here. I don't – I don't think he really meant to hurt me.' *This time*.

Shane was looking at her like she'd grown a second head, one with serious brain damage. 'It's *Jason*. Of course he meant to hurt you! Wasn't the gun pointed at your head a clue?'

He was right, of course, but – she'd seen the look in Jason's eyes, and it hadn't been the predatory glee she'd seen before when he was playing his little sadistic games. This had been flat-out desperation. She couldn't explain it, but she believed Jason.

This time.

Shane was still watching her with a frown. So

was Michael. 'Are you all right?' Shane asked, and folded his arms around her. The warm weight of his body pressed against hers, and she realised just how cold she felt. She was shivering, and her knees felt weak underneath her. *I could collapse*, she realised. *And he'd catch me.*

But she stayed on her own two feet, pulled back, and looked him in the eyes.

'I'm fine,' she said. She kissed him. 'Everything's fine.'

CHAPTER NINE

Eve hadn't said a word, but she'd allowed Michael to take her back inside once the cops had pulled away; she'd taken only one look at her brother as he'd been hauled off in handcuffs, but that had been enough. On top of the shock of her father's death, and the trouble with Michael, Eve didn't seem to have any emotion left to spare.

Through common consent, none of them went to bed. They didn't eat. The four of them crammed onto the couch, grateful for the warmth and the company, and put on a movie. A scary one, as it turned out, but Claire was glad to focus on someone else's problems for a change. Being hunted by a city full of zombies might have seemed like a relief in some ways – at least you knew whom to run from, and whom to run *toward*. She lay with her head on Shane's chest, listening more to him breathe than to the characters babbling at one another. His hand kept a slow, steady rhythm on her hair, stroking all her tension and fear away.

Eve and Michael didn't cuddle, but after a while, he put his arm around her and pulled her closer, and she didn't resist.

By the time the DVD menu came on after the credits, they were all sound asleep, and trouble was far, far away.

Fridays were usually good days, classwise; even most of the professors were in better moods.

Not *this* Friday, though. There was a weird tension in the air, along with the increasingly chilly bite to the wind. Her first professor of the day had lost his temper over a cell phone going off, and reduced some sophomore sorority girl to tears before exiling her from the class with a flat-out failing grade. Her second class didn't go much better; the TA had a headache, maybe a hangover, and was grumpy as hell – too much to bother slowing down as he sped through the lecture, or to answer any questions.

The only good thing about her third hour was that she was confident it would be over in *under* an hour. Professor Anderson had widely advertised today's supposedly pop quiz; only a complete coma patient wouldn't know to come prepared. Anderson was one of *those* professors – the ones who gave you plenty of chances, but the test was The Test, full stop. He gave only two a year, and if you didn't do well on both of them, you were screwed. He had a reputation for being a nice guy who smiled a lot, but he'd never yet allowed anybody extra-credit work, or so Claire had heard.

The history majors liked to call his class Andersonville, which was a not very funny reference to the Civil War prison camp. Claire had studied her brains out, and she was absolutely sure that she would ace the test, and have extra time left over.

She stopped off in the restroom, since she was a little early, and carefully balanced her backpack against the wall of the bathroom stall as she did her business. She was going over dates and events in her head when she heard a soft, muffled laugh from near the sinks. Something about it made her freeze – it wasn't innocent, that laugh. There was something weird about it.

'I hear there's a test in Andersonville today,' a voice said. A familiar one. It was Monica Morrell. 'Hey, does this colour look OK?'

'Nice,' Gina said, fulfilling her job as Affirmation Friend #1. 'Is that the new winter red?'

'Yeah, it's supposed to shimmer. Is it shimmering?'

'Oh yeah.'

Claire flushed the toilet, grabbed her backpack, and braced herself for impact. She tried to look as if she didn't care a bit that Monica, Gina, and Jennifer were occupying three out of the four sinks in the bathroom. Or that the rest of the place was deserted.

Monica was touching up her hooker-red lipstick, blowing kisses at her reflection. Claire kept her eyes straight ahead. *Get the soap. Turn on the water. Wash—*

'Hey, freak, you're in Andersonville, right?'

Claire nodded. She scrubbed, rinsed, and reached for the paper towels.

Jennifer snagged her backpack and pulled it out of her reach.

'Hey!' Claire grabbed for her stuff, but Jennifer dodged out of her way, and then Monica took hold of her wrist and snapped something cold and metallic around it. For a crazy second Claire thought, *She's switched bracelets with me. Now I'm Oliver's property...*

But it was the cold metal of a handcuff, and Monica bent down and fastened the other end to the metal post on the bottom of the nearest bathroom stall.

'Well,' she said as she stepped back and put her hands on her hips, 'I guess you'll be finding out just how tough the little general can be, Claire. But don't worry. I'm sure you're so smart, you'll just fill in those test answers by the power of your mind or something.'

Claire yanked uselessly at the handcuffs, even though she knew that was stupid; she wasn't going anywhere. She kicked the bathroom stall. It was tough enough to stand up to generations of college students; her frustration wasn't going to make a dent.

'Give me the key!' she yelled. Monica dangled it in front of her – small, silver, and unreachable.

'This key?' Monica tossed it into the toilet in the first stall and flushed. 'Oops. Wow, that's a shame. You wait here. I'll get help!'

They all laughed. Jennifer contemptuously shoved her backpack across the floor to her. 'Here,' Jennifer said. 'You might want to cram for the test or something.'

Claire grimly opened her backpack and began looking for something, anything she could use as a lock-pick. Not that she knew the first thing about picking locks, exactly, but she could learn. She *had* to learn. She barely looked up as the three girls exited the rest-room, still laughing.

Her choices were a couple of paper clips, a bobby pin, and the power of her fury, which unfortunately couldn't melt metal. Only her brain.

Claire took the cell phone out of her pocket and considered her choices. She wouldn't have been surprised to find out that Eve or Shane had experience with handcuffs – and getting out of them – but she wasn't sure she wanted to endure the questions, either.

She called the Morganville Police Department, and asked for Richard Morrell. After a short delay, she was put through to his patrol car.

'It's Claire Danvers,' she said. 'I – need some help.'

'What kind of help?'

'Your sister kind of – handcuffed me in a bathroom. And I have a test. I don't have a key. I was hoping you—'

'Look, I'm sorry, but I'm heading to a domestic-disturbance call. It's going to take me about an hour to get over there. I don't know what you said to Monica, but if you just—'

'What, apologise?' Claire snapped. 'I didn't say *anything*. She ambushed me, and she flushed the key, and I have to get to class!'

Richard's sigh rattled the phone. 'I'll get there as fast as I can.'

He hung up. Claire set to work with the bobby pin, and watched the minutes crawl by. Tick, tock, there went her grade in Andersonville.

By the time Richard Morrell showed up with a handcuff key to let her loose, the classroom was dark. Claire ran the whole way to Professor Anderson's office, and felt a burst of relief when she saw that his door was open. He *had* to give her a break.

He was talking to another student whose back was to Claire; she paused in the doorway, trembling and gasping for breath, and got a frown from Professor Anderson. 'Yes?' He was young, but his blond hair was already thinning on top. He had a habit of wearing sport jackets that a man twice his age would have liked; maybe he thought the tweed and leather patches made people take him seriously.

Claire didn't care what he looked like. She cared that he had the authority to assign grades.

'Sir, hi, Claire Danvers, I'm in—'

'I know who you are, Claire. You missed the test.'

'Yes, I—'

'I don't accept excuses except in the case of death or serious illness.' He looked her over. 'I don't see any signs of either of those.'

'But—'

The other student was watching her now, with a malicious light in her eyes. Claire didn't know her, but she had on a silver bracelet, and Claire was willing to bet that she was one of Monica's near and dear sorority girls. Glossy dark hair cut in a bleeding-edge style, perfect makeup. Clothes that reeked of credit card abuse.

'Professor,' the girl said, and whispered something to him. His eyes widened. The girl gathered up her books and left, giving Claire a wide berth.

'Sir, I really didn't – it wasn't my fault—'

'From what I just heard, it was very much your fault,' Anderson said. 'She said you were asleep out in the common room. She said she passed you on the way to class.'

'I wasn't! I was—'

'I don't care where you were, Claire. I care where you weren't, namely, at your desk at the appointed time, taking my test. Now please go.'

'I was *handcuffed*!'

He looked briefly thrown by that, but shook his head. 'I'm not interested in sorority pranks. If you work hard the rest of the semester, you might still be able to pull out a passing grade. Unless you'd like to drop the class. I think you still have a day or two to make that decision.'

He just wasn't *listening*. And, Claire realised, he wasn't going to listen. He didn't really care about her problems. He didn't really care about *her*.

She stared at him for a few seconds in silence, trying to find some empathy in him, but all she saw was self-absorbed annoyance.

'Good day, Miss Danvers,' he said, and sat down at his desk. Pointedly ignoring her.

Claire bit back words that probably would have gotten her expelled, and skipped the rest of her classes to go home.

Somewhere in the back of her mind, a clock was ticking. Counting down to Bishop's masked ball.

There was one comforting thing about the theory of complete apocalypse: at least it meant she wouldn't have to fail any classes.

Just when she thought her Friday couldn't get any worse, visitors dropped by the house at dinnertime.

Claire peered out the peephole, and saw dark, curling hair. A wicked smile.

'Better invite me in,' Ysandre said. 'Because you know I'll just go hurt your neighbours until you do.'

'Michael!' Claire yelled. He was in the living room, working out some new songs, but she heard the music stop. He was at her side before the echoes died. 'It's her. Ysandre. What should I do?'

Michael opened the door and faced her. She smiled at him. François was with her, both of them sleek and smug and so arrogant it made Claire's teeth itch.

'I want to talk to Shane,' Ysandre said.

'Then you're going to be disappointed.'

François raised his eyebrows, reached down, and pulled a bound human form from the bushes on the side of the steps. Claire gasped.

It was Miranda, looking completely terrified. Tied hand and foot, and gagged.

'Let's put it another way,' Ysandre said. 'You can let us in to talk, or we have our dinner alfresco, right here on your veranda.'

There was absolutely no right answer to that, Claire thought, and saw Michael struggle with it, too. He let the silence stretch for so long that Claire was really afraid Miranda would be killed – François seemed glad to have the chance – but then Michael nodded. 'All right,' he said. 'Come in.'

'Why, thank you, honey,' Ysandre said, and strolled in. François dropped Miranda on the wooden hallway floor and followed her. Claire knelt next to the girl and untied her hands.

'Are you OK?' she whispered. Miranda nodded, eyes as big as saucers. 'Get out of here. Run home. *Go.*'

Miranda stripped off the ropes around her ankles, scrambled up, and escaped.

Claire shut the door and hurried to the living room.

François had shoved Michael's guitar out of the way and taken the chair. Ysandre sat on the couch, as comfortable as if she owned the world and everything in it. 'How kind of you to ask us in, Michael. I didn't think we got off to a very good beginning. I want to start over.'

François laughed. 'Yes,' he said. 'We should be friends, Michael. And you shouldn't be living with cattle.'

'Is this all you have? Because if it is, I think we're all done.'

'Oh, not quite,' Ysandre said.

'They're making dinner,' François said. 'That's ironic, don't you think? When they let ours go.'

'These humans, all they do is eat,' Ysandre said. 'No wonder they're all fat and lazy.'

Shane came out of the kitchen. He wasn't surprised, Claire saw; he must have heard them. 'You're not invited,' Shane said. Ysandre kissed her lips toward him.

'Oh, Shane, I really don't care whether I am or not, and you aren't anywhere near powerful enough to make me leave,' she said. 'It's Friday, my love. You received the costume I want you to wear for tomorrow?'

Shane nodded unwillingly, like his neck had

frozen stiff. His eyes were more than a little crazy.

'You need to go,' Claire said to Ysandre, with a bravado she really didn't feel.

'What do you think, Michael? Do I?' Ysandre locked gazes with him, and there was something awful in her eyes. 'Do I have to go?'

'No,' he said. 'Stay.'

Claire gaped.

They make you feel things. Do things, whether you want to do them or not. Shane had said it, but Claire hadn't imagined that they could do it to other vampires. Even one as young and inexperienced as Michael.

'Michael!'

He didn't look at her. He seemed completely caught in the web of Ysandre's attraction.

Claire dug her cell phone out of her pocket. She hesitated over the address book.

'Deciding who to call for help?' François yanked the cell phone out of her hands and threw it across the room. 'Amelie won't thank you for distracting her from all her preparations. She's busy, busy, busy, making sure everything goes just right to welcome our beloved father properly.'

'Maybe you ought to ask Michael what to do,' Ysandre said, and laughed, showing fang. She pronounced it like *Michelle*. 'I'm sure he'll help dispatch us. So *fierce*, isn't he?'

Michael's eyes were slowly turning crimson.

They can make you feel things. Do things.

'Shane,' Claire said. 'We need to get out of here. Now.'

'I'm not leaving Michael.'

'Michael's the problem.'

Ysandre laughed. 'You really *are* clever, *ma chérie.*'

François snapped his fingers in front of Michael's face. 'Dinner's ready.'

Michael opened his mouth and snarled. Full fangs.

And he turned and fixed his gaze on Claire.

'Oh, crap,' Shane breathed. He grabbed Claire's arm. 'Kitchen!'

They retreated. Shane shoved the table against the swinging door, for all the good it would do, and they backed up toward the rear door.

Claire opened the refrigerator and took Michael's last two sealed bottles out of the back of the refrigerator. *Have to tell Michael to pick up more*, she thought, and how weird was that? Running short of blood was getting as normal as needing Coke or butter.

She was gibbering in her head, that was it. And yet, oddly calm.

Michael burst into the room and headed straight for them.

Claire stepped into his path, held out a bottle, and said, 'You're not one of them. You're one of us. One of us, and we love you.'

'Claire—' Shane sounded agonised, but he

didn't move. Maybe he knew it would have blown everything.

Michael stopped. His eyes were still blazing red, but he seemed to *see* her.

And the red flickered a little.

She held out the bottle.

'Drink it,' she said. 'You'll feel better. Trust me, Michael. Please.'

He was staring into her eyes.

And this time, she was the one who challenged him. *See me. Know what you're doing.*

Push her out.

His eyes flared white. He grabbed the bottle out of her hand, popped the cap, and tipped the bottle, guzzling the contents as fast as he could swallow.

He didn't look away.

Neither did she.

His eyes faded back to blue, and he lowered the bottle with a gasp. A thin line of blood dripped off his lip, and he wiped it with a trembling hand.

'It's OK,' Claire said. 'She got in your head. She can do that. She—'

Shane was gone. While she'd been so focused on Michael, he'd just...disappeared.

The kitchen door was still swinging.

It'll be easier for her the next time, Shane had told her.

Claire headed for the living room. Michael tried to stop her, but he seemed weak. Sick. She remembered how shaken Shane had been.

Why not me? Why doesn't she control me?
Maybe she couldn't.

Shane was sitting on the couch beside Ysandre, and his shirt was unbuttoned. Ysandre was running her hands up and down Shane's chest, tracing invisible lines, and as Claire watched, the vampire began to nibble on Shane's neck. Not seriously, as in not drawing blood, but little teasing nips. Licks.

Shane's face was still and blank, but his eyes were pools of panic. *He doesn't want this,* Claire realised. *She's making him.*

Claire threw the second bottle of blood at Ysandre. The vampire's hand came up unbelievably fast to snatch it out of the air before it made contact with the side of her head.

'If you're hungry, eat,' she said. 'And get your claws out of my boyfriend.'

Ysandre's eyes narrowed. Claire felt something brush at her mind, but it was like walking through a spider web, easily broken.

Ysandre flipped the cap from the bottle, sniffed it, and made a disgusted face. 'Don't be so possessive. Shane is at my command. The invitation said so.'

'He's at your command *tomorrow.* Not *today.*'

'How charming. So young for a lawyer.' Ysandre sipped from the bottle, gagged, and shook her head. 'Why your vampires subject themselves to this indignity is beyond my understanding. This is rancid. Undrinkable filth.' She threw the bottle back at Claire, who had no choice but to try to catch it; she did, but the contents splattered cold over her face and neck. 'Remove it from our presence.' Her eyes took on a horrible dull shine, angry and cruel. 'And clean yourself up. You're as useless as the hospitality you offer.'

'Get out,' Claire said. She felt the power of the house now, gathering like a storm around her. Rushing into the cool silence, crackling with energy. 'Get out of our house. *Now.*'

It exploded up through her feet, painful and shocking, and hit Ysandre and François like a bolt of invisible lightning. It knocked them flat, grabbed them by the ankles, and *dragged* them to the front door, which crashed open before they reached it.

Ysandre shrieked and clawed at the floor, but it was useless. In that moment, the house wasn't taking any prisoners.

It threw them out into the sun. François and Ysandre staggered to their feet, covered their heads, and ran for their car.

Claire stood in the doorway, spattered with cold blood, and yelled, 'And don't come back!'

The power cut off, and the sudden emptiness left her shaking. Claire clung to the door for a few seconds, long enough to see them drive away, and then staggered back to the living room. Shane sat on the couch with his shirt unbuttoned to the waist, head in his hands.

Shuddering.

'You OK?' she asked.

He nodded convulsively without looking up at her. Michael opened the kitchen door and came straight to her. He had a towel, and he scrubbed the blood off her face and hands with rough, anxious movements.

'How did you do that?' he asked. 'Even I can't – not on command. Not like that.'

'I don't know,' she said. She felt sick and shaky, and perched on the couch next to Shane. Shane was buttoning his shirt. His fingers moved slowly, and didn't seem very steady, either.

'Shane?' Michael stood next to him, and his voice was very gentle.

'Yeah, man, I'm fine,' he said. His voice was threadbare with exhaustion. 'She may own me, but she can't take possession until tomorrow night. I don't think she'll risk coming back here. Not just for me.' He looked up at Michael then, and Michael nodded tightly. 'I don't want to ask, but—'

'You don't have to ask,' Michael said. 'I'll look out for you. As much as I can.'

They bumped fists.

'I need a shower,' Shane said, and went upstairs. He wasn't moving like Shane, not at all – too slow, too heavy, too...defeated.

Michael had made the promise, but Claire was afraid – very afraid – that he wouldn't be able to keep it. Once they were away from this house, isolated and separated, nobody could stop Ysandre from doing whatever she wanted to Shane. To Michael. To *anyone*.

If Jason had been telling the truth when he'd come by the house looking to talk, then Oliver had had something to say. Maybe he still did.

Maybe, somehow, it would help Shane.

It was really the only thing Claire could think of that might help.

When she went to Oliver's coffee shop, she walked into more trouble, although it wasn't as obvious as Ysandre and François taking over the living room. In fact, it took Claire a few seconds to identify what was odd about what she was seeing, because on the surface it looked quite normal.

But it wasn't.

Eve was sitting peacefully across the table from Oliver, whom she'd sworn she'd rather stake than look at again. And whatever it was she was saying, Oliver was gravely listening, head cocked, expression composed. He had a very thin smile on his face, and his eyes were fixed on Eve's face with so much focus it made Claire's skin crawl.

She was going to draw their attention, standing like an idiot in the middle of the room, even as busy as the place was. She turned away, went to the coffee bar, and ordered a mocha she didn't crave, just to have some reason to be here. Eve was too deep into her own thing to realise Claire had come in, but Oliver knew; Claire could feel it, even though he hadn't so much as glanced her way.

She paid her four bucks and took her overpriced, yet delicious, drink to an empty table near the front windows, where there were plenty of students to cover her. She didn't really need to worry, though; when Eve got up and left, she walked straight out, and she didn't look right or left as she stiff-armed the door and stalked off down the street. She was wearing a black satin ankle-length skirt that reminded Claire of the inside of a coffin, and a purple velvet top, and she looked thin and fragile.

She looked vulnerable.

'Terrible, the lengths some girls will go to for attention,' Oliver said, and settled into a chair across from Claire. 'Don't you think her obsession with the morbid is a bit much?'

She didn't take the bait, just looked at him. The line of sunlight was very close to him, and creeping closer. In another few minutes, it would touch him on the shoulder. She knew he, like most older vampires, had partial immunity to sunlight, but it would still hurt.

Oliver knew what she was thinking. He glanced at the hot line of light and scooted his chair sideways, enough to buy another few minutes in the shadows.

'Why did you send Jason the other night?' she asked.

'Why do you think I sent him?'

'He said so.'

'Is Jason so reliable a source as all that? I thought

he was a crazed murderer who was stalking his
own sister.'

'What did you just talk to Eve about?'

Oliver raised his eyebrows. 'I believe that is Eve's
business, not yours. If there's nothing else—'

'Ysandre and Frangois just tried a power play at
our house. *In our house*, Oliver. Why did you send
Jason?'

Oliver was quiet a moment. He wasn't looking
at her at all; he was watching the people walking
outside on the street, the cars passing. His gaze
wandered over the students inside his shop, talking
and laughing. There was something odd in his
expression, as if – like Eve – he was suddenly aware
of his own vulnerability.

And that of others.

'I don't admit that I did send him,' Oliver said.
'But if I did, obviously I would have had a very good
reason, yes?'

She didn't answer. His gaze flashed back to her,
bright and very, very focused. 'I have never made
any secret of my desire for power, Claire. I don't
like Amelie, and she doesn't care for me, but our
games are honest ones. We know the rules and we
abide by them. But Bishop – Bishop is beyond all
rules. He would take our game board and overturn
it completely, and that I cannot have. Not even if I
gain in the process.'

The light dawned, finally. 'Bishop tried to
recruit you. Against Amelie.' Claire's blood chilled

a couple of degrees. 'You couldn't tell her directly. So you wanted to use Jason to tell me, and let me tell her.'

'Too late now. Things are moving too quickly to the edge. It's not within my power to halt it, or hers. Much less yours, Claire.'

Claire realised she was clutching the table in a death grip, and let go. Her fingers ached from the pressure. 'What were you talking to Eve about?'

Oliver's eyes fixed on hers, and he said, 'She is accompanying me to the feast.'

Eve was going to the masked ball. With Oliver.

Claire sat back, unable to think of a single thing to say for a moment, and then it hit her exactly what that meant. 'Does Michael know?'

'Frankly, I could not care less. Eve can explain it as and if she chooses; it's no concern of mine. I believe I'm finished assisting you with your inquiries, Claire. But if I might give you a piece of advice—' Oliver leant forward, and it put him completely in the sun. He didn't flinch, though the pupils of his eyes contracted to almost nothing, and his skin began to take on a definite pink tinge. 'Stay home tomorrow. Lock your doors and windows, and if you're a religious person, a little prayer might not go amiss.'

It was such a startling thing for him to say that Claire almost laughed. 'I'm supposed to pray? For who, you?'

Oliver didn't blink. 'If you would,' he said, 'that

would be comforting. I don't think anyone's done it in quite some time.'

He stood up and walked away. Claire sat for a while staring off into the afternoon sunlight, sipping a mocha long gone cold and tasting nothing at all. When a knot of big upper-class jocks asked her, none too politely, if she was done with the table, she left without any protest. She went for a walk, following the curve of streets without any real awareness of where she was, or where she might be going.

All these people. She was away from the college crowd now, and Morganville natives took advantage of the sunshine any way they could – sunbathing, working in their gardens, painting their houses.

And tomorrow, if Oliver was right, it could be all over. If Bishop succeeded in taking over from Amelie...

Claire realised with a start that the sun was slipping toward the horizon, and turned at the nearest cross street to head for home. She made it with the day still officially in the late-afternoon phase, although twilight was creeping in, but as she opened the gate and came through the walk, she realised that someone was sitting on the front steps waiting for her.

Shane.

'Hey,' he said.

'Hey,' she returned, and sat down next to him. He was looking out at the street, the occasional passing car. A breeze ruffled his dark hair, and the sunlight made his skin look like it had a faint brushing of gold.

God, he was so...perfect. And he was breaking her heart with the look in his eyes.

'So,' Shane said. 'I was thinking we should go out tonight.'

'Out?' she repeated blankly. 'Out where?'

He shrugged. 'Doesn't matter. Movies. Dinner. I'd take you to the local bar for a blow-out, but your dad might kill me.' Shane looked at her for a few seconds, then went back to his careful study of nothing. 'I just want to spend tonight doing something with you. Whatever it is.'

Because tomorrow, it could all change. It was the same eerie feeling Claire had felt walking around town: the feeling that the world was ending, and only a few people had a clue it was coming.

'Any place you've always wanted to go?' Claire asked.

'Sure. I play a great game of Anywhere but Here. You mean in Morganville?' He was quiet for a second, as if the question had caught him by surprise. 'Maybe. You up for a drive?'

'In whose car?'

'Eve's.' He held up the car keys and jangled them. 'I made her a deal. I get the car two nights a week; I do her share of the chores two more days. I'm exercising my rental coupon.'

'The sun's going down,' Claire felt compelled to point out.

'So it is.' He jangled the car keys again. 'Well?'

Really, he already knew what the answer would be.

They drove to a restaurant near the vampire downtown area – far enough that it had mostly human patronage, but still stayed open late. There was a lounge area with a dance floor, and a jukebox that played oldies. Shane had a beer he was too young to order. Claire had a Coke, and they spent a roll of quarters on choosing songs, one right after another.

'This is the biggest damn iPod I've ever seen,' Claire said, which made him choke on his beer. 'Kidding. I have seen a jukebox before.'

'The way you're feeding it, I'm not so sure. You think you picked enough songs?'

'I don't know,' she said. 'How many will it take to play all night?'

He put his beer down on the table, put his arms around her, and they swayed together as the songs changed, and changed, and changed.

And around them, Morganville slowly went quiet.

CHAPTER TEN

Saturday dawned cooler and windier, with a breath of chill cutting like metal.

Shane and Claire drove in just before dawn, exhausted but peaceful. They'd danced until the restaurant closed down, then drove, then parked. It had been sweet and urgent and Claire had almost, almost wanted it to go further...at least into the backseat.

But Shane had held to his word, no matter how frustrating that was for both of them, and she supposed that was still a good thing.

Mostly, she just wanted to get his clothes off and dive into the bed with him and never, ever come out. But he kissed her at her bedroom door, and she knew from the look in his eyes that he wasn't trusting himself that far with her.

Not tonight. Not even with the whole world changing.

Claire fell asleep just before dawn and slept right through sunrise. Through sunrise. Through lunch. She only woke up at all because the next-door neighbour started up his monster gas-powered lawn mower for the last trim of the season. It was like a gardening jet engine, and no matter how many pillows Claire piled on her head, it didn't help.

The house was eerily quiet. Claire put on her robe and shuffled down the hall to the bathroom. She tapped oh Eve's door on the way, but there was no answer. None at Shane's or Michael's, either. She took the fastest shower on record and went downstairs, only to find...nothing. No Michael, no Shane, no Eve. And no note. There was coffee in the pot, but it had long cooked down to sludge.

Claire sat down at the kitchen table and paged through numbers on her phone. No answer from Eve's cell, and Michael's rang to voice mail. So did Shane's.

'Hey,' Claire said when his recorded voice told her to leave her message. 'I'm – I just was hoping I'd see you. You know, this morning. But – look, can you give me a call, please? I want to talk to you. Please.'

She felt so alone that tears prickled her eyes. *The feast. It's today.*

Everything was changing.

A rap at the back door made her jump, and she peered through the window for a long time before she eased open the door a crack. She left the security chain on. 'What do you want, Richard?'

Richard Morrell's police cruiser was parked in the drive. He hadn't flashed any lights or howled any sirens, so she supposed it wasn't an emergency, exactly. But she knew him well enough to know he didn't pay social visits, at least not to the Glass House.

And not in uniform.

'Good question,' Richard said. 'I guess I want a nice girl who can cook, likes action movies, and looks good in short skirts. But I'll settle for you taking the chain off the door and letting me in.'

'How do I know you're you?'

'What?'

'Ysandre. She – well, let's say I need to be sure it's really you.'

'I had to uncuff you in a girl's bathroom at the university this week. How's that?'

She slid the chain loose and stepped back as he walked in. He looked tired – not as tired as she felt, but then she guessed that wasn't humanly possible, really. 'What do you want?'

'I'm going to this thing tonight,' he said. 'I figured you'd be going too. I was thinking you might need a ride.'

'I – I'm not going.'

'No?' Richard looked puzzled by that. 'Funny, I could have sworn you'd be Amelie's first choice to parade around at a thing like this. She's proud of you, you know.'

Proud? Why on earth would she be proud? 'What, like a pedigree dog?' Claire asked bitterly. 'Best in show?'

Richard held up his hands in surrender. 'Whatever, it's none of my business. Where is your gang, anyway?'

'Why?'

'It's my business to know where the troublemakers are.'

'We're not troublemakers!' Richard gave her a look. One she had to admit she deserved. 'Your sister's going, you know.'

'Yeah, I know. She's been preening around the house for days. Spent a fortune on that damn costume of hers. Dad's going to kill her if she gets anything on it. I think he's planning to return it.'

Claire waved the fresh coffeepot inquiringly, and Richard nodded and sat down at the kitchen table. She slid a mug over to him, and watched as he sipped. He seemed – different today. *Everything's changing.* Richard seemed more vulnerable, too. He'd always been the steady one, the sane Morrell. Today, he looked barely older than Monica.

'I think something's going to happen,' Claire said. 'Don't you?'

Richard nodded slowly. There were lines of tension around his eyes, and bags under his eyes big enough to hold changes of clothes. 'This Bishop, he's not like the others,' he said. 'I met him. I – saw something in him. It's not human, Claire. Not even a little bit. Whatever humanity he ever owned, he sold a long time ago.'

'What are you going to do?'

Richard shrugged. 'What the hell can I do? Stick with my family. Look out for the people of this town. Wish I was a million miles away.' He was quiet for a few seconds, sipping coffee. 'Thing is, I think we're going to be asked to promise him some kind of loyalty, and I don't think I can do that. I don't think I *want* to do that.'

Claire swallowed. 'Do you have a choice?'

'Probably not. But I'll do my best to keep people safe. That's all I know how to do.' His eyes skimmed past hers, as if he didn't dare to really look too deeply. 'The others are going, aren't they?'

She nodded.

'Did you know your parents are going?'

Claire gasped, covered her mouth with her hands, and shook her head. 'No,' she said. 'No, they're not. They can't be.'

'I saw the list,' Richard said. 'Sorry. I figured you were just on another page. I couldn't believe you were left off. That's good, though, that you can stay home. It's – I think it's going to be dangerous.'

He drained the rest of his coffee and pushed the mug back toward her.

'I'll watch out for your friends and your parents,' he said. 'As much as I can. You know that, right?'

'You're nice,' Claire said. She was surprised that

she said it out loud, but she meant it. 'You really
are, you know.'

Richard smiled at her, and even though she'd
developed a partial immunity to hot guys smiling at
her, thanks to Shane and Michael, some part of her
still went *Oooooooooh*.

'I'm hiring you as my press agent,' Richard said.
'Lock up and stay inside, all right?'

She saw him to the door and dutifully turned all
the dead bolts, since he was standing there waiting
to hear it. He waved and got back in his police
cruiser, and silently backed out of the drive to the
street.

Which was, Claire realised, eerily deserted.
Morganville was usually active in the afternoons,
but here it was prime walking-around time, and
she couldn't see a soul out there. Not walking, not
driving, not weeding a garden. Even the next-door
neighbour had powered down the mower and locked
up tight.

It was like everyone just…knew.

Claire booted up her laptop and checked her
e-mail, which was really more like checking her
spam. Today, come-ons from sad Russian girls
and Nigerian businessmen desperate to get rid of
millions of tax-free dollars didn't amuse her all that
much. Neither did random surfing or the *I'm Feeling
Lucky* Google feature. She had hours to kill, and her
whole body was aching with tension.

You could visit Myrnin. Myrnin's not going, either.

Oh, that was way too tempting. Myrnin was work. And work was a great distraction.

Richard told me to lock myself in. Yeah, but he hadn't said *where*, had he? Myrnin's lab was pretty safe. So was the prison where Myrnin was kept. And at least she'd have company.

'Nope,' Claire said. 'Can't do it. Too dangerous.'

Except it was still daylight outside. So, not nearly as dangerous as it could be.

The sensible side of her threw up its hands in disgust. *Whatever. Go on, get yourself killed. See if I care.*

Claire grabbed a few things and shoved them in the backpack – textbooks, of course, but a couple of novels that she'd been meaning to take to Myrnin, since he was always interested in new things to read.

And a bread knife. Somehow, that seemed like a wise thing to pack, too. She put it in her history textbook, like the world's most dangerous bookmark.

And then, with one last glance around the house, she left.

I hope I come back, she thought, and turned to look at the house as she fastened the front gate. *I hope we all come back.*

She felt like the house was hoping that, too.

It was a long walk to Myrnin's lab, but she wasn't in any danger, except from dying of the creepies. She saw one or two cars, but they were full of frightened, anxious people heading to some safe haven – work, home, school. Nobody else was outside. Nobody else was walking.

Claire followed the twisting streets of Morganville into a run-down older area. At the end of the street sat a duplicate of the Glass House – the Day House, where a lovely old lady named Katherine Day still lived. Today, her battered rocking chair was empty, nodding in the breeze. Claire had been kind of hoping that Grandma Day, or her fiercer granddaughter, would be hanging out; they'd have invited her up to the porch for a lemonade, and tried to talk her out of what she was doing. But if they were home at all, they were inside with the curtains drawn.

Just like everybody else in town.

Claire turned down the dark alley next to the Day House. It was bordered with tall fences, and it got narrower the farther it went. She'd come here by accident the first time, and on purpose ever since, and it still struck her as a terrifying place, even in broad daylight.

Grandma Day had known about Myrnin. She'd called him a trap-door spider.

Grandma Day, in Claire's experience, had been right about a lot of things, and that was one of them. As sweet and kind and gentle as Myrnin could be, when he turned, he turned all the way.

Claire reached the end of the alley, which was a rickety shed barely large enough to qualify as one room. The door was locked with a new, shiny padlock. She dug in her pocket and found her keys.

Inside, the shack wasn't any better – nothing but a square of floor, and steps leading down. What little light there was spilt in through the grimy windows. Claire grabbed a flashlight from the corner – she always kept a supply there – and flicked it on as she descended the steps into Myrnin's lab.

She'd half expected to find Amelie here, or Oliver, or somebody else – but it was just as she'd left it. Deserted and quiet, with only a couple of dim electric lights burning. Claire pushed aside the bookcase that stood against the right-hand wall – it was rigged to move easily – and behind it was a door. It was locked, too, and she got the keys out of the drawer under the journal shelves.

As she was unlocking it, she could have sworn she heard a rustle from the shadows. Claire turned, and felt the stupid impulse to ask who it was; all that stopped her was pure shame, and a determination not to be as stupid as the girls in horror movies. There was nobody here. Not even Oliver.

Instead, she slipped the lock from the door, took a deep breath, and concentrated.

The physics of Myrnin's special doorways still eluded her, although she thought she was beginning to understand the breakthrough he'd made in quantum mechanics...Of course, he didn't look at it scientifically; to him it was magic, or at least alchemy. *You don't have to know how something works to use it*, Claire reminded herself. It irritated her, but she was getting used to the fact that some things were going to be harder to figure out, and anything that had to do with Myrnin definitely fell into that category.

She swung open the door, which led to the prison on the other side of town. She'd looked it up on maps, measured the distance between Myrnin's hidden lab and the abandoned complex. It wasn't possible for there to be a door between the two, unless you seriously twisted the laws of physics as she understood them, but there it was.

And she stepped through and closed the door behind her. There was a hasp on this side of the door, too; she locked it up, just in case her imagination hadn't been running wild and someone was in the lab watching her. They'd have a hell of a time getting through, and with the nature of Myrnin's doorways, they probably wouldn't end up here if they ended up anywhere at all.

'Hi,' Claire said to the cells as she passed them; she didn't think any of the vampires really understood her, but she always tried to be kind. They couldn't help what they were – whatever that was. Insane, certainly. Some of them less than others, and those were the ones who made her feel sad – the ones who seemed to understand where they were, and why.

Like Myrnin.

Claire stopped in at the refrigerator and picked up supplies of blood packs, which she tossed into the cells from a careful distance away. She saved two for Myrnin, whose cell was at the end of the hall.

He was sitting on the bed, spectacles perched at the end of his nose. He was reading a battered copy of Voltaire.

'Claire,' he said, and put a faded silk ribbon between the pages to mark his place. He looked up, young and pretty and (today, at least) not entirely crazy. 'I've had the oddest thing happen.'

She pulled up her chair and settled in. 'Which is?'

'I think I'm getting better.'

'I don't think so,' she said. 'I wish that was true, but—'

He shoved a Tupperware container toward the bars of the cell. 'Here.'

Claire froze, eyeing the container doubtfully. 'Umm...what is that?'

'Brain tissue.'

'*What?*'

Myrnin adjusted his glasses and looked at her over their tops. 'I said, brain tissue.'

'Whose brain tissue?'

He looked around the cell, eyebrows raised. 'I haven't a lot of volunteers in easy reach, you know.'

Claire had a horrible thought. She couldn't actually bring herself to say it.

Myrnin gave her an evil smile.

'We are testing the serum, are we not? And so far, I am the only test subject?'

'That's *brain tissue*. How can you – ?' Claire shut her mouth, fast. 'Never mind. I don't think I want to know.'

'Truly, I think that's best. Please take it.' He showed his teeth briefly in a very unsettling grin. 'I'm giving you a piece of my mind.'

'I *so* wish you hadn't said that.' She shuddered, but she ventured close enough to the bars to fish out the container. Yes, that looked…grey. And biological. She checked to be sure that the top was firmly fastened, and stuck it in her backpack. 'What makes you think you're getting better?'

Myrnin picked up half a dozen thick volumes and held them out on the palm of his hand. 'I've read these in the past day and a half,' he said. 'Every word. I can answer any question you'd like about the contents.'

'Not a good test. You already know those books.'

He seemed surprised. 'Yes, that's true. Very well. How would you propose to test me?'

'Read some of this,' she said, and passed him a novel from her backpack. He glanced at the author's name and the title, flipped to page 1, and began. She watched his eyes flicker rapidly back and forth – faster than most humans could begin to comprehend words on a page. He was focused, and he seemed genuinely interested.

'Stop,' she said five minutes later. Myrnin obligingly closed the book and handed it back to her. 'Tell me about what you read.'

'It's rather clever of you to make it a novel about vampires,' Myrnin said. 'Although I think their avoidance of mirrors is a bit ridiculous. The main characters seemed interesting. I think I'd like to finish it.' And then he proceeded to recite, at length, the descriptions and histories of the characters as they'd been given in the first fifty pages...and the plot. Claire blinked and checked his facts.

All correct.

'See?' Myrnin took off his spectacles and stowed them in a pocket of the purple satin vest he was wearing over a white dress shirt. 'I am better, Claire. Truly.'

'Well, we really should wait to see—'

'No, I don't think so.' He stood up, lithe and strong, and walked to the bars.

He took hold of them and heaved, and the lock – the lock that was supposed to hold the strongest, craziest vampires – snapped loudly. He rolled the bars aside on their groove and stood in the open doorway, smiling at her.

'Are those for me?' He nodded at the blood bags lying on top of her backpack. She realised that she was clutching the book in white-knuckled fingers, barely breathing. *I hope he didn't remove some part of his brain that stops him from attacking me...*

'Yes,' she managed to say. She'd been intending to throw the blood to him, but somehow it didn't seem right. She picked up the first one and held it out.

Myrnin walked slowly toward her – deliberately slowly, making sure she got used to the idea – and took the plastic pack from her hand without so much as brushing her skin. He even turned away to bite into it, and although the sucking noises made her uncomfortable and a bit sick, when he turned around, there wasn't a speck of blood on him, or in the plastic packaging, either.

Claire held up the second one. He shook his head. 'No need to stuff myself,' he said. 'One is plenty for now.' Which was odd, too, because Myrnin was usually – how could she put it without making herself feel nauseous? – a hearty eater.

'I'll put it back,' she said, but before she could move, Myrnin had taken it from her palm. She hadn't even seen him move this time.

'I'll do it.' She shivered, listening and watching, but he was already gone into the shadows. She heard the creak of the massive refrigerator door open and close, and then suddenly he was back, strolling slowly out of the darkness. Arms crossed over his chest. He leant against the wall across from her.

'So?' he asked. 'Do I seem insane to you?'

She shook her head.

'You wouldn't tell me even if I was, would you, Claire?'

'Probably not. You might get angry.'

'I might get angry if you lied,' Myrnin said. 'But I won't. I don't feel angry at all right now. Or hungry, or even anxious, and that never seemed to leave me the last few years. The drugs you gave me, Claire, I think they're taking hold. Do you know what that means?' He flashed across the empty space, and when she was able to focus on him again, he was kneeling next to her chair, one pale hand gently resting on her knee. 'It means my people can be saved. All of them.'

'What about mine?' Claire asked. 'If yours get well, what happens to mine?'

Myrnin's face went carefully still and blank. 'The fate of humans isn't really my area of responsibility,' he said. ' Amelie has worked hard to be sure Morganville is a place of balance, a place where our two kinds can live in relative harmony. I doubt she'd change all that based on the outcome of this experiment.'

He could doubt it all he wanted, but Claire knew Amelie better. She'd do whatever was best for her own first, humans second. In fact, Claire wasn't altogether sure, but she suspected Morganville *was* the experiment – and an experiment would be ended when an outcome was achieved.

If this was the outcome – what happened to the lab rats?

Myrnin's dark eyes were glowing now with sincerity. 'I'm not a monster, Claire. I wouldn't allow you to be hurt. You've done us a great service, and you'll be looked after.'

'What about other people?' she asked.

'Which people? Ah, your friends, your family. Yes,

of course, they'll be safeguarded, as well, whatever happens.'

'No, Myrnin, I mean *everybody else*! The guy who makes hamburgers at the Burger Dog! The lady who runs the used-clothing store! *Everybody!*'

He blinked, clearly taken aback. 'We can't care about *everyone*, Claire. It isn't in our natures. We can only care about those we know, or those we're connected with. I appreciate your altruism, but—'

'Don't talk to me about *our natures*! We're not the same!'

'Aren't we?' Myrnin patted her knee gently. 'I'm a scientist. So are you. I have friends, people I care for and love. So do you. How are we different?'

'I don't suck my dinner out of a bag!'

Myrnin laughed. He showed no trace at all of fangs. 'Oh, Claire, do you imagine that eating slaughtered and mutilated animals is any less disgusting? We both eat. We both enjoy the company of others. We both—'

'I don't dig *brain tissue* out of my skull! Oh, and I don't kill,' she said. 'You do. And you really don't mind it.'

He sat back a little, staring into her face. The glow of sincerity took on a harder edge. 'I think you'll find I do mind it,' he said. 'Or else I wouldn't put up with this from—'

'From a servant? Because that's what I am, right? Or worse – a slave? Property?'

'You're upset.'

'Yes! Of course I'm – of course I'm upset.' She fought to keep it together, but she couldn't; the misery just boiled out of her like steam under pressure. 'I'm sitting here debating the future of the human race, and my friends and family are going to that party, and I can't protect them—'

'Hush, child,' he said. 'The feast. It's tonight, yes?'

'I don't even know what it is.'

'Amelie's formal recognition of Bishop. Every vampire in Morganville who is able will be present, all there to swear their obedience, and every one of them will bring a token gift.'

She sniffled, sat up, and wiped her face. 'What kind of gift?'

Myrnin's dark eyes were steady on hers. 'A token gift of blood,' he said. 'Specifically, a human. You're right to be worried for your friends, your family. He has the right to choose any human offered to him. The gesture is meant to be ceremonial – it's come down to us as a tradition from long ago – but it doesn't have to be.'

And Claire understood. She understood why Amelie had forbidden her to come; she understood why Michael had deliberately asked Monica Morrell instead of Eve.

It was chess, and the pawns were *people*. The vampires were playing with what they could afford to lose.

'You—' Her voice didn't sound steady. She cleared

her throat and tried again. 'You said that he could choose any human.'

Myrnin didn't blink. 'Or all of them,' he said. 'If he so wishes.'

'You know he'll do it. He'll kill someone.'

'Most likely, yes.'

'We have to stop this,' she said. 'Myrnin – why would she *do* this?'

'Amelie is not a brave woman. If the odds are against her, she will surrender; if the odds are near even, she will play for time and advantage. She knows she can't defeat Bishop on her own; not even she and Oliver combined can do it. She has to play the long game, Claire. She's played it all her life.' Myrnin's dark eyes were glowing again, and he began to smile. 'Amelie reckons her odds without me, of course. With me at her side, she can win.'

'You want to go. To the feast.'

Myrnin straightened his vest and brushed imaginary dust from his sleeves. 'Of course. And I'm going with or without you. Now, are you going under those circumstances?'

'I – Amelie said—'

'Yes or no, Claire.'

'Then...yes.'

'We'll need costumes,' he said. 'Not to worry, I know just the place to get them.'

'I look ridiculous,' Claire said. She also looked completely *obvious*. 'Can't we do something in, I don't know, black? Since we're supposed to be sneaky?'

'Stop talking,' Myrnin commanded as he applied makeup to her face. He seemed to be enjoying himself a hell of a lot more than the situation called for, and she felt doubt once again that his cure was really a *cure*. There had been a good reason Amelie said he shouldn't be at the feast; there'd been a good reason, too, for leaving him out of her calculations for war or peace.

But Claire knew Amelie too well. If peace meant it had to come at the price of a few human deaths, even ones that were dear to Claire, she'd count it an acceptable cost.

Claire didn't.

'There,' Myrnin said. 'Close your eyes.'

Claire did, and felt a soft brushing of powder over her face. When she opened her eyes, Myrnin stepped out of the way, and she saw some alien creature in the mirror reflecting back at her.

She *did* look ridiculous, but she had to admit she didn't look like Claire Danvers. Not at all. A white face that would have done Eve proud. Full red lips. Huge, black-rimmed eyes with funny little lines to draw attention to them.

A tight-fitting costume, top and tights, covered with red and black diamonds. A matador's hat. 'What am I supposed to be?' she blurted. Myrnin looked disappointed in her.

'Harlequin,' he said, and twirled like a crazy little girl. 'I am Pierrot.' Myrnin was dressed in white, and where her costume was tight, his was full, billowing around his body like choir robes with white pants beneath. He had an enormous white ruffle around his collar, and a white hat that looked like a traffic cone. The same manic makeup, which only made his dark eyes look wider and less sane. 'Don't they teach anything in your schools?'

'Not about *this*.'

'Pity. I suppose that's what comes of your main education flowing from Google.' He fitted something over her head. 'Your mask, madam.' It was a simple domino mask, but it was patterned in the same red and black as her costume. 'Can you do cartwheels? Backflips?'

She gave him a hopeless look. 'I'm a *science nerd*, not a cheerleader.'

'Pity about that, too.' He put on his own mask, which was plain black. He'd painted his face to match hers – dead white, huge red lips. It was eerie. 'Well, then, we have costumes. Now all we need is something to tip the scales in our favour, should things go badly. As I'm sure they will, knowing Bishop.'

They were in the attic of the Glass House, surrounded by what looked like centuries of... stuff. Claire had never been up here; in fact, she hadn't known there was an entrance at all. Myrnin had taken her to the hidden Victorian room, and then pressed a few studs on the wall to pop loose yet another secret door, which led through a dusty, cramped hallway and opened out into a vast, dark storage space. He'd found the costumes packed in a trunk that looked old enough to have been carried through the Civil War. The dressing table, where Claire sat, was probably even older. The *dust* on it looked older.

Myrnin wandered off into the stacks of boxes and suitcases and discarded treasures, muttering in what sounded like a foreign language. He began rummaging around. Claire went back to staring at herself in the mirror. The makeup and costume made her look alien and cool, but her eyes were still Claire's eyes, and they were scared.

I can't believe we're going to do this, she thought.

Myrnin popped up like some terrifying full-sized jack-in-the-box next to her, carrying a suitcase the width of Rhode Island. He dropped it to the wooden floor, where it hit with a shuddering thud.

'Ta da!' He threw it open and struck a heroic pose.

Inside were weapons. *Lots* of weapons. Crossbows. Knives. Swords. Crosses, some with crudely pointed ends.

Myrnin fished around in the chaos and came up with a dirty-looking bottle that had probably once held perfume, back around the Middle Ages. 'Holy water,' he said. '*True* holy water, blessed by the pope himself. Very rare.'

'What *is* this? Where did these things come from?'

'People who were unsuccessful in using them,' he said. 'I wouldn't recommend the vials of flammable liquid, the green ones. They do work, but you're as apt to kill your own allies as your enemies. Holy water will hurt, but it won't destroy. I would rather you were armed with nonfatal methods.'

'Why?'

'Even if we win, Amelie will be forced to bring to trial any human who kills a vampire. You know how well that ends.' Claire did, and she shuddered. Shane had nearly been killed for a murder he hadn't committed. 'So if there's any killing to be done, let me or another vampire do it. We're better suited in any case.' He folded cloth over his hand and picked up a medium-sized ornate cross with a pointed end, which he handed over with care. 'Self-defence *only*. Now, for me...'

Myrnin picked up a wickedly sharp knife and eyed the edge critically, then slipped it back into its leather scabbard. It went under his tunic and against his side.

He closed the lid on the suitcase.

'That's all?' Claire asked, surprised. There had been an arsenal just waiting for him.

'It's all I need. Time to go,' he said. 'That is, if you're certain you want to do this.'

'I'm sure.' Claire looked down at herself, and the tight costume. 'Um...where are my pockets?'

CHAPTER ELEVEN

The Glass House was on what Claire had come to think of as the Impossible Travel Network... Myrnin's doorway system led to a total of twenty places in town that she'd been able to identify, and one of them was in their living room. One, of course, was to the prison where he'd been making his residence lately. One was to the Day House, and she suspected most if not all the Founder Houses had similar connections.

There was also a doorway to Amelie's castle – or at least, Claire thought of it as a castle; she had no idea what it looked like on the outside. She didn't even know where it was in town. But inside, it felt and looked old and very, very strong. There were exits in the system to the university administration building, to the library, to the town hall, and to the Elders' Council building.

Which was where the ball was being held.

'I can't believe we're doing this,' Claire whispered as Myrnin contemplated the blank wall in the Glass House living room. 'Myrnin, are you sure? Maybe we should take a car or something.'

'This is faster,' he said. 'Not afraid, are you? No need. You're with me.' He said it with effortless arrogance, and once again, she had that flash of chilly doubt. *Was* he OK? He seemed to be stringing thoughts together just fine, but there was something...off. The sweet-natured Myrnin who normally emerged during his brief bouts of sanity was gone, and she didn't really know this Myrnin at all.

But he'd given her holy water and a cross, and he didn't have to do that. Besides...she needed him.

Didn't she?

It was too late for second thoughts. The area of wall where Myrnin was staring fluttered and melted into grey fog. The fog swirled, took on colour, and became darkness with a line of hot gold light barely visible at the bottom.

It looked like the interior of a closet.

'Come on,' Myrnin said, and extended his hand to her. She took it, and they stepped through together into the darkness. Behind them, she felt the portal seal itself, and when she turned to look, there was nothing there.

The place smelt like cleaning supplies, and as Claire swept her hand around, she came into contact with the wooden shaft of a mop. *Janitor's closet.* Well, she supposed it made arrivals a little less noticeable.

Except for the part about sneaking out of the janitor's closet.

Myrnin hadn't stopped. He reached out and turned the knob of the door, then eased it open just a crack.

'Clear,' he said, and opened it wide. He stepped out first. Claire hurried to follow, and shut the door behind them. They were in what looked like a utility hallway, plain white walls and dark red carpet.

All the doors were unmarked. And identical. Claire tried to count, to be sure she could find the room again.

'This way,' Myrnin said, and strode down the hallway to the right. His white tunic billowed as he walked, and he ought to have looked ridiculous in that traffic-cone hat, but somehow...somehow, he didn't. 'I should have let you be Pierrot, little Claire. Pierrot is known for his sweet, innocent nature. Not like Harlequin. Libitor frenzy, Claire.'

'What?'

'I said, I should have let you be Pierrot—'

'No,' she said slowly. 'You said *libitor frenzy*. What does that mean?'

'I said what?' Myrnin sent her an odd look. 'That's nonsense. Aqua lace that.'

She stopped dead in her tracks, and after a couple of steps on, he realised she'd been left behind and turned impatiently. 'Claire, iguana time.' *Claire, we don't have time.*

'Myrnin, you're not making sense. I – think the serum is wearing off.'

'I feel acting.' *I feel fine.*

'Can you hear yourself? What you're saying?'

He held up his hands. He couldn't tell that he was making word salad. *Neurological complications,* she thought, and wished she could talk to Dr Mills. *Of course, he did carve out part of his brain. That could have done some damage.* Then again, he'd been talking fine right up until these last few moments.

Claire tried to keep her voice as calm as possible. 'I think you need another shot. Please. I don't think we should wait to see how much worse you get, do you?'

Myrnin silently held out his arm and pulled up his sleeve. His exposed skin was alabaster pale, and as she took hold, it felt less like a human arm than soft leather over marble. Claire took out the small case she'd stuck in the waistband of her tights – the one Dr Mills had given her, with the syringe and vials of medicine. She'd practiced giving injections with the needle on an orange, but this was different.

'I'll try not to hurt you,' she said. Myrnin rolled his eyes.

Her hands trembled as she slipped the needle into the rubber stopper of the vial and filled up the syringe.

She squirted a few drops of the liquid from the needle and took a deep breath.

She hoped Myrnin would let her do this without a fight.

He didn't seem inclined to act out, at least not yet; he stood passively as she positioned the needle over the cold blue of his vein.

'Ready?' she asked. She was really asking herself, not him. He seemed to know that, because he smiled.

'I trust you,' he said.

She pushed, and the needle popped through his skin and slipped deep. There was a second of resistance against the surface of his vein, and then it was in.

She quickly pressed the plunger and yanked out the needle. A thin drop of blood marked where it had come out, and she wiped it away with her thumb, leaving a faint smear on his perfect skin.

She looked up and saw his pupils shrink to nothing, and a feeling of utter terror swept over her, freezing her in place. Myrnin's mouth was wide and red and smiling, and there was something about him that really, really wasn't at all right –

Then it was gone, as he blinked, and his pupils began to expand again to normal size. He shuddered and heaved a sigh.

'Unpleasant,' he said. 'Ah, there comes the warmth. Now, *that's* pleasant.'

'It didn't hurt, though?'

'I don't like needles.'

Which was funny enough to make her laugh. He frowned at her, but she kept giggling and had to cover her mouth with her hand as the laughter ratcheted higher and thinner, toward hysteria. *Get it together, Claire.*

'Better?' she asked him. Myrnin's arrogance was back, obvious in the look he sent her as she packed away the supplies.

'I wasn't *bad*,' he said. 'But I appreciate your concern.'

The hallway ended up ahead in a pair of white swinging doors, and Myrnin took her hand and practically dragged her toward them. 'Wait! Slow down!'

'Why?'

'Because I want to be sure you're—'

'*Compos mentis*? That's Latin, Claire. It means—'

'In your right mind, yes, I know.'

'I'm not babbling nonsense. And I don't think I needed the shot in the first place.' He sounded huffy about it. That was, Claire thought, the scariest part of it – Myrnin really couldn't tell when he was slipping away.

She hoped that was the scariest part, anyway. From the eagerness in Myrnin's face, she was afraid it might get a lot worse.

* * *

On the other side of the doors was the round foyer of the Elders' Council building, and it was *packed*. People stood talking, holding flutes of champagne or wine or something that was too red to be wine. All in costume, all masked.

'You were right,' she said to Myrnin. 'I think every vampire in town is here.'

'And every one brought a little human friend,' he said. 'But I think you're the only one who was told the true reason.'

Claire caught sight of Jennifer first, who was preening on the arm of François, Bishop's protégé. She was wearing a sixties costume of a tie-dyed halter top and tiny miniskirt, platform shoes, peace-sign jewellery. Her mask was an afterthought. Clearly, her whole costume's point was to show as much skin as possible without actually going nude. *Good job*, Claire thought. François clearly approved. He was dressed as Zorro, all in black satin and leather, with a flat Spanish hat.

Near Jennifer was Monica, who'd gone as Marie Antoinette, from low-cut bodice to wide skirts. She'd tied a red ribbon around her throat, which made Claire feel a little queasy, and had a miniature guillotine in her hand. She was clinging to the arm of...Michael. Who looked, even with the mask, like he wished he was far, far away and anywhere but next to Monica. *He* was dressed as a priest, in a plain black cassock and white collar. No cross visible.

Claire followed Michael's eye line across the

room to a tall scarecrow – straight out of the scariest cornfield movie she could imagine – and a girl dressed as Sally from Tim Burton's *Nightmare Before Christmas*...Oliver, and Eve. Eve looked like the perfect Sally – wistful, sad, stitched together by nothing but hope.

And she was staring at Michael, too.

Oliver, on the other hand, was ignoring her to focus on everyone else. Looking around, Claire slowly picked out a few more she recognised. Her mother wasn't anywhere to be seen, but her father was dressed in a bear costume, looking intensely uncomfortable as he stood next to a middle-aged woman – vampire? – dressed as a witch.

'Do you see Shane?' Claire asked Myrnin anxiously. He nodded toward the other side of the room. She'd already looked there, but she tried again, and after skipping over him three times, she finally figured it out.

Does your costume involve leather? she'd asked. And he'd said, *Actually, yeah, it might.*

It really did. It involved a leather dog collar, leather pants and a leash, and the leash was held by Ysandre, who was in skin-tight red rubber, from neck to thigh-high boots. She'd topped it off with a pair of devil horns and a red trident.

She'd made Shane her dog, complete with furry dog mask.

'Breathe,' Myrnin said. 'I'm not much for it myself, but I hear it's quite good for humans.'

Claire realised he was right; she'd been holding her breath. As she let it out, her shock faded, letting in a cascade of rage. *That bitch!*

No wonder Shane had looked so sick.

'She hasn't hurt him,' Myrnin said, speaking softly next to her ear. 'And you may be wearing the costume of Harlequin, but Ysandre is most definitely more of a devil. So be cautious. Bide your time. I'll let you know when we can engage with our enemy.'

Claire nodded stiffly. If she'd had any doubts at all about this, that was done now. She was going to get her friends and her family out of this, and she was going to personally take that leash out of Ysandre's hand and – do something violent with it.

'I'm ready when you are,' she said.

Myrnin shot her a mad, smiling look. 'Yes,' he said. 'I think you might be, little one.'

They stayed to themselves, watching the others, and although others eyed them curiously, no one approached. Claire asked – better late than never – if people wouldn't recognise Myrnin, even with the makeup, but he shook his head.

'I'm hardly a social fixture,' he said. 'Amelie, Sam, Michael, Oliver, a few more might know me by sight. But very few others, and none of them would expect to see me here. Especially as' – he twirled theatrically, the white tunic billowing out around him – 'Pierrot.'

Which made zero sense to her, since she still had

no idea who Pierrot was, but she nodded. Myrnin saw one of the vampire women nearby watching him, and made an elaborate low bow in her direction. 'Do a cartwheel,' he said under his breath to Claire.

'Do a what?'

'I would ask you to do a back flip, but I'm almost certain that would be a problem. Cartwheel. *Now.*'

She felt like a total idiot, but she fastened the elastic string on her matador hat under her chin and did a cartwheel, coming off it and bouncing to her feet with a bright, trembling smile.

People clapped and laughed, then turned back to their own conversations. All except Oliver, who stared intently.

But at least he kept his distance.

There was no sign of Bishop or Amelie, but Claire gradually identified most of the vampires she knew. Sam arrived, dressed as Huckleberry Finn, which went well with his red hair and freckles. He'd brought a girl Claire knew slightly from Common Grounds, one of Oliver's employees. Probably the one who'd replaced Eve when she'd quit. For Sam's sake, Claire hoped she was someone Oliver could afford to lose.

Miranda was there, dressed in ancient Greek robes with snakes for hair, and with her was a faded, small man in a Sherlock Holmes costume. 'Charles,' Myrnin confirmed when Claire asked. 'He always did have a weakness for the damaged ones.'

'She's only fifteen!'

'Modern standards, I'm afraid. Charles comes from a time when twelve was a good age to be married, so he takes your age-of-eighteen rules a little lightly.'

'He's a *paedophile*.'

'Probably,' Myrnin said. 'But he's not on Bishop's side.'

Sam spotted them, frowned, and gradually made his way through the crowd to them. Myrnin pulled off the comical bow again, but Claire was glad to note he didn't require a cartwheel this time. 'Samuel,' he said. 'How lovely to see you.'

'Are you – ?' Sam visibly checked himself, because the question had probably been, *Are you crazy?* and that answer was self-evident. 'Didn't Amelie tell you to stay away? Claire—'

'He was coming anyway,' she said. 'He broke the lock. I thought I ought to at least come along.' Which was a true – if cowardly – explanation of how they'd come to be standing here. Still, Myrnin gave her a look. One that clearly said, *Confess.* 'I probably would have done it anyway,' she said in a rush. 'I can't let my friends and my parents be here without me. I just can't.'

Sam looked grim, but he nodded like he understood. 'Fine, you've been here. You've seen. It's time to go, before you're announced. Myrnin—'

Myrnin was shaking his head. 'No, Samuel. I can't do that. She needs me.'

'She needs you to *stay out of it*!' Sam stepped up,

right into Myrnin's personal space, and Myrnin's eyes turned a muddy crimson. So did Sam's. 'Go home,' Sam said. 'Now.'

'Make me,' Myrnin said in a silky whisper. Claire had never seen him look so deadly, and it was terrifying.

She nudged him. Carefully. 'Myrnin. What happened to biding our time? Sam's not the enemy.'

'Sam would protect our enemy.'

'I'm protecting *Amelie*. You know I'd die to protect her.'

That sobered Myrnin up, at least to the extent that he took in a breath and stepped back. The white froufrou of the Pierrot costume made him look like the scariest clown she'd ever seen, especially when he smiled. 'Yes,' Myrnin said. 'I know you would, Sam. That will destroy you, one day. You have to know when to let go. It's an art the oldest of us have been forced to master, again and again.'

Sam gave them both frustrated looks and turned away.

The crowd had thickened, filling the circular room, and Claire heard a distant grandfather clock striking the hour. It seemed to go on forever in deep, sonorous bongs, and when it finished, there was silence in the room except for the rustle of fabric as people jostled for position.

The gilt-edged double doors to Claire's right opened, and a smell of roses drifted out. She knew that smell, and that room. A vampire's body had been laid in state on that stage. She and Eve and Shane had been terrorised there.

Not her favourite place, or her favourite memory.

'The lady Muriel and her attendant, Paul Grace,' said a deep, echoing voice near the door. It carried to all corners of the room. Claire craned her neck and saw a short, round vampire dressed as an Egyptian being escorted through the doors by a tall man dressed in Victorian costume. The man doing the announcing was standing to one side, a gilded book open in both hands, though he wasn't consulting it.

The maître d' of the undead.

'John of Leeds,' Myrnin whispered to her. 'Excellent choice. He was herald to King Henry, as I remember. Impeccable manners.'

The next name was already being spoken, and another couple moved forward. Claire couldn't see what was beyond the door from her angle, but she saw the glow of candlelight. 'It's going to take forever,' she said.

'Ceremony is part of the joy of life,' Myrnin said, and handed her a glass of something that sparkled. 'Drink.'

'I shouldn't.'

He raised an eyebrow. She put her lips to the champagne and tasted it – not sweet, not bitter, just right. Like light, bottled.

Maybe just one sip.

The glass was empty by the time she and Myrnin had drifted up to the front of the line; Claire felt hot and a little off-balance, and she was glad Myrnin had taken her arm. The herald, John, stood to Myrnin's left, and he seemed mildly surprised for a bare second, then said with his usual smoothness, 'Lord Myrnin of Conwy, with his attendant, Claire Danvers.'

So much for the subtle approach.

Heads turned. *Lots* of heads turned, and although vampires weren't given much to gasping, Claire heard the whispers start as she and Myrnin swept into the room. It was a cavernous, dark place set up ballroom-style, with round tables and chairs, and a large dais on the stage. Fine white linens. Floral arrangements on each table. Glittering glass and gleaming china. The entire room was lit by candles – thousands of them, in massive crystal displays.

It would have been magical, if it hadn't been so scary. The pressure of all that attention – hundreds of eyes watching their every move – made Claire's knees feel like bags of water.

Myrnin seemed to sense it. 'Steady,' he said softly. 'Smile. Head up. No sign of weakness.'

She tried. She wasn't sure how she managed it, but when he released her next to a chair, she sank down fast. They were at an empty table near the back of the room. As she looked around, she saw that Sam was seated not far away, and so was Oliver. Eve was with him, staring wide-eyed at Claire.

She couldn't see Michael. Unfortunately, she could see Shane all too clearly, because Ysandre was on the dais on the stage, and she'd brought Shane on his leash up the steps so that everyone could see him, too. They were seated at a long table on one side; François and his date were on the other.

Still no sign of Amelie, or Bishop.

Claire's father started to get up from his seat across the room, but the vampire with him took his arm and pulled him back into his chair. So the rules were no mingling, apparently. She wanted to go to him, very badly, but when she glanced at Myrnin, he shook his head. 'Wait,' he said. 'You wanted to play the game, Claire. Now we'll find out if you really have the gall for it.'

'That's my *dad*!'

'I told you, this will be a test of nerves. Yours are on display. Calm yourself.'

Fine talk from a guy who'd let his eyes turn red when somebody as unthreatening as *Sam* got in his face. But Claire concentrated on deep, slow breaths, and kept her gaze turned down, away from temptation.

'Ah,' Myrnin said, in a voice full of satisfaction. 'They're here.'

He meant, of course, Amelie and Bishop. Amelie entered first from the right of the stage, a glittering sculpture all in a white so cold it hurt the eyes. She'd come as some sort of ice spirit, which was appropriate in so many ways. Her platinum hair was woven into a crystalline tower, and she looked delicate and fragile.

On her arm was *Jason Rosser*. At least, Claire thought it was Jason. She'd never seen him after a bath and a haircut, but she recognised the stooped shoulders and the walk, if nothing else. He was wearing a hooded brown monk's robe. *She picked someone she could afford to lose, Claire thought. That's why she didn't pick me.* It should have made her feel better about being left out, but somehow, it didn't.

Bishop entered, stage left. He was dressed all in Episcopal purple, in – what else? – a bishop's costume, minus the cross. He even had the tall hat, the mitre.

On his arm, he had an angel. A woman dressed as one, anyway, with fine white feathery wings that were taller than she was, and swept the floor behind her.

Claire slapped both hands over her mouth to hold in the shriek that threatened to erupt.

It was her *mother*.

'Steady,' Myrnin said. His cool hand pressed her arm. 'What did I tell you? Control yourself! We have miles to go yet.'

She didn't want to listen to him. She wanted to get her mom and her dad, Shane and Michael and Eve. She wanted to get out of here, hit the borders of Morganville, and keep on going.

She didn't want to be here anymore.

Other guests filled in the remaining seats at their table, and two of them were Charles and Miranda. Miranda looked dreadfully young and pallid under her snaky hair and Greek robes. She sat next to Claire, and under cover of the tablecloth, reached for her hand. Claire allowed it. Miranda's felt as cool as Myrnin's, and clammy with fear.

'It's happening,' Miranda said. 'All the blood. All the fear. It's really happening.'

'Hush,' said Charles, seated next to her, and nodded at her plate. 'Eat. Beef will build your strength.'

Miranda, like Claire, picked at the prime rib on her plate. Claire tried a bite. It was good – smoky, tender, just the right warmth – but she had no appetite. Myrnin tucked into his with a frightening zeal. She wondered how long it had been since he'd had an actual meal, or wanted one. That led her to an erratic series of questions – were there vegetarians in the crowd? Did the vampires cater to food allergies? As she nibbled dully on the bread, Claire saw Amelie staring toward them. At this distance, it was impossible to really see her expression, but Claire was sure it wasn't pleased.

'I think Amelie's going to have us thrown out,' she said to Myrnin. He chewed his last bite of prime rib.

'She won't,' he said with absolute confidence. 'Aren't you going to eat that?'

Claire gave up and passed her plate. Myrnin began cutting up the meat.

'Amelie can't afford a scene,' he said. 'And no doubt it will amuse Bishop to have me here.'

He seemed odd again, almost happy. Claire eyed him doubtfully. 'Do you feel OK?'

'Never better,' he said. 'Ah, dessert!'

The servants – Claire never did catch more than a shadowy glimpse of them, so they must have been vampires – delivered exquisite little martini glasses full of berries and cream to each place. Berries and cream were something that even Claire couldn't resist. She ate the whole thing, in between staring at Shane to see if he was eating. She didn't think he was. He wasn't moving at all.

As after-dinner drinks were delivered – blood for the vamps, champagne and coffee for the haemoglobin intolerant – Claire felt her anxiety ratchet up another notch. There was murmuring in the room, a rising tide of it, and she felt the swell of excitement. 'Myrnin? What's happening?'

Miranda's hand grabbed hers again, squeezing so hard Claire almost yelped.

'It's coming,' Miranda said. 'It's almost over.'

Before Claire could ask what she meant, Myrnin touched her shoulder and said, 'They're beginning the ceremony.'

John of Leeds had come out of the wings behind the dais, and had taken up a post at a dark wooden podium. He was wearing a traditional herald's tabard, Claire realised, just like in books and paintings. She half expected him to pull out a long, thin trumpet.

He opened the book that he'd been holding outside the room instead.

'Behold,' he said in a deep, velvety smooth voice, 'there comes to us on this day one who is worthy of our fealty, and as one, we welcome him to our house.'

Bishop stood up. A curtain pulled back onstage, and behind it was a huge dark wooden throne, heavily carved.

Bishop walked up the steps to take his seat on it.

Claire's mother stayed where she was, at the table.

'What's happening?' Claire asked. Myrnin shushed her.

'As I speak your name, come forward with your tribute,' John said. 'Maria Theresa.'

A tall Spanish woman dressed in a glittering matador's costume rose from her chair, took hold of the man she'd brought to the feast, and escorted him up onto the dais. She bowed to Amelie and then turned to Bishop on his throne. She bowed again.

'I give you my fealty,' she said. 'And my gift.'

She looked at the man standing next to her. He seemed...stunned. Frozen.

Bishop looked at him and smiled. 'Princely,' he said. 'I thank you for your gift.'

And he flicked his fingers at them, and just like that, it was over.

'Vassily Ivanovich,' John of Leeds called, and the parade went on.

Nobody got killed. It was just like Myrnin had said...a token. A gesture.

Claire let out her breath. She hadn't even been aware how hard she'd been holding it, but her whole rib cage ached. 'He could kill them. Right? If he wanted?'

'Right,' Myrnin said. 'But he isn't doing so.' He looked grave and focused under his clown's makeup. 'I wonder what's stopping him.'

It was, Claire saw, going to stretch on for hours. She was glad they had seats, because standing would have been torture. As John of Leeds called each name, a vampire would rise and lead his or her human up to be presented to Bishop; Bishop would nod; and that would be it.

As life-and-death confrontations went, it was really boring.

And then it suddenly wasn't.

The first hint came when Sam mounted the dais with his 'gift' – he bowed to Amelie, but he only nodded to Bishop. Myrnin made a slight sound and leant forward, dark eyes intent, and Bishop sat up straighter in his chair.

'I welcome you to Morganville,' Sam said. 'But I'm not going to swear my loyalty to you.'

The hall went absolutely still, not even the little

rustles of fabric and clinks of cups on china that had been noticeable to that point. Amelie, Claire noticed, had moved closer to Sam than she had to the other vampires.

'No?' Bishop asked, and beckoned Sam forward. Sam obliged by one single step. 'Your lady will acknowledge me. Why won't you?'

'I have other oaths.'

'To her,' Bishop said. Sam nodded. 'Well, then, her oath to me will bind you, as well, Samuel. I believe that will do.' He eyed the girl. 'Leave the gift.'

Sam didn't move. 'No.'

Amelie murmured something to him, but it was soft enough that it didn't carry to Claire's ears despite the excellent acoustics of the room.

'She's my responsibility,' Sam said, 'and if you want a gift, take what Morganville offers you. Freedom.'

He reached in the pocket of his rope-belted Huck Finn blue jeans and pulled out a blood pack.

Ysandre leapt from her seat. So did François. 'You dare!' Fraçnois snarled, and knocked the blood pack out of Sam's hand. 'Take that filthy thing away!'

Ysandre grabbed hold of Sam's date by the hair and yanked her away. 'She's the tribute,' Ysandre said, 'and you have no right to deny her to him.'

'He has no right,' Amelie said. Every word was clear as crystal. 'But I do.'

Bishop's eyes locked with hers, and for a long, long moment, nobody moved.

Then Bishop smiled, sat back in his chair, and waved. 'Take her, Samuel,' he said. 'I find she's not to my taste, after all.'

Sam grabbed the girl's hand, shoved François out of the way, and descended the steps back to the banquet-hall floor. Murmurs bloomed in the darkness as he passed. He headed straight for the table where Michael sat, leant over, and said something. Michael replied, looking strained and a little bit desperate. Whatever the argument was about, it was ripping Michael apart to take the other side.

Sam yanked Michael to his feet, and this time Claire heard what he said. 'Just come with me!'

Whether Michael might have or not, it was too late, because John of Leeds said, 'Michael Glass of Morganville,' and everybody waited to see what the youngest vampire in town was going to do.

Michael took Monica's hand and walked to the dais. He mounted the steps, nodded to Amelie, and nodded to Bishop. Not much in the way of obedience either direction.

'Ah, the Morrell girl,' Bishop said. 'I've heard so much about you, child.'

Monica, the idiot, seemed pleased about that. She risked her tall wig by doing a deep curtsy in those mile-wide Marie Antoinette skirts. 'Thank you, sir.'

'Did I tell you to speak?' he asked, and transferred

his attention to Michael again. 'Your kinsman refused to swear fealty. What say you, Michael?'

'I'm here,' Michael said. 'But I'm not swearing anything.'

There was a long, tense moment, and then Bishop impatiently waved him offstage.

Monica dragged her feet, simpering at the big, bad vampire. 'What an *idiot*,' Claire muttered under her breath, and Myrnin chuckled.

'There are always a few,' he said. 'Thankfully.' The next vampire was already on stage. He was a little more politic than Michael – he welcomed Bishop as a guest to Morganville, but again, no pledges of loyalty. Bishop looked sour. 'Well, this is taking a turn for the interesting. I wonder how long he'll tolerate it.'

Not long, it seemed, because Oliver was next. And even though Oliver bowed, there was something forced about it. Something militant. Bishop sensed it.

'What say you, Oliver of Heidelberg?'

'I bid you welcome,' Oliver said. 'And nothing more.' He bowed again, mockingly. 'Your days of ordering us about are done, Master Bishop. Haven't you noticed?'

Bishop stood up. So did François and Ysandre. 'Bring your tribute,' Bishop said. 'And walk away, while I allow you to walk at all.'

And Oliver, the coward, dropped Eve's hand and left the stage. Abandoning her.

Michael, down on the floor, tried to go to her rescue, but Sam tackled him and held him down. 'Get off me!' Michael yelled, and the two of them rolled into a table and sent the expensive china and glasses flying. 'You can't let him—'

François and Ysandre were closing in on Eve like hunting tigers. And she was standing, petrified, caught in Bishop's stare.

Shane stood up and took off the dog mask Ysandre had made him wear. He walked over to stand next to Eve, unhooked the leash, and let it fall to the floor in a slither of leather.

'I'm so done with this crap,' he said, and extended his elbow toward Eve. 'How about you?'

'So done,' she agreed. 'Though I do love a good dress-up party. Can I have the collar when you're done with it?'

'Knock yourself out.'

They were trying to be cool, but Claire could feel the menace up there, the hair-trigger violence just waiting to erupt. And Shane couldn't win. He couldn't even hurt them. All he could do was get himself killed.

She fought to get out of her chair. Myrnin's hand crushed her shoulder hard, forcing her down again. 'No,' he said. 'Wait.'

'They're my *friends*!'

'Wait!'

He was right. Amelie stepped forward, between Shane and Eve and Bishop. 'They belong to me,' she said. 'They are not Oliver's to give.'

'That argument could be made for anyone in this town,' Bishop said. 'Will you deny me any tribute at all?'

She smiled slowly. 'I never said that. Be careful, Father. You sound desperate.'

Claire saw Bishop's eyes flare red, then white-hot.

Amelie didn't back down. She turned her head slightly, and nodded at Shane and Eve. Shane hustled Eve off the stage and down to the banquet-hall floor. François seemed to get some silent message from Bishop, because he backed out of their way.

Sam let Michael up, and in seconds, Michael was across the room to join them as Shane and Eve descended the stairs from the dais.

Sam followed. That made a small group in the no-man's-land in the centre of the tables on the floor.

'It's starting,' Myrnin said. 'We're at the tipping point now. He knows he's losing. He'll have to act.'

And John of Leeds said, in that perfectly calm voice, 'Lord Myrnin of Conwy.'

There was that head-turning thing again. Myrnin got up from his chair and held out his hand to Claire. His eyes were bright, a little too bright. A little too manic.

His smile scared her, and she didn't think it was just the makeup. 'Ready?' he asked.

She didn't really have a choice. She stood and put her hand in his, and walked toward the last thing in the world she wanted to do.

CHAPTER TWELVE

Going up the steps felt like the proverbial march to the gallows. Amelie stood to one side, glittering like a chandelier, and she was glaring at Myrnin with fierce displeasure.

He took her pale, perfect hand and kissed it. 'Oh, don't look so distressed, my old friend,' he told her. 'I'm perfectly fine.'

'No,' Amelie said. 'You're not. And you're about to be a good deal less so.' She turned to Bishop. 'I regret that Lord Myrnin is unwell. He must leave, for his own health.'

'He looks well enough,' Bishop replied. 'Let him come forward.'

'You fool,' Amelie whispered as Myrnin did his Pierrot twirl and ended in a dancer's perfect floor-scraping bow. 'Oh, my lovely fool.' Claire couldn't tell if she was appalled, angry, or sad. Maybe all three.

Bishop seemed amused. 'It's been years,' he said. 'And how have you fared, Myrnin?'

'As well as you'd expect,' Myrnin said.

'Pierrot. How...odd for you. You're much more the Harlequin, I should think.'

'I've always thought that Pierrot was the secretly dangerous one,' Myrnin said. 'All that innocence must hide *something*.'

Bishop laughed. 'I've missed you, fool.'

'Truly? Odd. I haven't missed you at all, my lord.'

That stopped Bishop's laughter in its tracks, and Claire felt the fear close around her, like suffocating cold. 'Ah, I remember now why you ceased to amuse, Myrnin. You use honesty like a club.'

'I thought it more like a rapier, lord.'

Bishop was all done with the witty conversation. 'Will you swear?'

And Myrnin said, shockingly, 'I will.' And he proceeded to, a string of swearwords that made Claire blink. He ended with, ' – frothy fool-born apple-john! Cheater of vandals and defiler of dead dogs!' and did another twirl and bow. He looked up with a red, red grin that was more like a leer. 'Is that what you meant, my lord?'

Claire gasped as hands closed cold around her throat from behind. She was pulled backward. It was Ysandre holding her, and the vampire woman bent to whisper, 'Yes, please do struggle. I lost your boyfriend before I could get a taste. I'll have you instead.'

Claire didn't hesitate. She reached under her

tunic, got out the ancient glass perfume bottle that Myrnin had given her, and thumbed off the cap.

And she dumped the holy water right on Ysandre's head.

Ysandre screamed in registers so high the crystal on the tables shivered. She spun away clawing at her hair, shedding drops that landed on François, who was moving toward her. He screamed, too. Where the drops touched, they ate away into skin. Claire stared, appalled. She'd hurt them, all right. Badly.

Myrnin laughed, deep in his throat, and took out the thin, sharp knife he'd worn at his side. As Bishop advanced on him, he cut at him, still laughing.

He connected.

It was a minor little wound to Bishop's arm, barely a nick, but Clare saw the cut on the older vampire's robes, and a thin film of blood on the knife.

Bishop looked surprised enough to stop to examine the damage to his costume.

Myrnin's laughter ratcheted higher and higher, and he twirled again, faster, almost a blur.

'Myrnin!' Claire yelled. She was backing away from Ysandre, burnt and furious, who was stalking toward her. She tripped and fell flat on her back. 'Myrnin, *do something*!'

He stopped twirling and looked at the bloody knife in his hand.

'I told Sam before, you have to know when to let go,' he said. 'It's time, Claire.' He blew her a kiss, and leapt over the table.

And ran away, shrieking with laughter, still holding the knife. Right out of the hall.

For a few seconds, nobody moved. Claire stared at Ysandre, who seemed just as surprised, and glanced at Bishop.

Who flicked his fingers against the cut in his robe, and chuckled.

'My fool,' he said, almost fondly. 'Madmen are the laughter of God, don't you agree?'

He sat down on his throne, smiling. 'Ysandre, leave the child. I'm inclined to allow our friends their small acts of defiance tonight.'

'She burnt me!' Ysandre snarled.

'And you'll heal. Don't whine like a kicked dog. It's no more than you deserve.'

Amelie, Claire realised, hadn't moved at all. Not even when Claire's life had been in danger. Now she did, leaning down to help Claire to her feet.

'Enough of this,' she said. 'You've had your fun, Father. End this.'

'Very well,' he said. 'It's time for the test, my child. Swear fealty to me, and it will all be over.'

'If I swear fealty, it will never be over,' Amelie corrected him. 'I never have sworn an oath to you. Did you really think tonight that would change?'

His cold, cold eyes narrowed. 'Blood traitor,' he said. 'Murderous witch. Do you welcome me to your little town? Do you grant me leave to walk your streets and take your peasants? I don't think you dare. You know me too well.'

'I grant you nothing,' she said. 'I won't swear loyalty to you. I won't give you welcome. I won't give you *anything*, Father.' It didn't seem possible, but as Claire watched her, Amelie seemed...human. Vulnerable. Fragile and waiting to be broken.

'You will give me one thing if you want to keep what you've built here,' he said. 'I want my book. The one you stole as you rolled me into my hasty grave, *daughter*.'

She froze, eyes widening. Amelie, who couldn't be surprised, had been completely taken for a ride this time. 'The book.'

'You think I want your pathetic town? Your ridiculous peasants?' Bishop's contemptuous gaze swept over Claire, over the room beyond. 'I want my *property*. Give it to me, and I'll leave. There. Now all our cards are up, child. What say you?'

'The book isn't yours,' Amelie said.

'I took it from the dead hands of a rival,' Bishop said. 'That makes it mine. Right of conquest.' He gave her a cold, slow stare. 'The same way you took it from me, if you remember, except that I wasn't quite dead enough. A pity you didn't make sure, eh?'

It was all going wrong. Myrnin had run away, and he was supposed to stay, supposed to fight. Amelie couldn't do this on her own; he'd said it himself.

The other vampires were all standing by and letting it happen.

'Amelie,' Bishop said, 'I'll destroy you if you

refuse. Don't you know that? Haven't you known it from the moment I came to town?'

Claire moved up beside her. 'She wants you to leave,' she said. 'You need to go. Now.'

Bishop laughed. 'A threat from a little yapping dog. Will you make me, mongrel?'

'No,' said Sam Glass. He jumped from the banquet floor up to the table in one lithe, easy motion, and then down to stand on Amelie's other side. 'Not by herself, anyway.' He'd taken off his Huck Finn straw hat, but even if he'd been wearing it, his expression was one that demanded to be taken seriously.

Michael joined him, crossing the distance with a leap, while Eve and Shane took the stairs.

There was a second's breathless pause, and then others began to move. Oliver. Monica. Charles and Miranda.

Claire's dad came up to take her mother's hands and lead her off to the side, out of danger.

More kept coming.

The vampires and humans of Morganville stood together, crowding the stage in front of Bishop, Ysandre, and François. Not all of them – but more than half the room.

'You're not welcome here,' Oliver said, '*Master* Bishop. This is our town. Our people. It's time for you to leave.'

'A rebellion,' Bishop said. 'How refreshingly modern.'

He nodded to Ysandre and François. François

yanked Jennifer out of her seat on the dais.

Ysandre feinted toward Shane, then grabbed hold of Jason Rosser and sank her fangs deep into his neck.

Pandemonium. Sam and Michael both hit François, bearing him backward as he tried to get his teeth into a screaming Jennifer, and Claire lost sight of them almost immediately. Bishop was on his feet, struggling hand to hand with Oliver.

Amelie, eyes the colour and hardness of diamond, grabbed Ysandre by the back of the neck and yanked her backward, away from Jason.

'My property,' she snapped, and held Ysandre at arm's length as she hissed and struggled. 'Boy. *Boy!*' She bent over Jason, her pale fingers touching his face.

Jason opened his eyes. He was crying, Claire thought, but then she saw his face, and she knew that wasn't crying at all.

That was *laughter*.

'Sucker,' he said.

'No!' Claire cried, but it was too late.

Jason took a stake out of the folds of his brown monk's robe and stabbed Amelie, right in the heart.

Everything stopped.

Amelie staggered backward. The wooden stake in her chest looked unreal, obscene, wrong.

Amelie was invulnerable. Couldn't be hurt.

A rim of blood spread into the white cloth

around the stake, growing before Claire's eyes.

Sam screamed. He abandoned François as Amelie fell, and caught her, easing her down to the wooden stage. The look on his face – Claire had never seen that much pain, ever.

Oliver punched Bishop so hard that the old man staggered backward and fell over the side of the throne; then Oliver moved to Amelie's side.

'No!' Oliver snapped as Sam took hold of the stake to pull it out. 'She's old. She'll survive until we get her to safety. Take her!'

And then he turned as Jason lunged at him, crazy-eyed, with another stake. Oliver grabbed him in midair and snapped his arm with an effortless twist, tossing him across the stage to crash into François, who had Michael down on the ground.

'Mom! Dad! *Get out of here!*' Claire yelled. Her dad beckoned her to come with them, but she shook her head. She wasn't leaving her friends behind. Not the way Myrnin had left her.

Her parents got out, all the way out the door. Others were running, mostly the ones who'd elected not to go up against Bishop in the first place. Claire saw Maria Theresa slipping out the side door, tugging her human tribute by the arm. He looked horrified, and he was trying to break free.

Out in the darkness, she heard screaming.

Amelie blinked, pulled in a breath, and whispered something to Sam. He looked up at Claire, and his face was as hard and pale as polished marble. 'Endgame,' he said. 'Bishop's counterattack.'

Claire looked out and saw that some of those who'd held back were turning on their humans, or attacking other vampires. Bishop had brought his own sleeper agents with him, and it was only a matter of time before they made their way up to the stage. It was going to be a free-for-all.

Michael joined them. His clothes were ripped, and he had a bloodless cut along one cheekbone.

'Get them out of here!' Oliver yelled to him. 'Now!'

Oliver lunged for Bishop, drove the older vampire back against the throne, and reached into his scarecrow costume. He pulled out a long, needle-pointed dagger, and shoved it through Bishop's chest to pin him to the wood.

It annoyed Bishop more than hurt him. Bishop wrenched free and pulled the dagger out, then backhanded Oliver so hard the other vampire went completely off the stage and out into the darkness of the banquet hall.

'Sam!' Michael yelled. Sam gathered up Amelie in his arms and jumped off the stage. Most of the others followed him. Michael grabbed Eve and Shane, and Claire turned to follow as they clattered down the stairs.

Ysandre stopped her.

'Not so fast,' she said. Her voice no longer sounded like a purr; it was a growl, low and vicious. '*You* I want.'

Claire fumbled for a weapon. She came up with a fork from a fallen place setting, and stabbed it into Ysandre's arm. The vampire yelped, plucked it out, and fastened her hand around Claire's throat, bending her back over the table. Claire couldn't breathe. She battered at the vampire's iron hand, and tried to twist free, but it was no use.

She was dying.

Oliver hit Ysandre in a flying leap. He knocked her into Bishop, and they both went down. Before they hit the floor, he'd grabbed Claire's wrist and pulled her toward the stairs. She wasn't moving fast enough for him. He scooped her into his arms, and the world blurred around them.

Vampire speed.

Screams smeared into noise, and Claire heard crashes and sirens, and then nothing.

Strange, to feel safe in Oliver's arms.

When she woke up, her head was in Shane's lap, and he was stroking her hair. She heard the hushed murmur of voices. 'What—' Her throat hurt. Hurt a *lot*. And her voice sounded funny.

'Hey,' Shane said, and smiled down at her. It didn't look right, that smile. 'Don't talk. We're home – we've got everything secured. It's OK.'

She doubted that. She could hear sirens outside, racing past on the street. Voices inside the house, lots of them. She tried to sit up, but Shane held her back. 'Sam's upstairs with Amelie, in the rec room.' Which was Shane's term for Amelie's hidden lair. 'The city's in lockdown. Bishop had a lot of people on his payroll already. Lots of surprises. He's been busy.'

She mouthed, *Who's here?*

'Yeah, well, we've got guests tonight,' he said. 'Couldn't get them to their own places, so they're taking refuge here. Your mom and dad are right here—'

And there they were, pushing Shane out of the way. Mom was crying as she stroked Claire's face. Her dad was more stoic, but his face was flushed and his jaw was tightly clenched.

'How you doing, kiddo?' he asked.

'Fine,' she whispered, and pointed at them.

'We're just fine, sweetheart,' her mother said, and kissed her on the forehead. She was still wearing the long white dress, but the angel wings looked battered and off centre. 'When Oliver brought you in, I thought – I thought it was too late. I thought—'

They'd thought she was dead. Claire felt guilty, even though passing out hadn't been her idea, exactly. 'I'm OK,' she managed to say. She tried to swallow, and found that was not just a bad idea; it was a *terrible* idea. She coughed. That hurt worse.

Pitiful.

'Oliver?' she whispered. Her dad nodded to someplace behind the couch, where she was stretched out.

'On the phone,' he said. 'He's quite the take-charge guy, isn't he?'

The lights in the house went out, and people screamed. Almost immediately, flashlights clicked on; Eve and Shane had them ready, and so did Michael.

'Calm down,' Michael said. 'Everybody relax. The house is secure.'

Nothing was secure from Bishop, Claire wanted to tell him. Ysandre and François had been here, and they'd get in again if they wanted. The gloom felt thick and oily around her. If there were ghosts in the house – other than the one Michael had been – they were coming out in force tonight, drawn by the fear and fury.

'Hey,' Eve said. She was standing at the front windows, looking out. 'Something's on fire out there.'

A fire truck roared by, screaming, chased by a fleet of patrol cars. *Busy night for city services*, Claire thought dizzily. She got up, despite her mother's attempts to keep her flat. The room spun a little, then steadied. She joined Eve at the window. Eve put an arm around her and hugged her, eyes still on the fire. It was a big one, maybe three streets away. Flames were leaping a dozen feet into the air.

'How you doing?' Eve asked her.

Claire gave her a silent thumbs-up, and saw Eve smile.

'Yeah, you went all Spartacus up there. I was proud, you know. Well, until you kind of got your ass kicked.'

Claire tried to choke out an indignant 'Hey!'

'OK, so, maybe not your fault.' Eve hugged her again. 'Holy water. Nice touch. I was almost impressed.'

'Whose house?' Two words, Claire managed in one whisper. That was progress. 'On fire?'

'I think it's the Melville house.' Eve angled for a different view. 'Crap. I see some more. This isn't good.'

Michael joined them. 'It's part of Bishop's plan,' he said. 'Or at least, that's what I'd guess. Create chaos. Keep Amelie off-balance.'

Claire bet the power failure was all part of the plan too. 'How many are here?'

'In our house? About thirty.' Eve rolled her eyes. 'Half of them vampires. Great, huh? After all that.'

Claire stared at her. 'Thirty?'

Eve nodded. 'What?'

'Makes us a good target.'

'She's right,' Michael said. 'We need to stay alert.'

Shane pressed in next to Claire. He was still wearing his leather pants, but he'd thrown on a grotty old Marilyn Manson T-shirt that looked rescued from the bottom of the laundry bag.

She didn't care. She collapsed against him, and felt his arms go around her, and just for a second, it was all right.

'Killer rabbit,' Shane said fondly, and kissed her. 'What's with the outfit?'

'Harlequin,' she croaked. 'Myrnin—' The memory of what Myrnin had done came flooding back. He'd taunted Bishop. He'd set Amelie up to take the fall, and he'd *run*. He'd left her there, too, to die.

'That's Myrnin? The crazy one? Claire. How could you trust him in the first place?' Shane cupped her face in his hands. 'He talked you into it, didn't he?'

Not exactly. She'd *wanted* to believe Myrnin. She wanted to believe in that sweet, innocent soul that she glimpsed in him from time to time – but now she wasn't at all sure it even existed at all.

Or if it had, maybe her cure had destroyed it.

'I couldn't—' Claire tried to put the words together, but it was too hard, and Shane's eyes were too forgiving. He kissed her, and even under the circumstances, with her parents *right there*, with a house full of vampires and half of Morganville in danger, she thought she could stand here all night and all day, in his arms.

'I know,' he murmured, with his damp, sweet lips on hers. 'I know.'

She almost thought he did.

'Sorry to break this up,' Michael said dryly from behind Claire, 'but I'm thinking we need to do a little perimeter patrolling.'

'Not a bad idea,' Shane said, and stepped back, 'if they're torching houses to drive people out in the streets. Easier to pick them off that way, I'll bet.'

'Exactly.' Michael handed him a crowbar. Shane twirled it and captured it under his arm. 'Like

Claire said, we're a good target. All the Founder Houses are. I'll take the back; you go to the front.'

'I'll do it,' Claire offered. Shane and Michael both grabbed her arms and towed her back to the couch, where she was unceremoniously dumped. 'Hey!'

Shane turned to her parents. 'Make sure she stays in.'

'We will,' her mother said, and sat down beside Claire. 'Honestly, Claire, what are you thinking? It's dangerous out there!'

That was exactly what Claire was thinking, in relation to Shane. But she knew that in her present condition, she wasn't much use. Not for this, at least.

'Bathroom,' she sighed, and there was no arguing with that. Her parents exchanged a look. Dad shrugged.

'I'll go with you,' Mom offered.

'Mom, I'm old enough to go to the bathroom alone.' Her voice was getting stronger all the time; she only had to hesitate a couple of times getting all that out. She still sounded like she had a pack-a-day cigarette habit, though. But husky was sexy, right?

Mom had her doubts about the whole old-enough theory, but she stayed where she was, on the couch. She and Dad exchanged shrugs. Claire stepped around a knot of strangers – all vampires, with cool, suspicious eyes – and took the stairs.

Miranda was sitting on the landing with her Medusa-snaked head cradled in her hands. 'Hey,'

Claire said, and hunkered down next to her. 'You OK?'

Miranda nodded. 'Told you,' she said. 'Blood. Fire. It's all going away.'

'Can you see anything about us? About the house?'

Miranda shook her head. 'Too tired.' She sounded like it – almost catatonic, slurring her words. 'Head hurts.'

'Come on,' Claire said, and got Miranda to her feet. 'I've got a bed. No reason somebody shouldn't be using it.'

She saw the girl tucked in, already dozing off, and then – as she'd promised Mom and Dad – visited the bathroom. There was a line. Once that was done, she felt free to investigate other options.

She'd never promised to come right back.

The way she wanted to go was blocked by one of Amelie's bodyguards – the one who'd nodded to her during an earlier visit, in fact. He was marginally less stone-faced than the rest of her staff, but definitely intimidating. Claire looked up at him, well aware that the bruising around her throat was turning purple.

'Can I go up?' she asked. The bodyguard seemed to consider her for a long second before giving her a nod and moving aside. He knocked. The hidden door popped open, and Claire slipped inside and closed it behind her.

There was another vampire bodyguard at the

foot of the stairs, and he wasn't as friendly, but after a whispered conversation at the top of the stairs, he let her go up.

Upstairs it was only Amelie, lying in a frozen waterfall of white silk on the couch, and Sam, and Oliver.

The stake was still in her chest, and her eyes were open and blank.

Oliver snapped at Claire the second she cleared the stairs. 'Go away!'

She nearly did, but Sam jumped in quickly. 'No,' he said. 'She's earned the right. She was the first one to stand next to Amelie, not you. Not even me.'

Oliver seemed harassed, but he refocused on Amelie's still, pale face. His long fingers were on her temples, unexpectedly gentle. He'd stripped off his scarecrow costume, or most of it, but there were still bits of straw in his hair, and smudges of greasepaint on his skin.

He leant close, staring into her open eyes, and held there. Seconds ticked by, and Sam waited.

'Now,' Oliver whispered.

Sam grabbed the stake and pulled, one swift yank. Amelie's body followed it upward in a spasm, and her mouth opened wide. Her vampire teeth glittered, sharp and deadly in the light.

She didn't make a sound.

Sam looked tormented. Oliver was whispering something, too faint for Claire to catch, and he bent his head so close to Amelie's they were almost touching. When Sam reached out toward her, Oliver looked up and shook his head sharply. Sam froze.

'Take her,' Oliver said, and removed his hands from her head. Sam quickly took over, sliding into his place. Oliver skinned back his grey shirtsleeve, took in a deep breath, and put his forearm to Amelie's mouth.

Claire flinched as Amelie bit deep. Oliver didn't. Sam's gaze alternated between Amelie and Oliver, looking for something Claire didn't quite understand, and then he let go of Amelie and grabbed Oliver's arm to pull it away from her.

Oliver staggered and collapsed, and covered his eyes with both hands. The open wounds on his arm trailed blood drops, pattering on the floor, then slowing. Stopping as he healed.

Amelie blinked and turned her head toward Claire. She looked dead, except for the fact that she was moving; her eyes were still fixed, pupils gone wide, and her skin was an eerie blue white.

'The girl,' she whispered. 'Must go. Hungry.'

Sam nodded and looked over his shoulder at Claire. 'Go get her some blood,' he said. 'There should be some in the refrigerator.'

And Claire realised with a shock that there wasn't. They were all out of blood.

'Crap,' Shane breathed as they stood together looking into the fridge. The shelves held leftover chilli, some pasta stuff, hamburger patties. Enough for them, for a couple of days. Not enough for anywhere near the number of people in the house, even for the humans. 'Are you thinking what I'm thinking?'

'I'm thinking we have about fifteen vampires and no blood,' Claire said. 'Is that it?'

'No, I was thinking we're out of chips. Of *course* that's what I was thinking.' Shane moved some condiment bottles again, in a three-time-loser search for some elusive hidden blood bottle. 'Did I say *crap?*'

'More than once, yeah. Shouldn't you get back outside?'

'I traded shifts with a vampire. Better to have them walking around in the dark than us, you know? Besides, the fewer of them there are in here right now—'

'The better,' she finished. 'I don't disagree. But Sam said Amelie needs to feed, and that means blood. She's not the only one, either. What about the Donation Centre?'

'They don't deliver,' Shane said, and then snapped his fingers. 'Wait. Wait a minute. Yes, they do.'

'What?'

He spun away and picked up the phone from the cradle on the wall, then put it back down. 'Dead.'

Claire took out her cell phone. 'I've got a signal.' She pitched it to him, and watched as he punched a number. 'Who are you calling?'

'Pizza Hut.'

'Loser.'

He held up a finger. 'Hey, Richard?' Not, Claire noticed, *Dick*. This situation had upgraded him to full-name status. 'Listen, man, we've got a situation here at the Glass House.'

Claire could fill in the other half of the conversation from Richard Morrell almost verbatim. *What do you think I have, with the town going crazy?*

'We're out of blood,' Shane said. 'Amelie's wounded. You do the math, man. A little home delivery service from Morganville's Finest wouldn't hurt right now.'

Whatever Richard said, it wasn't encouraging.

'You're kidding,' Shane said, in an entirely different tone. A worried one. 'You're not kidding. Oh my God.' A short pause. 'Yeah, man, I get it. I get it. OK, right. Take care.'

That, she thought, was definitely the most civil she'd ever heard Richard and Shane. It was almost friendly.

Shane folded up the phone and threw it back to her, and his face was a study in self-control.

'What?'

'Donation Centre's burning,' he said. 'How do you feel about blood drives?'

The Bloodmobile arrived in front of the house exactly fifteen minutes later – glossy, black, and intimidating. It came with a flanking guard of squad cars and police wearing protective vests who took up posts on either end of the street.

Claire looked at the clock. It was nearly four a.m. – still hours until dawn, although the fires were making it hard to tell day from night. The Morganville Fire Department was outmatched. Whatever serial arsonists Bishop had employed were definitely doing their jobs.

Claire wondered what Bishop was doing. Waiting, probably. He didn't really have to do anything else. Morganville was coming apart, with strikes at the communications hubs, the Donation Centre, and – as she heard by word of mouth from some of the others – the hospital. So far, the university seemed safe. There was a blood supply on campus, but it would be tough to get to in the chaos.

Michael went out to meet the vampire driving the Bloodmobile. He came back shaking his head. 'Nothing left,' he said. 'He'd already dropped off the day's collections at the Centre. There's nothing in storage. He says he's heard the supplies at the hospital have been sabotaged, too.'

'Unless we go door-to-door and gather up bottles and bags, that's all there is,' said the stern-looking vampire. 'I *told* the Council there should be more backup supplies.'

'What about the university storage?'

'Enough for a couple of days,' the Bloodmobile driver said. 'I don't know of anything else.'

'I do,' Claire said, and swallowed painfully as

they all looked at her. 'But I need to get permission from Amelie to take you there.'

'Amelie's not in any shape to give permission. What about Oliver?'

Claire shook her head. 'It has to be Amelie. I'm sorry.'

The Bloodmobile driver looked tired and very frustrated. He pinched the bridge of his nose. 'Fine,' he said. 'But before she can begin to give consent, she needs feeding. And I need donors.'

Eve, who'd been uncharacteristically quiet, stepped forward. 'I'll do it,' she said.

'Me, too.' That was Monica Morrell. She stripped off her heavy Marie Antoinette wig and dropped it on the ground. Claire thought about what Richard Morrell had told her about the mayor wanting to return the costume for credit, and almost laughed. So much for that plan. 'Gina! Jennifer! Get over here! And bring everybody you can!'

Monica, as imperious as a real French queen, put her ability to threaten and intimidate to good use for a change. Within ten minutes, they had a line of donors ready, and all four Bloodmobile stations were working.

Claire slipped back inside. The vampires were all facing the windows, watching for surprises. Most of the humans were outside, giving blood.

She faced the blank wall in the living room, next to the table. *Got to do this fast.*

It faded into mist, and she stepped through

and was gone almost before the portal opened.

She stepped out into the prison, reached under her Harlequin top, and pulled out the sharpened cross that Myrnin had given her. *Use it only in self-defence.*

She was ready to do that.

Myrnin's cell was empty, and the television was on and tuned to a game show. Claire checked the prison refrigerator. There was a good stockpile of blood there, if she could get it out where it was needed.

Myrnin could be anywhere.

No, she thought. Myrnin could be only in about twenty places in Morganville, at least if he was using the doorways.

She went back to the portal wall and concentrated, formed the wormhole tunnel to the lab, and stepped through.

And there he was.

He was feverishly working, and every lamp and candle in the room burnt at full capacity. He hadn't stopped to change, though he'd lost the cone-head cap somewhere; as Claire watched, he got one of his full white sleeves too close to a candle and caught it on fire.

'*Cachiad!*' he blurted, and ripped off his sleeve to throw it on the ground and stomp out the blaze. Irritated, he stripped off the whole billowy top and dumped it, too.

He looked up, half-naked, wild, and saw Claire watching him.

For a second neither of them moved, and then Myrnin said, 'It's not what you think.'

Claire stepped away from the door. She swung it shut and clicked the padlock shut. 'If you didn't want anybody coming after you, you should have locked up.'

'I don't have time for this, and neither do you. Now, do you want to help me, or—'

'I'm done helping you!' she shouted. Her abused voice broke like shattered glass, and she heard the raw fury bleed out. 'You *ran*! You left us all to *die*!'

Myrnin flinched. He looked away, down at what he'd been doing at the lab table, and she saw that he'd prepared a number of slides. 'I had my reasons,' he said. 'It's the long game, Claire. Amelie understands.'

'Amelie got staked in the heart,' she said.

His head slowly rose. 'What?'

'Bishop bought off her tribute, Jason. Jason staked her.'

'No.' It was a bare thread of sound. Myrnin shut his eyes. 'No, that can't be. She knew – I told her—'

'You *left her to die*!'

Myrnin's legs failed. He slid down to his knees and buried his face in his hands, silent in his anguish.

Claire gripped the cross, holding it at her side, and walked toward him. He didn't move.

'Is she alive?' he asked.

'I don't know. Maybe.'

Myrnin nodded. 'Then it is my fault. That shouldn't have happened.'

'And the rest of it *should have*?'

'Long game,' Myrnin whispered. 'You don't understand.'

There was a chessboard, a familiar one, set up in the corner where Myrnin normally read. A game was frozen in mid-attack. Claire stared at it, and for a second she saw the spectre of Amelie sitting with Myrnin, moving those pieces in white, cold fingers.

'She knew,' she said. 'She helped you. Didn't she?'

Myrnin stood up, and Claire held up the cross between them. Myrnin didn't so much as look at it. She pushed it closer. Maybe it was a proximity thing?

Myrnin closed his hand over hers, and took the cross away. He held it on the open palm of his hand.

No sizzling. No reaction at all.

'Crosses don't work,' he said. 'We all pretend they do, but they don't.'

Her mouth was hanging open. 'Why?' Great. Her last words were, as always, going to be questions.

'Obviously, it keeps people from moving on to things that *will* hurt us.' Myrnin lifted his eyebrows, but the dark eyes below them were cautious and sad. 'Claire. I wasn't *supposed* to stay.

I was to provide a distraction, get my sample, and leave.'

'Sample.'

He pointed toward the lab table, and what he'd been doing. Claire saw the silver gleam of the knife he'd carried to the feast – clean now, no trace of blood.

But there was blood carefully mounted and fixed on glass slides, ranks of them.

'Bishop's blood?'

Myrnin nodded. 'We've never been able to obtain a sample from any vampire beyond Morganville. As far as we knew, there *weren't* any vampires beyond Morganville. Look.'

Claire didn't trust him. He stepped back, far back, and indicated the microscope with an apologetic bow.

'Mind if I hold this?' she asked, and grabbed the knife.

'So long as you keep it pointed away from me,' he said. The weight of it eased her jitters a little, but it still took her several tries to look into the microscope long enough to focus, instead of checking his position.

When she did, she immediately recognised the difference.

Bishop's blood cells were – for a vampire – healthy.

She stepped back and stared at Myrnin. 'He's not infected.'

'It gets better,' Myrnin said, and nodded toward the ranks of slides. 'Try number eight.'

She switched out the slides. 'I don't see any difference.'

'Exactly,' he said. 'That is my blood, mixed with Bishop's. Now check number seven – my blood, alone.'

It was a nightmare. Worse than Claire had ever seen it. Whatever the serum was doing to Myrnin, it was destroying him.

She checked slide eight again.

Slide seven.

'He's the cure,' she said.

'Now you see,' Myrnin said, 'why I was willing to risk everything and everyone to be sure.'

Myrnin's health failed again after another hour – longer than Claire would have given him, based on what she saw under the slides. When he started tiring and mixing words, she unlocked the prison door and took him back to his cell.

'Damn,' she sighed, remembering the broken door. 'We need to move you.'

That took some time, although she grabbed only what Myrnin pointed out as essentials – clothes, blankets, the rug, his books. By the time she'd gotten everything put into the next cell, and replaced the ancient filthy bunk with the clean cot, Myrnin was in the corner of the room, curled into a ball. Rocking slowly back and forth.

She approached him as carefully as she could.

'It's ready,' she said. 'Come on. I'll get you something to eat.'

Myrnin looked up, and she couldn't tell if he'd understood her until he scrambled to his feet and waved her out of the way with a trembling hand.

He closed the cell door and tested the lock, then slumped onto his bed.

'Amelie,' he said. 'Take care of Amelie.'

'We will,' Claire promised. She handed him a blood pack – not threw, handed. 'I'm sorry. I didn't understand.'

His nod was more of a convulsive tremble. His gaze was drawn to the blood, but he forced it back to her face. 'Long game,' he said. 'Use what Bishop wants. Let him think he's winning. Play for time. Bring the doctor.'

'Dr Mills?'

'Need help.'

'I'll get him here somehow.' Claire didn't want to leave Myrnin, but he was right. There were things to do. 'Are you going to be OK?'

Myrnin's smile was, once again, broken, but beautiful. 'Yes,' he said softly. 'Thank you for trusting me. Thank you for believing.'

She hadn't, really. But she did now.

As she turned away, she heard him whisper, 'I'm so sorry, child. So very sorry I left you.'

She pretended not to hear.

CHAPTER THIRTEEN

The portals were more confusing now, because the power was out in Morganville. Most places were completely dark, and no matter how hard Claire concentrated, she couldn't pull up three of the destinations at all.

Which meant, she supposed, that they no longer existed.

She focused on the surroundings of home, but again got darkness. She heard people talking, though, and caught a glimpse of candles being lit.

Eve's face caught by the glow.

Home.

She was getting ready to step through when something hit her from behind, silent and heavy. She lost control of the portal as she crashed forward, screaming. She heard Myrnin, far behind her, call out, 'Claire? Claire, what's wrong?'

She thought it was one of the inmates, until she

felt a hand wind deep in her hair and lips brush her neck.

She heard Bishop's mocking laughter. 'Thank you,' he said. 'For leading me to my fool.'

He threw her through the portal.

She hit the floor on the other side and rolled, then scrambled up and threw herself at the wall. It didn't open for her. She battered at it with her fists.

Nothing.

Claire turned, because it didn't feel like home. Darkness and utter silence.

'Hello?' No answer. 'Shane? *Mom?*'

She wasn't at the Glass House. Bishop had screwed up her destination when he'd thrown her through the portal, and she had no idea where she was.

Half-sobbing, Claire felt her way across the room. Her fingers brushed soft cloth, and she pulled. *Curtain*, she thought. She tugged, and caught a glimmer through a window.

Orange light.

Claire pulled back the curtains of the window, and looked out at Morganville, burning. It gave her enough light to see the inside of the room where she was standing. It was the same as the Glass House living room in shape, so it had to be a Founder House...one of the thirteen, then. But which one? Not Grandma Day's; she'd been inside that one, and it had been crammed with furniture. This one was piled with boxes...

Claire's gaze fell on the familiar outline of a couch. She walked to it and brushed her hand over the soft curve of the arm. There was a slightly stiffer patch near where it joined with the back, where she'd spilt a soda two years ago but hadn't ever quite gotten the stickiness out.

Some of the boxes in the corner were labelled CLAIRE.

It was Mom and Dad's new house.

Claire mapped it in her head. This house was to the northwest, so if she went to the mirror of her own bedroom, she ought to be able to see toward the Glass House. She wasn't sure what that would get her, except maybe a better idea of what her chances were to get back.

But she needed to see it. To know her friends and family were OK.

There was a house on fire that direction, but it was the same one that had been burning earlier. The Melville house. Claire couldn't make anything out past the blaze except a few faintly lit windows.

They were, she thought, still safe.

A police car raced toward the fire, lights flashing, and Claire slapped her forehead in frustration. 'Idiot,' she muttered. She'd lacked any pockets to put her phone, so she'd stowed it inside her hat.

Thanks to the elastic band, the silly little matador cap was still on her head.

Claire breathed a sigh of relief as she dug the phone from the hole in the lining, and dialled Richard Morrell.

'I need a ride.'

Richard was in the middle of a cell phone rant about how he wasn't her taxi service, and how important it was to keep city services moving, when he screeched his patrol car to a halt at the curb just outside. Claire jumped down the steps of her parents' house and raced for the car door as he threw it open.

She made it, slammed the door, and locked it. Richard looked her up and down. He no longer seemed pressed and perfect; he was smoke-stained, tired, and rumpled, and he was the most lovely thing she'd seen.

'What the hell are you supposed to be?' he asked.

'Harlequin.'

'Isn't that a Batman villain?'

'I thought you were in a hurry.'

Richard slammed on the gas, and the car screeched away from the curb. 'Strap in,' he said absently. She fastened her seat belt. 'So. Nice night for you?'

'Peachy,' she said. 'You?'

'Fantastic.' He jerked the wheel and nearly spun the car as he took a right-hand turn. 'There are two of Amelie's vampire buddies at the power station right now, refusing to turn on the lights. And three

of them made us stand by while the Donation Centre
burnt. You have *any* idea what's going on?'

'The long game,' Claire said. He sent her a look.
'Not really, no. But in chess you create openings to
make your opponent move the wrong way.'

'Chess,' Richard said in disgust. 'I'm talking
about *lives*. Kid, you're starting to scare me.'

'I'm scaring myself,' Claire said. She didn't feel
like a kid. She felt a million years old, and very
tired. 'Just get me home.'

Because she was going to have to tell Amelie that
she'd just left Myrnin, alone, at Bishop's mercy.

Amelie was sitting up when Claire arrived,
escorted in by Richard Morrell, who was instantly
pounced on by his sister and father for hugs and
information. She didn't look good, but she looked
alive.

Sort of.

Claire didn't have any sympathy for her.

'Myrnin,' Claire said. 'You used him.'

Sam, sitting on the arm of Amelie's chair,
frowned at her. 'Don't. She's very tired.'

'Yeah, well, we've all got problems.' Claire shook
off Michael's hand, too. 'Bishop's blood is the cure.
You and Myrnin were right.'

Amelie's expression didn't change. She looked
cold, remote, unreachable.

All of a sudden, Claire felt a wild urge to hurt
her. Badly.

So she did.

'Bishop's there,' she said. 'He's got Myrnin.'

Amelie's eyes focused on hers, and all of Claire's fury melted away. 'I know,' Amelie said. 'I can feel it. We knew it was a risk, using Myrnin as a stalking horse, but something had to be done.'

'You can't leave him there. You can't.'

Amelie sighed. 'No,' she agreed. 'I can't. I still need Myrnin, very much. It's far too early in the game to sacrifice him.'

Claire swallowed hard. 'Do we mean anything to you? Any of us?'

Amelie looked around the room. At the humans, all wearing purple elastic bandages at their elbows, the sign they'd given blood to save her. At the other vampires, all waiting for commands.

'You mean everything to me,' she said. 'The survival of my people, and yours, is all I have ever wanted, Claire. It's why I came here. It's all I've worked for.' Her eyes grew chilly, and some of the old Amelie came back. 'I would sacrifice Myrnin for it. Oliver. Sam. Even myself. But it's not enough.'

Everyone in the room was still. Shane moved up next to Claire, and she was aware of Eve and Michael just behind her.

But Amelie was staring right at *her*.

'What will you sacrifice, Claire?' she asked. 'To win?'

'It's not a game,' Claire said.

Amelie inclined her head. 'True. It is war. And now we have to fight for all of our lives.'

Claire linked hands with her friends.

'Then tell us what to do.'

Amelie was quiet for a moment, and then she stood. Claire thought that only those who knew her, really knew her, could tell what that cost.

She raised her voice to carry to every part of the room.

'Our forces must be split,' she said. 'We must not lose the Founder Houses, the Bloodmobile, the university, and Common Grounds. We *will hold.* Those who follow Bishop have been promised the freedom to hunt. Those of us who are strong enough will deny them that right. Those who are prey will be armed to defend themselves. *This is not optional.* All humans will be armed and taught how to strike a vampire.'

'There's no going back from that,' Oliver said. His voice was neutral. His expression wasn't. 'You're giving them too much.'

'I'm giving them equality,' Amelie said. 'Do you wish to argue the point with me now, of all times?'

Oliver, after a heart-stopping second, shook his head.

'Then go,' Amelie said. 'Oliver, Eve, go to Common Grounds and hold it. Sam, choose defenders for each Founder House. At least two vampires and two humans per house. Michael, Richard – go to the university. I will call the regent – you'll have all you need.'

Her gaze moved to Claire. 'I need you with me,' she said. 'We will fetch Myrnin.'

'Bishop's there,' Claire reminded her.

'I'm well aware. We will take precautions.'

Shane cleared his throat. 'You're not going anywhere without me.'

'I'm afraid we are,' Amelie said. 'I have a very special job for you, Shane Collins.'

'I'm not going to like this, am I?'

She smiled.

'Didn't think so,' Shane finished under his breath.

'You will be in charge of the Bloodmobile,' Amelie said. 'And one other thing.'

'Like the Bloodmobile isn't bad enough?'

Amelie reached in the pocket of her crystal-specked robes, and pulled out a small leather-bound book.

It looked really, really familiar. It was the book that had gotten them in such trouble before – the book Bishop wanted.

'You'll be in charge of this,' she said, and held it out to him.

He took it, and as he did, Claire realised what Amelie had done.

She'd just made Shane the bait.

Acknowledgements

Couldn't have happened without Sondra Lehman, Josefine Corsten, Sharon Sams, and my friends at LSG Sky Chefs.

Thanks also to Lucienne Diver and Anne Bohner, without whom…well, you know!

The Morganville Vampires series
so far...

Check out our website for free tasters and exclusive discounts, competitions and giveaways, and sign up to our monthly newsletter to keep up-to-date on our latest releases, news and upcoming events.
www.allisonandbusby.com